Dirty MAFIA SINNER

DIRTY MAFIA KINGDOM BOOK TWO

MICHELE MANNON

DIRTY MAFIA SINNER

ISBN 979-8-9947836-1-0 (special edition paperback)

Published by: 3M Productions
Easton, Pennsylvania 18042
michelemannon@gmail.com

Cover Design: Deranged Doctor Design
Editor: Nia Quinn

www.MicheleMannon.com

We flung ourselves off the edge of the cliff and built our wings on the way down."

~ Ray Bradbury

THE AIR CRACKLES with tension as the stranger holds court across the bar.

I can't take my eyes off him. All evening, I've soaked in his power like a bubble bath until I've absorbed every ounce.

This man radiates control mixed with an undeniable dark charisma as, one after another, men dare strike up a conversation. Exchanges are brief and to the point, before the next brave victim steps forward and is treated to an equal share of scrutiny and contempt.

My reaction is puzzling. Not attraction, per se, though he is handsome, tall with broad shoulders, short dark hair and high cheekbones. Not fear, despite the sense he sees beyond the perfect makeup, black dress, and high heels, straight to my hollow core. Not disinterest, which is how I regard almost everything these days.

I steal another glance, which he returns with a bone-chilling ferocity. Adrenaline races through me, and suddenly, everything seems brighter.

"Drink?" a server asks, drawing my attention. I stand between the bar and a cluster of pub tables set up for tonight's event. It's the perfect place to observe, and where I can avoid conversations on either side.

I return an empty champagne flute to the server's tray and, flashing him a weak smile, take another. He nods and continues on, and I return my attention to the man across the bar.

Except he's gone.

Loss rushes in. He disappeared, just when I decided the solution to my problems isn't spending months coddled and pitied, but the exact opposite. Beneath his scrutiny, I feel alive, *awake*. Like I've been jarred out of a long tumultuous slumber a different version of myself.

I move across the open space, desperate to catch sight of him, until I'm standing in the middle of the club. Clusters of people surround me like jet bumpers in a pinball table. Minutes tick by as my eyes bounce from group to group until it's obvious that my stranger has escaped me.

Once more, Fate's lifted me high and then dropped me like dead weight.

I take a fortifying sip of champagne and swallow back my disappointment. It's for the best. I'm not a reckless person. My life was orderly and safe until events not within my control sent me spiraling. Pursuing a powerful man like him? Clearly, I don't know which way is up anymore.

Laughter filters across the space. A few groups over, my best friend, Emily, and her boyfriend and my new boss, Ciro, are in a large group, giddy and in high spirits, pleased as punch at all the attention. Tonight is the groundbreaking celebration for the new Riverview Casino on Brooklyn's waterfront. Ciro's business, C&C Enterprises, won the lucrative contract. "Money coming in like you wouldn't believe," Ciro likes to boast. If the family rumored to be building the casino saw the chaotic state of his office, they'd think twice about his managerial abilities.

I moved to New York City a week ago at Emily's prompting. Ciro needed a bookkeeper with strong organizational skills, and I needed an escape. What better place to fade into obscurity than New York, right?

My grandparents discouraged me. They distrust Ciro. Too ambitious. Too loud. Trouble written all over him. I don't disagree. But how long can a person survive abject numbness before forgetting how to breathe altogether?

Ciro insisted all C&C Enterprises' employees attend the club event. So here I am.

I glance around once more, then softly shake my head in defeat. "Dwelling on what you couldn't control, Riley," my therapist back home in Marietta, Ohio, liked to remind me, "will inhibit what you can control going forward."

Easy for her to say when her entire world hasn't imploded.

Light catches on my champagne flute, and a kaleidoscope of fireflies dance across the glass. An illusion of light within this dark club. A trick of the eye. A reminder that life, time, *love* are fleeting.

I lift my glass, desperate to capture the light for a little longer. Because at heart, I'm an optimist. It's just that Fate's been too cruel for me to be hopeful about anything anymore.

Out of nowhere, my elbow's jarred, and then everything happens in slow motion. A tall, leggy blonde brushes by, swinging her handbag as she passes. The crystal flute in my hand goes flying. Champagne rains down on me as the glass shatters on the hard concrete floor. The woman walks away, oblivious. Whatever illusion of control I thought I had slips.

It's not my ruined dress or the champagne dripping from my face, or even the alarm in several guests' expressions that sends me into a panic.

Gucci.

Her handbag was vintage Gucci.

The room tilts, and fireflies cloud my vision. Bitter pain pierces me, and my breathing shallows. I clutch my hands over my heart, fearing the fragmented pieces might come tumbling out.

Breathe, Riley. It's a panic attack. Over a stupid designer handbag, nothing more.

I glance around. Great, a few people are staring. New York was supposed to be a fresh start, and now I've caused a scene at a work event.

Move ... run.

My knees buckle as I stagger forward. But I don't go down, and push on. One foot. Then the other. Push. Push. Push. Onward in the direction of the women's restroom.

I tuck my chin and make a broad circle around Emily and Ciro, then cross the floor. No one but a handful of unlucky strangers witness my downward spiral right here in the middle of the casino's groundbreaking ceremony.

What doesn't kill you makes you stronger, right? But what happens when the closest people to you die? Does the same rule apply? Will you suddenly be gifted some fucked-up superhero powers now that you've experienced the worst Fate has to offer? If so, I could use them right now.

Take-me-to-the-bathroom power, *activated.*

"Honey, you're ..." someone cries out in alarm. I keep moving and don't acknowledge her, not even when she finishes her sentence. "... *bleeding.*"

I don't want attention, pity, or concern. I want the cold embrace of comfortable oblivion to swallow me whole.

Finally, I reach the restroom and hurry inside, pushing into an empty stall before doubling over with my hands on my knees, hyperventilating yet fighting for control.

Focus on your breath.

Everything will be okay.

No. Not okay. Never okay. Lower your expectation to nearly bearable.

Slowly, ever so slowly, I relax and regain some semblance of normalcy.

I stay like this for a while. Women enter, occupy the stalls next to me, wash their hands, then leave. And little by little, my mind calms enough to plan.

Wash my face. Fold my hands over my ruined dress and hide the champagne stain until I can make it to the exit. Go home and drink a cup of tea. Earl Grey tea—it's good for the immune system.

Plan in place, I exit the stall and approach the mirror to assess the damage.

Champagne-soaked hair frames my sticky face. I wash it away while nausea rolls through the pit of my stomach. *Damn overpriced designer handbags.*

I dry my face and decolletage with a few paper towels. More towels, less and less stickiness. The process continues until I can press a hand to my cheek and remove it without a soft sizzle similar to the noise slime makes when you roll it in your palm. By the time I'm finished, my hands have stopped shaking.

I consider my next steps and then retrieve my cell phone from my dress pocket and text Emily.

> Riley: Broke my heel so headed home. Talk
> tomorrow.

Do I feel bad about lying? Not really. Emily doesn't believe nonmilitary people can suffer from PTSD. Heck, I spent days online researching my diagnosis to better understand how psychological trauma is at the heart of these illogical reactions. There's no chance in hell I'll share my panic attack, especially not how it was triggered by a designer handbag. As far as Emily is concerned, I'm the same girl who completed her best friend's calculus homework and reasoned with her about why her current flavor-of-the-month didn't deserve her tears.

Unfortunately, the list on Ciro could be turned into a book, one I began mentally compiling only this week.

With my composure fully in place, I exit the bathroom and make a beeline for the front entrance. I cross the club and exit onto the street without issue, and as luck would have it, a large white car sits waiting at the curb.

Thank heavens. I hurry forward, pull open the door, and climb into the backseat. "I'll pay you double if you take me home now," I tell the Uber driver. "I live five blocks away. You'll be back in time for whoever hired you." It's a bold move. But logical, considering it's a win-win situation for both of us.

I feel his stare from behind his dark sunglasses.

"Please get me out of here," I softly insist, pulling the door closed behind me. "Tonight's been difficult." His head turns toward the side-walk, and I glance out the window, trying to track what's captured his attention.

My gasp fills the car. It's him. My stranger. He's exited the club and is outside the vehicle, standing a few feet away, frozen mid-side-walk and shooting daggers at the driver.

Oh, sweet hell. I've stolen his Uber.

"Get out," the driver snaps.

I look away from his scowl to the stranger's harsh stare.

"Listen and listen carefully. Either leave or I'll toss your ass inside the trunk and take you for a ride you'll regret."

I search the car dashboard for his Uber credentials, so I can report him for threatening a customer.

Which is why I don't notice the stranger's approach until the back door's jerked open. I jump at the same time the driver begins violently cursing. The stranger bends his head, and our eyes lock.

Rage fills his dark blue eyes. He's every bit as intimidating this close as he was from across the bar. Everything stills as he skims his eyes over me, from my long legs to the hem brushing my knees, across my tight waist—made even smaller by my frequently skipped meals—to my chest. With narrowing eyes, his attention lingers there, like he can see my heart beneath my left collarbone, rumbling like the epicenter of an earthquake, and is fascinated by it. And the longer he stares, the stronger the quaking becomes.

"For Christ's sake, this is your last warning," the driver bellows. "Get yourself gone."

Despite my downward slide tonight, I'm not reckless, and not one to debate with ornery drivers or steal rides from dangerous men who radiate power like a nuclear warhead. Not in less intimidating circumstances, and most definitely not now. I scooch toward the door like the good girl my mother raised me to be.

Except, it's too late. The intimidating stranger is already climbing into the car.

As he settles into the seat and adjusts his long legs and suit jacket, I don't say a word. And neither does the driver.

The tension inside the car grows with each passing second while I discreetly inch my way toward the opposite door.

Seconds turn into a minute before he speaks. "This is a surprise." His tone's deep with a raspy growl.

I stare at my lap yet still feel the driver's glare through his sunglasses.

"Drive. Or is there anyone else you'd like to offer a ride?"

Lord. If sarcasm were a weapon, the stranger's tongue would be lethal. I swallow hard and inch further away. My earlier assessment is correct—he gets off on taking hearts and crushing souls.

"No one else," the driver replies, unfazed. Far from the man who threatened to toss me into the trunk moments ago.

Five blocks.

Sit quietly. Avoid attention. *Survive.*

I frown at the thought and shoot a glance at the man next to me. Mercifully, his attention's turned toward the club.

"Where to?"

I jump at the driver's question, then blush. I'm the reason the car sits idle at the curb. In a soft voice, I rattle off my address.

The car pulls into the street and then silence descends like a steel trap.

I pretend to study my hands, but this man has enraptured me all night, so instead, I peer at him beneath my lashes. Black shoes polished to perfection. Long legs encased in an expensive designer suit tailored to fit his body. A rich leather belt with a gold buckle. White dress shirt neatly pressed and silk navy tie, both visible beneath his suit jacket. Is he a Wall Street executive? An investor with a stake in the new casino? His harsh manner and authoritative vibe suggest so.

I glance at his profile.

Dark hair. Clean-shaven jawline. Tightly drawn lips, as he thumbs his phone and skims through messages.

Ignoring me completely.

He's the whole package, a present wrapped in thorns.

I look out my window. What did I expect? Flirtation? An indecent proposal? Look at me. My hair is damp, and my dress reeks of champagne. My makeup is now nonexistent and my mental state questionable. Making it to my apartment without any more issues is the new plan. *Be thankful he's preoccup—*

"You're bleeding all over the car."

I stiffen with surprise, then spin toward him. He continues scrolling through his phone, as if he didn't address me.

"No I'm not."

"I must be imagining it."

I glance at one bare arm and then the other, remembering the woman's screech earlier.

Pain shoots through me, and I gasp. He's poked a fingertip into a gash on my lower calf. I'm horrified as he shows me his bloody finger.

"How did that happen?" I mutter, alarmed. I was that focused on my appearance, I missed an injury? *No one except your aging grandparents care about you now, Riley. If you don't take care of yourself, no one will.*

I force back tears while he watches me intently.

An uncomfortable silence follows.

"Open your mouth."

His deep commanding tone sends shivers up my spine. Without thinking, I obey.

"Eyes on me while you suck it clean."

I blink, at first not comprehending. Then, why he's demanding I do such a thing hits me; *this man enjoys playing with broken things.*

Call it shock, weariness, fatigue or *recognition*—of who I am and who I want him to be—whatever it is has me testing the theory.

I lean in and then wrap my lips around his digit.

The metallic taste of blood is less surprising than his reaction. His eyes deepen to an impossible blue, the color of a Midwest summer sky after a storm's torn through. Energy radiates through me. It's like I'm sucking the power clean off his finger. It's dangerous and heady, and far, far beyond the definition of extreme.

I haven't crossed the line; I've blown it out of the stratosphere. And yet, I push harder, suck harder until his nostrils absolutely, positively flare.

The driver clears his throat, breaking our connection and ruining the moment. How long has the car been parked in front of my building? I free his finger and turn toward the driver.

"Get out while you can." Something in the driver's tone makes me wonder if I'll actually be able to get out, but I reach for the door handle, then the door falls open, and my fear fades.

I can't help but glance over my shoulder at my stranger.

He's back on his phone. For a moment, I'm certain I'm already forgotten, until he draws the same finger I sucked on across his lips.

Ignored, maybe.

Forgotten, not at all.

I hesitate. A desperate desire for more of whatever this dangerous man has to offer has me thinking the unthinkable.

Before it has me asking the unimaginable.

"Do you want to come upstairs?"

NEVER IN MY life have I been so reckless.

I glance over my shoulder at the stranger as we climb the stairs to my fourth-floor walkup. Random acts are not my thing, and I'm shocked I invited him in.

My friends back home joked how my house was the nicest in town, yet they hardly saw the inside. I had my reasons for keeping my family life private. But the truth is I'm great at being the shoulder others cry on yet struggle asking for help myself. Not that this stopped the Big-Hearts-with-Big-Mouths back in Marietta politely inquiring about my mental condition after "The Tragedy," believing talking about what happened will fix me.

Just for a little while, I want to give no fucks. Tonight, every fiber within me is awake. And, if the man behind me gets off on playing with broken things, guess what? Tonight's his lucky night.

"All these apartments are vacant?" His gravelly tone breaks the silence and echoes through the stairwell.

"Yes. My unit was the first one renovated. The rest are under construction."

"You live alone in the building?" Lord, his voice is sexy, even while laced with disapproval.

"My best friend was supposed to be my roommate." We reach the top-floor landing, and I find my key. "But she moved in with her boyfriend. I've only been in New York City for a week and haven't had the time to find another roommate."

We fall quiet as I unlock the door. Then we step inside and into the kitchen, and I flip on the light.

"This is the lock?"

My lips draw tight. Ciro's LLC owns the building and was renovating it as a flip, up until C&C Enterprises won the casino contract. Progress has slowed, yet the workers completing the renovations still show up sporadically for a few hours' work. I requested a better lock, but Ciro dismissed my concerns, reminding me about the expensive, high-tech keypad and the overpriced security cameras installed in the main entrance. "No place safer in Brooklyn," he informed me, blowing me off.

"That's the lock," I reply, a bit unnerved by the stranger's unwavering regard.

"The construction crew all women?"

"All women? No."

"You can't be that stupid."

The insult shocks me like a blast of ice water in the face. *You wanted to feel something, Riley. And he delivered.* I wait for my anger to surface. Because he's correct, a five-year-old could pick the lock.

His eyes bore into me as he leans casually against the door, radiating a heady combination of arrogance, power, and danger. My wildly thumping heart competes with the warning bells in my mind. I should feel insulted and demand he leave. But I won't. The tension between us crackles, powerful enough to dissolve his harsh words and strip away my common sense.

"You're right," I murmur, and he blinks in surprise. "The lock needs replacing."

His blue eyes are like the deepest sea, turbulent and unrelenting, dragging me into uncharted territory, as he studies me. But there's no warning when he prowls forward, forcing me to step backward until I'm against the bathroom door, facing the entry. He places a hand to my right and draws in close, caging me. His head tips, and I gasp as his warm tongue touches below my ear. He smells like lemon and spice. Looks like a wet dream. And everything about him feels ... *right*.

I must be losing my mind.

My lips part with a small gasp as he licks a trail across my jawline. "Why did you invite me inside?" he growls. A shiver races up my spine at his husky tone.

"You know why," I whisper.

"You want me to fuck you." Statement, not question.

I nod. Except how do I tell him it's not just that? How do I invite a complete stranger—even one so shockingly handsome—to overpower me with sensation, play with each and every shattered piece within me, and make me feel alive?

His eyebrows pinch as he reads my expression.

"Please," I beg.

He cups the back of my neck and holds me still while ever so slowly drawing a finger, like a knife blade, across my throat. To strike fear? To intimidate? To force me to squirm and push him off me?

It's a dangerous game we're playing. Even so, excitement licks up my spine as I act on instinct alone and tilt back my head, offering him my throat.

His grin catches me by surprise. Arrogant. Dangerous. Sexy beyond words.

His thumbs press against my throat. "Ever orgasm like this?"

Wide-eyed, I shake my head.

"Oxygen restriction heightens the pleasure."

I'm at a loss for words. Don't most men steal a kiss or grab ass as part of foreplay? Lean into it with charm and intent? "Erotic asphyxiation," I murmur. "The brain releases endorphins and adrenaline, causing a drug-like high."

His eyes pierce me, and my body warms beneath the intense scrutiny. Finally, he steps back. Loss sweeps over me, but it's temporary.

"Take off your dress."

My hands shake, yet I manage to reach behind me and unzip my black dress. It slides down my body and pools at my ankles. Leaving me in a flimsy lace bra and matching thong with a triangular patch that barely covers my sex.

"Holy fuck."

His hungry gaze rakes over me while I stand frozen and he looks his fill. His reaction is reassuring, and Lord knows I need more than a flash of his wicked grin to counter the fact I'm slightly terrified.

He removes his belt and unbuttons his pants. Wow, is this really happening? Before I can change my mind, he's spinning me around and pushing me belly-first into the door. My heart beats against the wooden panel. Rat-tat-tat. Rat-tat-tat. Every pulse is dialed into him.

My arms are pulled back, and expensive leather wraps around my wrists.

"Wait," I protest, reality crashing in. Oh God. He's binding my wrists. What was I thinking, relinquishing control to a complete stranger?

He nudges a thigh between mine, spreading them. "Stop fighting what we both want."

"And what's that?" I squeak.

"Your surrender."

He rips off my thong and pushes two fingers inside me. My walls clamp around them like a vise grip. "Wet, just like I thought." He finger-fucks me without mercy, and I stretch to accommodate him, feeling deliciously wicked despite the sting.

"I wasn't expecting this sweet pussy to be so fucking tight." He scrapes my earlobe between his teeth and then softens the bite with a lick.

There's a rustle behind me, then foil crackling.

I brace myself as he slides his cock across my slit. Everything stills except for my shaking body. He hooks an arm around me, and I jerk in surprise when he pinches a nipple. "Shhh," his silky hush warns. "Let me play." He cups my breast in his palm like he's weighing it, and his erection thickens against my center. Pain mixes with plea-sure, his touch rough and then gentle while he pinches and strokes one nipple and then the other.

"Cazzo, I'm tempted to fuck your beautiful breasts right here on the floor."

Warmth gathers at my core, and I bite my lip, wondering if he can feel my excitement, but then stop thinking altogether when his hand slides down my stomach. His fingers glide across my clit and I buck beneath his firm touch.

He laughs. "That's right. Beg me for it."

"Please ..."

"Please what?" he demands, not quite serious, not quite friendly. "Say it."

"Make me submit."

Everything stills. He thought I was going to say, "Fuck me." It's obvious I've surprised him.

"You're goddamn perfect," he mutters like he's struggling to believe it. Like I'm not the only one who's lost her mind.

He wraps his fingers around my throat, then squeezes and shoves his cock so hard into me, I'm forced up onto my toes.

I struggle for balance and breath, and to accommodate his enormous size. Because he's *huge*. And I'm practically a virgin. My one fumbling boyfriend was more an experiment than my forever person.

His arm pushes into my stomach, and he holds me in place while he slowly withdraws, only to thrust into me one more. I see stars. From the controlled press of his fingers or from the forceful fucking I'm taking, it's hard to know.

"You won't walk straight for weeks when I'm done with you." His dirty promise echoes around the kitchen.

"Go on, then," I recklessly insist. "Make me crawl."

A long pause follows. Clearly, I've surprised him once more. Then he mutters, "Fucking perfect," and proceeds to live up to his naughty promise.

He fucks me like it's a religious experience, cursing and grunting and groaning against my neck. Months of nothingness unravels into aching need. I've never felt this full, this worshipped. And, although I've never orgasmed from sex—aside from my own experimental touches—my body responds like it was custom-made for him.

The hand at my throat drops to my breast, and as he rolls his palm over it, I swear his erection thickens deep inside me.

My body begins to shake. "Oh my God," I chant. "Oh. My. God."

"Come before I say you can"—he pinches my breast in warning—"and I'll spank you until your ass burns."

I whimper; failure is likely. I've been spiraling all night, invited a stranger home for sex and let him bind my arms and choke me. My self-control is just another broken part of me.

"Christ's sake, not like this." Withdrawing, he lifts me by the hips and spins me around, before settling me against the door and himself back inside me.

My elbows brush the trim.

"Wrap your thighs around my waist."

I hiss as I readjust so my inner thighs straddle his hip bones, drawing him impossibly deeper and making obeying him that much more difficult.

His hungry gaze lifts from my breasts to my face.

"What's your name?"

I blink. "Riley."

Seconds pass until it becomes obvious. "Aren't you going to tell me your name?" I say.

"Doesn't matter. I'm fucking you senseless, then tossing the condom into the trash and leaving."

Every twisted part of me breaks all over again. Because as infuriating as he is, I want his kind of dirty. "Why ask my name if you're fucking and running?" I insist.

He snorts. "Leaving. Not running."

"It's the same thing."

"It's not. Running would imply you mean something to me. You don't."

Ouch.

I squirm, and he hisses. His cock is still hard as steel.

"Do it," I demand. Surprising him, and myself. "Finish, and then stroll on out of here."

Without warning, he grabs me by the throat. To intimidate me? To show me who is boss?

I don't understand what possesses me. Maybe it's tonight's panic attack. Maybe I've lost so much, walking the ledge between life and death feels normal. Maybe it's simply curiosity ... At this point, I'll take pleasure, even the risky sort, over anguish any day. Acting on instinct, I tilt my head back and dare him with my eyes to squeeze harder.

And he does.

Until my eyes tear up.

Until there's a shift between us, this tiny fragile thing, this pull neither of us can deny.

"Christ's sake." He curses and drops his hand to grasp my ass. Hiding his face in my breasts, he pulls me onto him and drives into me like a man possessed.

I'm bound and at his mercy. Moving with him while we fall into a quick rhythm. "Oh God," I cry out, my body knowing what it wants even if my mind doesn't. "Please," I whisper. "I'm so close."

"Fucking hell," he groans. "I want to destroy this tight pussy. Fill you with so much come, you'll be drowning in it."

His dirty words have me begging. "Please. Say yes. I don't care if you leave afterward. I don't care if you fuck my breasts on the kitchen floor. My entire body is on fire. I never ..."

"Never what?" he demands.

"I need to," I plead, avoiding his question. "*Now.*"

He stiffens. "Jesus Christ."

"What are you doing? Don't stop."

"You asked for it."

I'm bounced into the air, just to the point where his bulbous tip rests at my entrance. Perched in this position, the seconds feel like minutes, until he relaxes his hold and my full body weight descends onto him. I take his massive erection in one brutal fall and swear my womb is crying.

"Ahhh," is all I manage, the sweet, painful building tension picking up where it left off. If he repeats that move again, I'll shatter.

"Look at me."

I open my eyes, not even realizing I closed them.

"Ask me if you can come."

"Can I come?"

"No."

If my wrists weren't bound, I'd slap his smug face.

He pulls me into his chest without breaking stride, flexing his hips and driving me wild, because he's so mind-shatteringly deep. "I'll do anything," I cry out, desperate. "What do you want from me?"

"What you promised earlier."

I struggle in his arms, tension coiling like a spring seconds away from snapping. My mind races, trying to solve the riddle so we can put an end to this game.

"Submit like a good girl, then you can come all over my dick."

How can a man be this beautiful and so filthy? I groan and plead with him with my eyes. *Please. I need this more than you'll ever know.*

"Count to three."

I blink as he lifts me once more, then hastily begin to count. "One. Two." He relaxes his arm and flexes his hips, and I nearly pass out, completely forgetting to say three while I erupt around him.

"Yeah, Riley," he groans. "So fucking good."

My name lingers in the air as his thrusts become more violent. Then he jerks deep, holds still, and curses in Italian against my neck.

You never forget your firsts; first day at school, first A, first car, first backseat kiss, first drink, first loss, first one-night stand, *first orgasm.* But anchored against his hard chest, with his lips suckling my neck and his cock still inside me, I realize something else about firsts —they always, always end.

And, as warned, he does just that.

Without a word, he withdraws and sets me on my feet to his right, then disappears inside the bathroom. I stand on shaky legs, the toilet flushing and water running. We don't speak when he returns, fresh and composed, and cold ... so brutally cold. Like he's utterly unaffected by what transpired.

I'm frozen, stunned. *What were you expecting, a high-five?*

He opens the door but then pauses to glance over his shoulder. Like he's about to ask for my number. Like I'd consider repeating tonight's insanity, even as I'm thanking God I'm alive and not a victim of my recklessness. I mean, he's leaving while my wrists are still bound.

But I don't regret tonight. He's given me something more to dwell on than sadness and remorse. A dirty, filthy memory. Of a time when I relinquished control and felt more alive than I have in years.

My eyes lock on his face.

His rake over my body.

But instead of asking for my phone number, my cold, cavalier hookup demands something utterly baffling.

"Get the goddamn lock fixed."

HE'S NOT COMING.

My one-night stand, who turned into consecutive Friday nights and then into every night over the course of a few weeks. It was hardly the beginning of a meaningful relationship. People talk in healthy relationships. He said hello and goodbye, and between, fucked me six ways to Sunday. His touch was addictive. *He* was addictive.

His late-night visits became less frequent until they stopped entirely.

Three weeks now.

It's over.

I curl a tea bag around a spoon. It's two in the morning, a bad time for a caffeine fix. Except, I can't sleep, so what does it matter?

He left that night after our wild fling, and I thought that was the end of it. Then, a few days later, a man in an expensive suit showed up at my apartment to install a new lock. Ciro—when I approached him later about it—was dumbfounded, and I realized he was the wrong man to thank. Not fully comprehending I'd soon be doing so in person.

My buzzer rang, waking me. It was well past midnight, but I scrambled from bed to answer the door, believing guilt had driven Emily to come over to apologize for a fight we'd had over dinner. That, or because she'd left Ciro. Because who else would show up at this hour?

Except it wasn't Emily standing there, eyes smoldering and daring me, just daring me, to comment on his return. As if his presence didn't make my throat go dry and words impossible. He came every Friday night, then practically every night until his visits stopped altogether.

Now, it's over.

I squeeze the amber liquid from the tea bag. The tea's too hot, but I drink it anyway, welcoming the burn and the reminder that even something outwardly innocent like tea can still hurt you.

The things we did, the boundaries he pushed …

He was everything I didn't know I was searching for.

Liquid sloshes across my T-shirt and kitchen floor. "Great," I mutter, setting everything on the counter before tearing off the shirt to rinse it in the sink. Once finished, I grab a towel, get onto my knees, and wipe up the mess, blindly making wide swooping arcs to reach liquid I can't see while I work.

Why is it so dark in here?

Big windows bookend my apartment's railroad-style layout, with plenty of natural light filtering in. The kitchen and small functional bathroom sit on one end, the living area square in the middle, and my bedroom on the other side. With renovations ongoing and the other apartments vacant, it's quiet at night.

"You live in a newly renovated NYC apartment rent-free," Emily informed me after I finally commented on how she'd bailed on being my roommate. One minute, she was crying over catching Ciro snorting coke like a character straight out of the movie *Scarface*, and in the next—after I suggested she move in with me "as planned"—she was defending him and attacking me. "Everything always has to be about poor, poor Riley, doesn't it?"

This from a friend who'd picked me up from the airport, dropped me off at the curb, informed me there'd been a change in plans and she'd moved in with Ciro, then, blurting out the entry code, drove off without the slightest remorse.

I'd stood on the sidewalk, in an unfamiliar city, in front of an unfamiliar building, two suitcases at my side and my one connection to home abandoning me. Left behind with an emptiness eating away at me.

"He could charge *thousands*."

"Is that why you're dating him?" I snapped, unleashing an anger that had been brewing for months. "For his money?"

Her claws came out to sink into my jugular. "I liked you better when you barely talked."

I stood up from the table, wavering somewhere between being the wrecking ball and the wrecked. "We'll talk when you're ready to hear the truth," I said in a flat voice before walking off.

But maybe I have changed. Still broken, yet not entirely defenseless.

I submitted to him yet discovered an inner strength long absent from my life.

With a sigh, I sit back on my haunches and toss the towel at the sink. "Why did he have to end it so soon?"

A grunt disrupts the quiet. A muffled sound, which has me falling backward. I search for the source, and find it at my kitchen table, a shadowy figure seated in the dark.

My eyes shift toward the door.

"Don't." *His* voice.

Fear quickly changes to indignation. "How long have you been sitting there?" The kitchen curtains are pulled closed, shrouding the table in darkness. I can barely make out his features.

I stand, arms folded, very aware how naked I am, wearing nothing but a skimpy red thong.

He doesn't respond. Typical. What else should I expect from a man who so reluctantly offered me his name. *Al*—that's all I got. "I wasn't expecting you."

"I know."

Three weeks, and he knows?

"Come here."

My stomach dips as I stand rooted in place, my hesitation shrouded by worry, because *that* voice is nonnegotiable. Yet he disappears and then reappears, and all he has for me is "I know"?

"Riley." His tone's laced with warning.

I close my eyes in defeat.

"Please."

Not once, in all the time we've spent together, has he ever used that word. I'm the pleaser. He's the taker. And never is the dividing line crossed.

He doesn't deserve my obedience, though I worry how he'll react if I completely disobey, so I meet him halfway, shuffling by him to open the kitchen curtain. Moonbeams dance across my skin, though he remains obscured by shadows.

"How did you get inside?"

"Used my key."

"What?" I gasp. "You have a key to my apartment?"

He counters my question with one of his own. "I've failed, haven't I?"

"Failed?" I stare at him, incredulous.

"At corrupting you."

A shiver races up my spine. That voice. That tone. He makes me forget my own name. "No," I whisper.

"Let me see," he orders. "Unfold your arms."

My skin heats beneath a flush. What a picture I must have made, bare-chested and crawling around on the floor. His lips have crisscrossed every inch of my body, so why this crippling shyness?

"Show me what you're hiding, baby."

Baby. The word feels like a soft caress from this harsh, no-nonsense man. Did he feel my absence, as much as I missed him?

I drop my arms, and my D-cup-size breasts bounce free. On my small frame, breasts this size appear bigger. And he, freakishly, loves them. Is borderline obsessed with them.

"Come here."

I step closer. My mema's crystal cocktail glass on the table, alongside a nearly empty whiskey bottle I don't recognize.

He had a few drinks the night we met, but I've never seen him drunk.

"What's wrong?"

His midnight black hair's mussed, like he's been running fingers through it. Scruff darkens his chin like he's forgotten to shave. I've memorized even the curve of his lips, the cupid's bow of his upper lip softening the rigid set of his bottom lip. I focus on the upper one, the antithesis of the steely force I've grown accustomed to.

How little I know about him, other than he thrives on control, domination, and filthy, dirty sex. He's always well-groomed, hair smoothed back and face baby-bottom smooth.

But tonight ... something's upsetting him.

"Say something."

"I'm here."

"I didn't notice," I quip. Such a liar. Because I notice everything about him. The spicy lemon cologne he wears. The tension sizzling between us. His face, body, enormous dick. The way Italian bleeds into his words, especially when he's bossy or extra dirty in bed.

"This is the last place I should be." He drops my cell phone onto the table with a clatter. Why did he have it? Was he scrolling through it?

As his comment registers, my earlier irritation reignites. Am I some magical, big-breasted siren who's lured him in? Does he actually believe, after weeks of relinquishing complete control, I have power over him?

"Then go," I respond, and mean it. I might beg him to fuck me, but I won't plead with him to stay.

The silence between us builds to a crescendo.

"You make my life impossible."

It's the only warning I get.

He lunges, knocking over his chair as he grabs me by the waist, hauling me off my feet, then rolling me back across the kitchen table. His arms wrap around me as he nuzzles his face between my breasts.

"I didn't mean it." I weave my fingers through his hair. Soothing him. Comforting him. "I've been waiting for you."

"Riley." He growls my name against my skin.

In moments like this, he allows me inside. Deepening our connection in a way words never could. His vulnerability as tangible as my fragile heart. I sensed the shift in him the week before his late-night visits stopped. Relentlessly overpowering me every way he could was normal but wrapping me in his arms afterward and praising me until I fell asleep was new.

What changed to make him stop coming?

His lips find my nipple. I smirk—they always do. God, I missed his mouth on me. Teeth scrape flesh, followed by pain softened with pleasure. I arch into him, relinquishing myself completely.

"Cazzo," he mutters then tenses. Just like that, everything shifts. "This shouldn't be this fucking hard."

His admission guts me. He doesn't *want* to want me. "You're breaking up with me." Hurt catches on each forced word.

He steps back—an answer in itself—and I hop off the table.

Tipping my chin up, I dare look at him. And immediately wish I hadn't.

His dark, brooding gaze locks on my face. Almost as if he was looking at a puzzle piece without a puzzle present to solve. Almost like we never stood a chance, but somehow we find ourselves in this moment.

"It's complicated," he grinds out.

"Explain it to me, then."

He stares at me. One second. Two. Then, he scowls and a steel wall slams down so hard between us, my teeth rattle. *Not today, Riley. Not ever.*

He disappears into the connecting bathroom. The faucet runs, and I listen to him splashing water on his face. I stand frozen. One part wanting him to leave; one part desperate for him to stay.

He returns, as cool, calm, and collected as the man I invited home that first night.

Silence thickens the air, but it's me who breaks it.

I pull my shoulders straight and draw on every ounce of pride remaining. "Am I just a fuck to you?"

"And if I say yes?"

His callous question is a punch in the stomach. This isn't within the rules of the games we play. This isn't me being a good girl or him pushing my boundaries. I might willingly, even eagerly, relinquish power, but what I won't do is be some doormat he can walk all over. "Go on. Leave. I've survived worse than you."

He frowns.

With a shaky hand, I gesture toward the door. If there's anything I know how to do, it's endure.

Everything pauses.

"Goddamn you," he growls, and before I can guess his intent, I'm swept into his arms and carried toward the bedroom.

SUNLIGHT FILTERS in between the blinds, waking me. A smile carves my lips. Late-night hours and early-morning summer sunshine might not play nicely together, but shades of my old self are resurfacing. Every day I wake up stronger than the day before.

Even if every blessed muscle in my body aches.

Last night was incredible.

He carried me to bed, undressed me, laid me down on the mattress, and with a surprising gentleness, showered my breasts, neck, and lips with kisses.

Then, he made love to me.

You never know someone completely, do you? They dress in a

certain style or move in a familiar fashion. Act in ways you grow accustomed to and sometimes, intentionally, say things to evoke a reaction. You label everything to derive meaning; husband, boyfriend, lover, or gullible, naive, innocent. Life is orderly that way, with no space for shades of grey.

But do you truly know them?

Because life is shrouded by greyness. And often, you don't realize it exists until it's too late.

Just consider my father's perfect fiancée. So popular and pretty. So young, too—a few years older than me. Yet look what she did. Look at the life she took and the one she destroyed. Look at the woman she devastated.

I shake off the last thought. What I'm learning—what *he's* taught me—is when you live a life without pain, you'll never truly know pleasure.

"Good girl." "Look how well my greedy girl takes my cock." "Come for me, Riley." He was gentle after weeks of aggressive fucking. I gave myself to him completely, and never felt so alive. But I'm not alone in sensing the shift in our relationship or how the bliss from one sweet comment could offset his typical filthy sex-talk.

"You feel like home."

Did he really say it, or was it a dream?

I roll toward the sunlight but don't notice him right away. He's seated in a chair pulled up next to the bed, hunched forward with elbows on thighs while he studies me.

"Couldn't sleep?" I sit up and secure the bedsheet around me.

He shakes his head.

Whatever was bothering him still plagues him, doesn't it? "What's wrong?"

"Tell me a secret no one else knows."

This is what he's been contemplating all this time? "Like what?"

"Something you're not proud of. A dirty little secret."

I stiffen as his request knocks the wind out of me. Weeks of carefully piecing my heart back together only to be asked to voice the impossible. "Will you tell me your name first?" I demand, deflecting. Because, before *I* reveal the darkest corner in my life, he should offer me the simplest pieces of himself—his full name. "Al is an abbreviation. Is your name Albert? Alex? Allen?"

"Al is all you need to know."

"You feel like home," Albert, Alex, or Allen had grunted in my ear. Or was it my imagination, desperate to move our relationship forward?

I stare at him. So cold to the eye. So proud and confident. So distrustful ... suspicious, even. Like I'd ever betray him. "You can trust me, you know."

"Trust isn't the problem."

I wait for him to elaborate, and then give up. It's clearly up to me to deepen our connection, as hard as it may be. "My dirty little secret is my father's fiancée shot him and then herself over a Gucci bag. She was upset about a canceled credit card. She spent so much money, more than my father could afford. The newspaper headlines called her *'The Baby-Faced Murderess.'* It made national news." Even to my ears, my admission sounds clinical and cavalier, like I'm discussing a balance sheet that doesn't add up.

"Cazzo!" he exclaims, with more expression than I've ever witnessed from him. He straightens, prepared to battle. To defend me. Except the war's already over, and I ended up on the losing side.

He waits for me to continue, but I pause. This kind of hurt can only be addressed in spurts and is better said like I'm listing facts off paper. "Stephanie shot my father in the head. He died. I was left with my grandparents."

"It doesn't bother you?"

"It does. I found them. Pieces of their brains were splattered across the white tile entryway. It was dark when I entered the house, and I slipped and fell, not understanding at first what caused me to lose footing ..."

"Jesus Christ. Come here, baby."

I spring from the bed and climb onto his lap. He pulls me in tight, and I snuggle into his arms.

"The first thing I noticed was her handbag."

Silence descends. It's always the damn bag that does it. They say speaking your truth will set you free. And Lord knows, I've done everything I can to avoid discussing what happened. All the busybodies back in Marietta can attest to it, as can the therapist I left behind.

I draw in a breath and then let everything out. "What hurts me the most and what I most feel guilty about is that I'm so fucking angry at him. Because he asked her to marry him and never told me. Stephanie and I despised each other—we were briefly in the same accounting class at college until she was caught cheating and dropped out, which said a lot about her character. But still, what father gets engaged without telling his only child? I found out about the engagement in the news."

He goes rigid beneath me, and I immediately worry I was too honest. He asked for a dirty little secret. I gave him the weight of my fucked-up world.

"I said too much ..."

"And your mother?" he asks, surprising me. "Where is she?"

"She passed from cancer when I was fifteen. It's just me and my grandparents now." I snuggle further into his arms. It's true you never get over losing a loved one, even if you're angry or feeling abandoned. Anguish may subside over time but missing them never fades away. "Have you ever lost someone?" I croak.

"My mother. Drug overdose. My father didn't know we existed until we showed up on his doorstep. He was twenty. We were five."

I do the math, but don't comment on the obvious. He's opening up, and we've reached an enormous milestone. "You have a sister?" I ask instead.

"Brother."

I consider that for a second, curious if they're close. I'm a single child but imagine if I had a sibling, we'd be best friends. His tenderness last night makes me think he's a good brother. That he protects those close to him. "You never really know a person, do you?" I whisper.

"No. You don't."

"Can I tell you something else?"

He's quiet for a few seconds too long. "Go on."

"You're the best kind of hurt."

He tenses for the briefest moment like I surprised him. Then he tightens his arms around me and confirms the feeling. I'm completely and utterly vulnerable right now yet feel safe in his embrace. When was the last time I felt so protected? Months? Years?

I relax into his arms, and we fall quiet, offering our heavy words space to settle. After a long while, I break the silence. "Ready for my darkest secret?"

"Fuck no." His chest rumbles. "I need a whiskey shot for this?"

I turn in his lap and rest my head on his shoulder so I can see his face. "I faked an orgasm."

His eyes flash.

I almost laugh. He thinks I meant with him.

"When?" he growls.

I'm tempted to lie. To press his buttons. After he loved on me all night and well into the morning, in full command and with me in full compliance, as every ache, bruise, and whisker burn applauds him for it, it's comical he'd question his prowess.

"Riley," he grinds out. Like he doesn't *know*.

I rise up and kiss his drawn lips. "With my ex-boyfriend back in Marietta," I clarify. "I faked them."

"Why?"

I sigh. "I didn't want him to feel bad."

"Them. More than one?" He scowls. Like an injustice has been served—on my behalf or not, it's difficult to decipher.

"All of them."

"Madonna!"

I smile at his expression. "He was madly in love with me. It was easier to pretend than to embarrass him. We only had sex a couple of times." My first love, except I always knew something was missing. Too sweet. Not *bossy* enough. "We never experimented."

"My greedy girl never got oral?"

"Nope." I flush. "No spankings. No handcuffed to the bed."

"That stupid kid didn't go down on your sweet pussy?"

"Never."

He stares at me, much like he did hours ago, like I'm an enigma he's struggling to figure out. Something within my expression causes him to stiffen, and then, with a look intense enough to burn steel, he demands, "And the others?"

"Others?"

His jaw slackens, his expression almost *pained*.

It's not how I anticipated he'd react. He thinks I'm a good girl, and I am. Trouble came calling for my parents, not me. I follow the rules. I choose right over wrong. The few white lies I've told were to protect someone's feelings from being shattered. I told my boyfriend we were breaking up because of me. Part white lie, part truth, though until I met *him*, I didn't truly understand what was missing. Orgasms, yet more.

A wave of shyness grips me, but I owe him the truth. "The other can spark an orgasm with the crook of his finger."

He stands and places me on my feet so quickly, I get whiplash. Then, he begins to pace. To the wall, and back to the chair. Back and forth. Wall. Chair. His broad chest, tapered waist, massive cock, and well-formed thighs on full display. No one could doubt his masculinity.

But his curses set me on edge. "Jesus Christ. Fuck. Cazzo."

I watch him, alarmed, as he thrusts his fist through the drywall.

What in God's teeth? He's losing his shit.

"What's the matter?"

He ignores me and heads for the kitchen. I hear the refrigerator open, and then seconds later, ice falling into a glass.

This worked up over a discussion about orgasms?

"Riley," he bellows. He *never* raises his voice. "Bring me my clothes."

Hurt washes over me. I shared my soul with him. Who does he think he is?

My feet won't move, but my mind races. He was tender and attentive. Loving, I'd dared to believe. Only we've circled back to where we started last night.

Like a robot, I pull on a robe and scoop the clothes piled on the floor into my arms. The hole in the wall competes with the one unraveling within my heart.

His eyes skim over me when I enter the kitchen.

Not cold, but hot. Like a fire rages within yet he's helpless to stop it. He shoots back a whiskey, then without a word, without an apology or explanation, takes the pile from my hands and disappears into the bathroom.

When he reemerges, he's not alone in his rage.

I feel foolish. It's one thing to be on your knees and begging to be fucked. It's another to be as intimate as two people can be, only to get fucked over. Eleven weeks of emotional whiplash, and my heart can no longer bear it.

Tears fall, but I swipe them away.

Back to me, he drinks straight from the bottle, before slamming it on the table, turning and stalking toward where I wait by the door. He moves to open it.

"Say it," I exclaim.

His jaw tightens.

"Say it." I rise on my toes and get in his face. "We're over. Give me that much."

His jaw tics. One second passes. Two.

On three, he nudges me aside and exits into the hallway.

He couldn't do it.

Damn him. Why didn't he say it?

CHAPTER 2

Alessandro

"YOU END IT?"

The backseat buckles beneath my weight as the waiting Cadillac purrs to life. This SUV is a reward from my father for a job well done, customized to my exact specifications—from the climate-controlled seats and leather-trimmed doors to the UL 757 Level-8 bulletproof windows.

The Riverview Casino project will be profitable in its first year, thanks to the strategic state tax incentives program I designed, recently approved by New York Governor Robert Amato. The Famiglie are eagerly awaiting their cut. After all, nothing breeds loyalty like a steady flow of illicit cash, and nothing impresses them more than securing a high-profile politician on our payroll.

Riverview is the first casino in the East Coast expansion plan. My father's dominance grows as I dot every I, cross every T and carve a giant X through my life, paying the steep price for his ambitions. When you're the heir to the next *capo di tutti capi*, Sebastiano Beneventi, everything comes at a cost—even control over your own future.

My fist tightens around the door handle. "I did what I had to do."

Tommaso cuts me a disapproving look in the rearview mirror. My father threatened to kill my bodyguard, occasional driver, and sometimes best friend if he didn't watch my every goddamn move. A threat Tommaso is taking seriously, considering how my father is on a murdering spree. Because of it, our *famiglia* is on lockdown. A risk that, tonight, I ignored.

"Took you long enough," he comments.

I harden my gaze.

He shakes his head, and then pushes on with psychoanalyzing mine. "You defied an order."

I don't react, especially not to obvious bullshit.

His attention doesn't falter. "To end it, right?"

I lock eyes with him, rage pulsing through my veins. I should be the son shooting coke up my nose like I'm the character inspiration for *The Wolf of Wall Street*. Rehab beats this rigidly disciplined lifestyle any day.

It was never meant to be.

Months ago, in front of what used to be the *Twelve* Famiglie, my father ordered Renzo to execute Emilio Conti's uncle. Conti, a low-ranking mafioso, thought he ruled Atlanta. The arrogant bastard secretly placed his uncle on a local gambling board, unaware it would soon be replaced by the new East Coast Gaming Commission, with good old Governor Amato at the helm and my father pulling the strings. My old man dragged Conti's uncle out of a car trunk to expose the deception. Conti, that stupid *cazzo*, denied knowing the man. Aware all eyes were on him and waiting to see who'd come out on top, my father—ever the opportunist—signaled my brother to pull the trigger.

And Renzo froze.

So, I grabbed the gun and shot the bastard. From that moment on, I stepped into the shoes my twin was supposed to fill.

That sensitive shithead.

You'd *think* that would have been enough to earn my father's respect? But I have a better chance of capturing a lightning bolt. No matter what I do—turn a profit, murder, *obey*—it isn't enough. I could be the next Thor, and he'd say I missed an opportunity to be Hercules. While my wild, wicked, overindulgent twin—the Joker, for sure—remains his favorite.

The SUV is a step forward. My old man not only *will* respect me one day, but he'll also scratch his head and wonder why it wasn't always so. No woman—no matter how tempting her pussy or how exquisite her submission—is worth sabotaging my legacy. If not respect, I still deserve something for my sacrifices.

"*I survived worse than you,*" she said.

Clueless about who she was talking to and how insignificant she is in my life.

End things before anyone discovers the truth. "Right," I mutter.

"You were in there a long time."

I raise a brow. "You asking for better compensation for your time?"

"No." Pause. "Just saying, I was surprised."

"Surprised?"

"This isn't your typical style."

Hardcore is what he means. I get off on dominating my partners in every way imaginable. Bondage. Breath-play. Kinky scenes, where the balance of power always leans my way. Yeah, I fuck my partners; it's the reward after intense play. My cold demeanor even translates outside the bedroom into my daily life; my assholery is that legendary. What I don't do are sleepovers, cuddles and mother-fucking kisses. Make them beg, make them relinquish control, and after I've had my fill, leave. I'm notorious for it.

I never make repeat visits just to hear her sweet voice.

"If you want a blushing innocent," Tommaso persists, "you can get that in Rhode Island."

I glare at him, and his eyes flash—he knows damn well he's six seconds shy of my fist in his face. The bullshit reminder must be payback for my making him wait in the SUV all night. "Let's get out of here."

He doesn't move.

I raise an eyebrow.

"Your apartment is secure. You can bring her back to Soho."

Just the idea makes my suit unbearably warm. Suddenly feeling suffocated, I unbutton the collar, my grip on my thoughts softening as my cock hardens at the suggestion. Her tied to my bedpost. Her tight cunt milking my cock. Her glazed green eyes bright with wonder.

I push down the emotions. "Easy pussy. I'll find a replacement once shit's settled."

"Right."

"Just drive."

Tommaso shifts the Cadillac into gear, and we pull away from the curb. I scowl at my muddy shoes. I left her building using the back door, avoiding the camera I discovered in the front entrance—filming my every goddamn move until I wizened up—then cut through the adjacent yard and exited onto the street around the corner, where Tommaso was waiting. He usually parks on her street, but with the larger new SUV, parking is easier a block over.

"For what it's worth, I liked her," he informs me. A man who cage-fights for fun and beats the living crap out of men for money. His father worked for mine, and we've known each other since child-hood. Never once has he expressed liking anyone or anything.

I flex my fingers, the memory of her rich auburn hair—wound around my hand while her soft whimpers fill the air—flashing through my mind. Everything innocent in the world wrapped up by my darkness.

"All your likes should be focused on pleasing me." Shifting, I remove my suit jacket and toss it onto the seat. A scrap of red silk falls free. I immediately scoop it up and roll the material in my palm. "Know what else I'd like you to do?"

"No, boss."

A heavy weight pulls deep inside my chest as I stuff the thong back inside my suit pocket. "Never mention her again."

Silence descends as he turns the corner and then stops at a red light at the intersection of her block.

Frustrated, I slide the jacket onto a coat hanger, but as I shift positions, movement flickers down the street.

Two men, midblock, on the sidewalk outside her building.

"See them?" I demand.

"Yeah. It's a big fucking city with a lot of people. Probably nobody."

I don't miss the doubt within his tone. As we watch, the men climb her stoop and disappear inside.

The fuck?

"Turn."

"Boss, we're in lockdown," Tommaso warns, as if I need reminding. "We should head back to Soho until the all-clear."

I push open the door and jump out of the SUV.

"Shit, Sandro. Wait."

I storm down the block and reach for my gun. Except it's wedged into the backseat cushion where I left it earlier—because I didn't want to alarm her.

Goddamn it. Amateur move. Another reason I should have stayed away.

The SUV jumps the curb and then cuts me off on the sidewalk. The passenger door flies open. "How about we drive by and then around once more? Check the video feeds before we charge inside?"

I curse beneath my breath. Tommaso's right. The famiglia is on lockdown after my father took a chain saw to a rival capo. Better to know what the situation is before going in blind, especially now. Besides, my man replaced the shitty lock on her door for the same high-security one I've on my apartment door. Fort fucking Knox. No one is breaking in. I climb back into the passenger seat.

"Glad you actually listened," Tommaso mutters.

The drill is familiar because we've completed the same routine each visit. A quick drive past her building to assess neighborhood activity and take plate numbers, before we circle the block, then run those numbers while pulling up video feed from the hidden cameras I had installed.

Weeks ago, Tommaso ran a background check on the LLC that owns the building. A group of investors, who came up clean. No mafiosi connections. Nothing off. Flippers looking to turn a quick profit, though progress on the building is slower than shit. He wanted to dig deeper, but I said it was a waste of time. What was the point since I was ending things?

Problem is addiction runs in the family. My father's addicted to power. Renzo's addicted to excesses and extremes, be they sex, drugs, or motherfucking rock 'n' roll.

And I'm addicted to her.

Fuck.

"Lights on in a third-floor unit," Tommaso comments, pulling into the same spot we vacated minutes ago. "Your girl said the construction crew has been knocking around the unit beneath hers, right?"

"It's Saturday morning, asshole. No beer-belching construction workers are on site this morning. If they are, I'll hire them on the spot." I run my hand across my chin. "You check the feed?"

"Not up yet." He glances at me. "Your call."

My father says good instincts make for good decisions. Renzo's accepted this advice as a challenge to prove him wrong, instinctively reaching for highs through poor decision-making. But I learned the hard way my father's right. The day I shot Conti's uncle, I ignored instinct, and allowed my godfather—our capo di tutti capi—to fill my cup with wine from his estate. "In celebration of your first kill," he boasted, slapping me on the back, then praised me for having the balls to do it. "Hai un bel coraggio, mio figlioccio." I was blinded by my godfather's praise, so much so I got piss-ass drunk and missed the most important meeting of my life.

My destiny was *mine,* up until that point.

"Drive around the block once more."

Hand on the wheel, Tommaso does as directed, fiddling with the feed as he drives. When we turn the corner back onto her street, the app finally loads.

I fall forward as Tommaso slams on the brakes. "Shit."

My gaze drops to the video. Two men are barreling down the stairs side by side. In *suits*.

A pit forms inside my stomach.

"And we're out of here," Tommaso exclaims.

My hand finds the door. "You think?"

"Yeah, I think. Mafiosi, for sure." We glance up at the same time, just as the two men are racing from the building. "Count yourself lucky they missed you."

Shit ... Riley ...

His fingers clench around the gearshift.

"No. Wait." I take out my cell, press her number, and thrust the phone at him. "Warn her. Tell her to get out, and to use the fire escape. Capisci?"

"What?" Confusion fills his expression. "Are you fucking insane ..."

Ignoring him, I grab a gun from the glove compartment, then push the door open and jump from the SUV.

Why would those two goons run from her building after being inside for five minutes? The answer's unclear. What is clear is there's no good reason for them to visit her building on a fucking Saturday morning, and minutes after I left.

I'm almost to her building when everything turns to shit. Bullets ricochet off the pavement by my feet, coming at me from behind. With a glance over my shoulder, I spot my SUV idling diagonally across the street and blocking a white van trying to drive around it. Men in suits swarm the street, using my fucking vehicle for target practice.

No way, motherfuckers.

I spin and fire, hitting two men in the chest.

"Found him," someone behind me shouts. "He's here ..." I pivot and shoot him in the head, shutting him up permanently.

My body tenses. This is an ambush.

And I fucked up.

Enraged, I start shooting at random. Killing as many men as I can, before I'm overtaken and slammed to the pavement.

A vicious beating ensues, but I give as good as I get. Every dirty trick I learned as a teen I execute with relish. Broken noses. Two fingers jammed into a man's eye sockets. I even rearrange a stronzo's balls and dick.

Every man is out for the knockout.

Except one.

Through the curses and flesh hitting flesh, I hear a click, and then through the blood, I stare up at a barrel.

Fucking terrific. This is how I'm going out? Before my goals, my ambitions, my desires are fulfilled? Before I can step out of the great Sebastiano Beneventi's shadow?

I disobeyed an order by coming here last night. Was it worth it? Her eager smile. My dirty hands all over her. So innocent. So corruptible.

So *over*—it had to be.

"Go on," I taunt. "Shoot."

"You were supposed to be dead." He grins.

This is it.

BOOM.

The ground shakes, and a plume of dust fills the sky. The man drops his gun, and it bounces on the sidewalk near my head. I grab it, and then shoot him in the stomach, his expression filled with surprise.

I stare at the plume, trying to make sense of it.

And then, it clicks.

Ah, fuck. Riley.

Men grab me. I'm dragged from the sidewalk into a white van.

I spring to my feet and lunge at the driver as he accelerates.

Something hits the windshield ... not something, someone.

Tommaso.

He holds on but loses his grip when the van takes the corner. He slides off the hood and out of sight.

My vision clouds as I'm wrestled to the floor.

It was *her* building that exploded.

Riley.

Please tell me you did as you were told.

Riley

I DRIFT in and out of sleep until my cell phone rings.

The clock reads 6:30 a.m. Too early for Ciro to be calling in a panic. My grandparents and friends are asleep. Aren't telemarketers prohibited from making calls this early?

Fear has me scrambling for my purse. If this is some sort of family emergency ... My hand shakes as I dig it out and then answer it before the fourth ring. "Hello?"

"Listen carefully," a harsh voice says. "Exit your apartment using the fire escape. Leave now, or you'll die."

Disconnect.

I stare at my phone, dumbfounded.

A prank call—it has to be.

Still ... something in the stranger's tone ... an urgency ... has me moving.

I grab my robe and purse, then climb out onto the fire escape. If I had neighbors, I'd be quite the sight, naked with wild hair and puffy eyes, outside their windows as I clamber down the steel steps.

For a brief second, I contemplate pausing to slip on the robe. This must be a prank, the telephone version of Ding-Dong Ditch. Besides Emily, Ciro, and Albert/Alex/Allen, and my weekly phone call to my grandparents, I haven't spoken to anyone else, not since my father's death. How would this man even get my number? Why would he warn me?

Al was scrolling through my phone earlier. But that wasn't his voice warning me to flee. Besides, he walked out on me nearly twenty minutes ago. And I don't believe I'll ever hear his voice again.

Loud pops fill the air.

Gunfire. A barrage of bullets, coming from the street in front of my building.

Oh, sweet heaven. What's happening?

Now I'm moving. My hands and feet slip and slide on the steel as I descend the last few steps, only to reach a landing stretching out over the building's grassy backyard.

I consider the drop, and how I could sprain an ankle or break a leg if I land awkwardly.

This is New York City, where big-city violence happens. The street violence and strange phone call are likely a coincidence. And given the gunshots, it'd be safer inside. With the new lock, anyone trying to enter would have to bust down the door.

But what if you're wrong?

A quick plan forms. Once in the yard below, I'll slip on my robe, call the police, and wait hidden in the backyard while the violence unfolding out front is resolved. When it's safe, I'll walk around to the front entryway. Type in the code and use my apartment key to reenter my apartment. Then, I'll laugh about flashing booby at my nonexistent neighbors and panicking over something just as ridiculous as a Gucci bag.

I release my purse, and it falls to the ground. Fingers wrapped around the lowest rung, I stretch my body and dangle my legs. Then,

I let go, dropping like a sack of potatoes, hit the ground, and then tumble onto my buttocks so hard, the wind's knocked out of me.

I'm sprawled on the grass and peering up at the sky when it happens. A loud, earth-shattering boom. The ground shakes. Bricks fall. Within seconds, flames shoot out of a window overhead.

Wait.

No. No. NO.

Not any window: the apartment window directly below my own.

MY FIRST THOUGHTS when I gain consciousness are of her.

Her, in the shower, pinned against the glass with my arm around her waist and fingers laced through her long auburn hair. Her quivering and so fucking ripe for my corruption.

She glances over her shoulder, but I'm not having it. I want her immobile and completely, utterly under my control. I press my chest against her back, and then thrust my erection between her thighs, the tight fit making me even harder. "Beg me to fuck you like this."

"Yes. Please ..." she croaks.

I tug her hair. "Say it."

"Please fuck my thighs."

I graze my teeth across her pale skin and then, in a moment of weakness, nuzzle her ear. Because, before I die, I need my name on her lips.

Say my name. Say, "Alessandro, fuck my tight little body."

Alessandro, please.

Palms on the glass, I cage her. "Brace yourself." I thrust forward, violently and without reservation, and she submits, giving me everything I dreamed of in a partner, and more.

"What's he saying?" A voice cuts through.

"Who gives a shit?" another man replies. "Make sure the ropes are tight."

Reality sets in with a vengeance. *My name on her lips. It was a dream.*

It was all a dream.

"You said he was inside the apartment," the first man—Dead Man One on my list—continues.

"I swear. He was inside all night. Must've left while I went for coffee," Dead Man Two responds.

The worst kind of pain washes over me, the kind you bring upon yourself. *These stronzos were following me.*

"Home Depot opens early." The ropes around me tighten. "Send Giovanni to buy a chain saw."

Darkness creeps in.

Until nothing else remains.

***

THE NEXT TIME I come to, I'm more alert and better prepared. I recognize Dead Man One's voice immediately. "You positive this is Alessandro Beneventi?"

"Been watching him for weeks."

"Yeah, and we've a situation now because of the shit job you've done."

Although I'm desperate for a good look at their faces, I force myself to relax like I'm still unconscious and listen. Because whoever is behind this hired morons to kill me.

A light flashes.

"What are you doing?" Dead Man Two demands.

"Sending a picture to our contact to confirm his identity."

"You're really taking some coked-up asshole's word over mine?"

Dead Man Two kicks something and it skitters across the room. "I told you already, it's Beneventi's son."

"It better be, or we're dead."

The tense silence is broken by the ping of a text alert.

"Cigorelli confirms it's him."

Ciro Cigorelli? The Riverview Casino construction manager? You've got to be shitting me.

As a native New Yorker, Cigorelli knows the ins and outs of New York construction better than anyone. I took his nothing company, C&C Enterprises, and put it on the map. I made that fucker rich. Why would he want to kill me when there are more lucrative casino jobs on the horizon?

These idiots must have it wrong. Cigorelli might have a coke habit, but he's a full-blown money addict—and I'm his primary dealer.

Unless someone made him a sweeter offer. Unless Ciro fucking Cigorelli thinks he can play both sides and cash in from me and the mafiosi behind this.

Benny Manocchio's men probably got to him. The mafioso capo my father hacked to pieces. His men are notoriously vindictive—who isn't?

Which is why my father ordered a lockdown.

Dead Man One interrupts my thoughts. "Why'd Beneventi come back?"

I will myself not to react and attempt bodily harm on these assholes until I've a better grasp of the situation.

As for why ...

Riley ... *fuck.*

"Don't know. Don't care," Dead Man Two mutters. "We have him now. But do we kill him first before chopping him up?"

I wait for his answer, at an obvious disadvantage.

Finally, Dead Man One speaks. "Naw. How about we record it and send it as our gift? He'll enjoy it, and maybe overlook your screwup."

My skin burns with rage. Who will enjoy it? Which delusional mafioso believes he'll survive after killing me?

"Jesus Christ," Dead Man Two mutters. "I'm gonna need another cup of coffee for this."

Footsteps approach. Without warning, I'm punched in the face. Somehow, I manage to not retaliate and stay limp.

"No worries this time. He's out cold," Dead Man Two comments. The weak-ass punk will pay for that.

Footsteps retreat, and a door slams.

If my lips weren't swollen like a clown, I'd smile. The stupid stronzos left me alone?

I pry my eyes open but can only see out of one.

Motherfuckers.

Light filters in through a basement window, enough for me to take stock of where they've left me. I'm inside an empty, unfinished basement with a cement floor and thick cement block walls, an exposed-pipe ceiling, a steel door, and little else.

I test the ropes around my arms and thighs. Tight, with little slack, though I knew this already.

It's a shitty situation to be in for most. But for a kid who grew up playing with his brother in the Beneventi family dungeon, this is just a carnival funhouse. Renzo and I had this game where we'd take turns locking each other inside one of the steel-barred cells. There was always only one way out, and we'd time how long it took to escape. Renzo's methods were predictable because he believed I'd overthink it—which, for a while, I did. I crafted elaborate challenges, hiding clues in layers to drag out the process. Yet, Renzo always made it out. Life's a game to him, and he's been slipping past one inescapable trap after another ever since.

The real question is, are these men methodical overthinkers like me, or simpletons like my brother?

They left me for a cup of coffee—simple it is.

I test the ropes, chair creaking. No slack, but it doesn't matter, the answer's so fucking obvious. Feet planted, I lean forward and stand, the chair rising with me, and then using my full weight, I fall back onto it. It collapses, the wood coming apart beneath me as I land on my back with a thunk.

Pain shoots through me like acid burn.

I push through it, knowing the odds aren't in my favor yet. Freeing myself, I toss aside the rope and grab a piece of wood, slowly and meticulously sharpening the end of a chair leg against the cement floor. The remaining shards I pile on the windowsill, blocking out the light.

Armed and ready, I press myself against the wall to the right of the door, waiting.

It's time to teach a lesson in what not to be—overconfident, stupid, weak. I'm the son of a monster, making me one in my own right. That's why you never fuck with a Beneventi.

The longer I wait, the harder it is to stay conscious, and the angrier I get.

How did this happen? How could I allow myself to be watched? Ambushed?

Finally, the distinct growl of a chain saw interrupts the silence.

Coming in with guns blazing, are they?

Just as well.

The door is unlocked, and Dead Man One, Dead Man Two, and the man with the chain saw—Giovanni—rush in.

"Why's it so dark in here?" Dead Man One hollers over the noise.

With 1980s horror music setting the scene within my mind, the carnage begins. Door kicked shut, I bludgeon Giovanni first, driving my weapon into his neck. He gurgles, and his hands reach for his throat.

The chain saw sails through the air like a torpedo, and then slices through Dead Man One's torso like deli meat. He drops his cell phone, and his innards spill out onto the cement floor.

I pick the chain saw up and turn toward the last man still standing.

Shaking, Dead Man Two backs into the wall. Panicked by how

easily I gained control, though he should be more concerned about punching me earlier. Though he'll survive a few more minutes.

Because a dead man can't talk.

I crash a fist into his face and gain immediate satisfaction when his nose breaks. Chain saw off, I demand answers. "You work for Bible Belt Benny?"

He cups his nose. "Who?"

Stupidity must run in the Manocchio bloodline. "Benny fucking Manocchio."

"Jesus, that Benny?" he stutters. "No. Never met him."

Something he said earlier seeps in between anger and intent. Something from their earlier conversation. *Why did he come back?*

"How long have you been following me?"

He holds up his hands. "I'll tell you everything if you give me your word I'll walk out of this room alive."

"Tell you what. I'll give you my word, and I'll buy a cup of motherfucking coffee as a thank-you."

I catch his nod.

"Six weeks."

My entire body stiffens. "You've been following me six motherfucking weeks?"

"Not following, exactly. Just waiting outside the apartment for your arrival. After the last three weeks, we didn't think you'd show your face again."

Amateurs. Them. *Me.*

How did I miss this? How did I allow my routine to become so freaking predictable?

"Lucky for you, you left the building before our guys could fire up the explosion. They turned the entire apartment on the third floor into a gas bomb. Used special sheetrock and window corking to block out air so the carbon monoxide could build up and ignite quicker."

Fuck. This was a planned execution weeks in the making, well before my father butchered Bible Belt Benny. Who would have believed he'd be that cunning? But something else they said earlier flickers through my thoughts. *"We'll send the video as our gift? He'll enjoy it, and maybe overlook your screwup."*

He—singular. Which of Benny's men would enjoy viewing my murder the most?

"What were your orders?" I grind out through clenched teeth.

"To violently kill Sebastiano Beneventi's sons." He pauses in indecision, while his words ring in my ears.

For the second time today, fear sets in for someone other than me.

Sons. Plural.

Renzo.

"Who? Who ordered the hit?" Except I know the answer.

"We don't directly work for him ..." His eyes grow into saucers. "But he's a big-time mafioso from the South."

Everything slides into place. "How far south?"

"Georgia."

"Atlanta?"

Dead Man Two / Last Man Standing nods.

A low-ranking member of the Eleven Famiglie orders the hits. A man my father ousted from Atlanta. The man whose uncle I murdered, and whose business partner my father *sawed into pieces.*

Emilio Conti.

"Where is he?" The room sways. The adrenaline spike's fading, but I push on. "Where is Conti?"

"Don't know."

"And he paid that rat Cigorelli to report on me?"

Last Man Standing swallows hard. "Well, yeah ..."

I pick up the chain saw and grab Last Man Standing by the neck, my vision clouding as dark shadows move to overtake me.

Not yet.

Not fucking yet.

I drag Last Man Standing out of the room onto the basement landing and start up the chain saw. We Beneventi will have quite the reputation after I'm done.

He recoils in terror. "You promised not to kill me."

"I promised"—I lean in to yell in his face—"you'd walk out of that room alive. Now shut up so I can go buy that celebratory cup of coffee."

Blood covers me from head to toe by the time I'm done. Then, I escape into Brooklyn's mean streets. Only for darkness to drag me under a few blocks away.

―――――

Riley

"IT'S A MIRACLE YOU SURVIVED."

Emily tosses her purse onto the counter, and then drops into a seat at the kitchen table. My hands shake as I stir mayonnaise into the shredded chicken, celery, and almonds mixture. They haven't stopped shaking, not during the cab ride to her apartment, not during my troubled sleep on her couch, not during this morning's police interview. I nearly *died*.

If it hadn't been for that phone call …

"I missed your chicken salad."

Her comment seems so normal. Something we'd discuss when life was sunshine and roses. "I can toast the bread if you want? You always like a bit of crunch."

"You don't need to do this."

I place two slices into the toaster. "You convinced Ciro I can stay here. And I'm wearing your clothes and makeup."

I escaped with nothing but a silk robe and the contents of my purse: a wallet with my new NY driver's license and credit cards, my passport, a checkbook, cell phone, touch-up makeup bag, birth control pills, tampons, and a box of Altoids. And keys to an apartment that no longer exists.

But what I lost is irreplaceable—him.

Even if I wanted to, without his full name, I'll never find him.

You escaped with your life, Riley. Be grateful for that.

I plate two pieces of white bread and spread chicken salad evenly across both.

"What did the police say?" she asks.

"It was a gas leak," I reply.

"Told you so. They happen all the time."

The toast pops, and I quickly fix her sandwich, then place the plate before her. She's right, gas leaks are common. And when I told the police about hearing gunfire, they said it was likely gang activity and under investigation.

I sigh. "You should have heard the gunfire, Em. It sounded like an old spaghetti western."

"It's a miracle you survived."

"Yeah, it is," I reply softly, taking my sandwich to the table and sitting across from her. The explosion, the gang activity, living and working for a drug addict—New York isn't for me. Emily was kind to offer me a place to stay, especially with our strained relationship. But Ciro is a disaster, spiraling out of control. Last night, he didn't even come home. Emily cried most of the night, and I was too shell-shocked to comfort her. Even if I suggest she return to Marietta with me, she'll just make excuses for him.

But I'm leaving. Fate gave me a firm shake, and I finally woke up. Life is precious, and I've wasted enough time merely existing.

"Did you get a police report?" she asks between bites.

"It's on the counter."

"Ciro needs to give it to the insurance company for review." She sighs. "I spoke with him this morning. He's furious because they want proof he actually owns the building before discussing filing a claim, and his name isn't listed on the LLC paperwork." She chews. Clueless. So clueless about the man she's dating. "Like Ciro would be paying workers under the table to renovate the apartments if it wasn't his building. Can you imagine?"

Yes. Yes I can. If there's a corner to cut, her boyfriend has his scissors ready. Except I don't say this. "Whose name is on the paperwork?"

"Three goombahs who do odd jobs for him, but who have Wall Street connections. Ciro says like attracts like, and that he hopes to rent the refurbished apartments to their broker buddies, who'll pay top dollar."

I frown. "So, Ciro doesn't *own* the building."

"Aren't you listening. He does. He has to prove it to the insurance people, is all."

Am I surprised? Not in the slightest. It's only been twenty-four hours, and he's already submitted a claim. He didn't return last night but is up early to file an insurance claim? I bet he doesn't even own the building. Those three goombahs better smarten up. Lord knows what this is about or what Ciro's hiding, but I call bullshit.

Don't get involved. You won't be around for the fallout.

With I sigh, I say, "If his name is on the deed, that should solve the problem."

"The deed. If he can find it ..." Emily clasps her hands. "Will you explain it to him?"

I blame it on stress and fatigue, but I grimace.

She sees it right away, and her face flushes with anger. "You know, he could have asked you to check into a hotel."

My throat tightens. How can she be so callous after what I've been through? "He wasn't here and hasn't been home."

Never mind how out of control, how paranoid, how psychotic Ciro has acted these past few weeks, or how horribly he's treated her —vanishing for days on end, coming and going at all hours, abusing substances like a child consuming candy—Emily always makes excuses for him.

She tosses her half-eaten sandwich onto the table. "Not everyone's a Stephanie."

"What?" How cruel can she be, bringing Stephanie into an argument?

"You walk around like a zombie," she snidely continues. "Avoiding relationships and trusting no one. In your eyes, everyone's a Stephanie in the making. Especially Ciro."

"That's not true."

She laughs cruelly. "Name one relationship you've made outside ours."

"I've had relationships." A relationship ... a fling. But for some reason, I kept it from her. Maybe because our friendship is so emotionally one-sided? Is that why I accepted her invitation to move to New York? Because she's the one person who barely notices my struggles? A friend more worried about missing my chicken salad than about my emotional well-being?

"None," she stresses. "Because in your twisted psyche, Ciro is a villain, when he's been nothing but kind."

"He calls me Triple B," I burst out, Stephanie's name triggering me in the same way her stupid handbags do.

"He told you this a thousand times. He isn't making fun of your breast size."

Three weeks after I began my job at C&C Enterprises, he began calling me Triple B. I took offense, because what else could he possibly mean? Emily caught him harassing me during one of his coke-binge episodes. "What?" He tossed his hands up in the air like the nickname made perfect sense. "BBB—Beautiful Beneventi Bait."

"Beneventi?" Emily asked. "As in—"

He kissed her on the mouth and ended the conversation.

The Beneventi family owns the casino. That's all I know about them. Is it a work thing? C&C Enterprises is employed by them?

You can Google them once you're home.

Home. Right. Since we're arguing about Ciro, I should break the news. I draw in a breath. "I've made a decision—"

And she starts crying.

My anger evaporates.

"He's quitting coke and getting sober, once construction is complete," she proclaims between sobs. "He promised."

Does she actually believe this bullshit?

"And ... I'll tell him not to call you that name anymore."

"This isn't about that, or him ..." It's about me. Me, making peace with the Tragedy. Me, accepting I'll be hearing the name Stephanie a lot when I return home, but I'm ready for it. This is about me, and my fresh start.

"I want to help him so bad. What do I do, Riley?"

Dump him.

Move home with me.

Chase happiness, not despair.

"I'm on your side, Emily. Always."

She stares at me with big tear-filled eyes. "Really?"

I choke on air. Dizzy and delusional. "We have the summer to figure it out," I offer. Sealing my fate.

I can't abandon her to the likes of Ciro.

I owe her, and unfortunately him.

Three months. Then I'll quit and return home, in time for fall classes.

Three months to convince her he's not worth her tears.

CHAPTER 4

BEEP. Beep. Beep.

I blink slowly, groaning as the pain slices through every part of me—my head, my body, my pride.

"Finally decided to grow a set of balls, huh?"

The voice is unmistakable. I force my good eye open, and sure enough, it's Renzo. And I'm in a hospital room, tangled in a mess of tubes and wires, hooked up like Frankenstein's monster with the relentless beeping of machines echoing in my ears. The pain is sharp and unyielding, cutting through the haze of medication.

"Shit," I mutter.

"Shit is right. You'd better have your story straight before Father arrives."

I turn my head in the opposite direction. My brother is seated in a chair he pulled up beside my bed. Alive—and not a sitting duck in the rehab center my father had him locked away in.

"There's a hit …"

"Yeah. Mafiosi showed up at the center, looking for me." He flashes me a weak smile. "But I'd had enough of vinyasa yoga, green smoothies, and Sergeant Dickwad and his hellish goons. I'm not fucking military material."

Military or mafia material. Renzo can whup ass—and we often go at it—but his heart's butter, when this lifestyle requires ice.

The softhearted prick.

"Where am I?" I croak, my voice shit.

"Providence Hospital."

Rhode Island, from some urine-infested New York side street? I don't remember anything after I escaped.

"Does he know?" I demand with all the strength I have.

"About the hit ... well, yeah." He rolls his eyes. "Didn't he just butcher Bible Belt Benny? Benny's men were bound to retaliate ..."

"Does he know I was ambushed?" I burst out, interrupting his wrong assumptions.

"You mean is Father furious you ignored the lockdown?" He grins like a madman. "Oh, yeah. If I were you, I'd get my story straight, and fast."

The cords attached to me tangle as I shift in bed. I hate them. I hate feeling weak and vulnerable. Most of all, I hate that my father knows I'm responsible for this, that I was nearly killed, that I made our family look weak.

"You look ready to strangle someone," my twin comments.

"Lean closer, and you'll find out."

He laughs. "For what it's worth, I'm proud you showed some balls. You ... disobeying an order? Not being the great Sebastiano Beneventi's bitch? I didn't think you had it in you."

"Call me a bitch once more," I grind out, "and you'll be lying in this bed."

"And offer Sergeant Dickwad an opportunity to haul me back to Maine? Not on my life."

His life ...

Thank fuck Renzo broke out of rehab when he did. "You know a lot about everything yet nothing about what matters right now. It wasn't Benny's men who issued the hits. It was Emilio Conti."

"That bottom-feeder?"

"Conti's been planning to kill me for weeks." My admission's a festering wound I keep scratching and scratching, my carelessness forming a vicious scar. A reminder of my weakness. A reminder to my father I'm not mafia material.

"Jesus. Stop projecting sad puppy vibes."

I glare at him with one eye, to little effect.

"Conti is patient and methodical. Look how long it took him to nearly gain control over Atlanta with that stunt he pulled with his uncle? That bastard plotted his move for months. I wouldn't be surprised if he had men watching you at the casino."

My fingers curl into a fist. Luckily, my perceptive brother doesn't notice. I'll deal with Ciro fucking Cigorelli before anyone, especially my father, uncovers the full truth.

Renzo flips his wrist, glances at his watch, then stands.

"Where do you think you're going?" I demand.

"Same place he'll insist you lie low for a while. While he counters rumors and saves face. Can't have Sebastiano Beneventi's heir kidnapped and nearly beaten to death. What will the famiglie think?"

It infuriates me that he's right. That Italy is exactly where he'll want me. Hiding away like a bitch while he does damage control. I own a villa in Sardinia. A place to blow off steam or get an Italian-style blow job, and more. My playground. My escape. And now, the great Sebastiano Beneventi will ruin that, too.

"You'll be staying in Sardinia?"

"And stare at your miserable face day and night?" He chuckles. "Fuck, no thank you. I'm not ready to sober up yet."

I stiffen, imagining Renzo high, untethered, and wandering Rome's seedy side. Vulnerable. "Conti's still out there."

"Father's men can't find me. What makes you think that bottom-dweller will do any better?"

"Drugs will rot your brain, asshole."

"While you, brother, rot your soul for him."

"Fuck you."

"And fuck you back."

I grit my teeth. "You think Sergeant Dickhead was difficult? Wait until I recover, because I'll personally hunt you down and go cold turkey on your ass. Capisci?"

"Game on, asshole." He pats my arm. "I hope she was worth what you're about to undergo."

Her name's Riley.

"I've my own fires to deal with, so I won't be sticking around to watch you burn. But I'd appreciate it if you don't mention to Father I was here."

I roll an eye. "Are you a moron? His men are all over the hospital." It's an assumption based on experience. Sebastiano Beneventi might be the highest-ranking capo next to our godfather, Don Lucchese, but as our father, he'd risk his life to protect us.

"Watch and learn, Sandro. Watch and learn."

With a groan, I force myself to a seated position, as Renzo heads to a window, pops it open, and disappears.

The Joker and goddamn Flash, rolled into one.

The room falls quiet ... *almost.*

Beep. Beep.

I frantically claw at my chest, which sets the machines off.

Two nurses race into the room. Screams mix in with the noise. "Sir! Stop! You can't do that."

I stagger to my feet.

Emilio Conti is a dead man.

I shove the medical monitor and send it crashing into the wall, then totter toward the door. Slow and unsteady, the race lost before it begins.

Two large, burly men in suits easily intercept me. I pop the first man in the chin, catching him by surprise. "Move out of my way." My words slur, and my legs grow heavy like I'm carrying extra weight.

"Your father's on his way."

No shit, Sherlock. That's why I'm on my way out. Conti is mine.

I have to end his miserable life before my father does. Redeem myself. Prove I'm worthy. I'm tempted, so tempted, to rat out my brother. Give my father's men something to focus on other than holding me back.

A needle is thrust into my arm.

Damn it. I should have expected this.

"That motherfucker won't get away ..." I'm pinned to the bed and then sedated. I struggle against the binds pulling tight across my body. Pure, unrequited rage fills me.

You fucked up, Sandro.

Beep.

Better get your story straight.

I WATCH my father's arrival through slitted, swollen eyes. He hits a wall, surprising me. His style's more ticking time bomb than grenade toss, a calculated fury that's nevertheless terrifying to witness.

Two nurses bolt from the room.

"Get a guard posted outside who doesn't reek like fucking sauerkraut," my father snarls into his cell phone. Only an Italian loyal to the Beneventi famiglia is trusted enough to stand watch over his son, keeping everyone out—and me in this damn bed.

He knows I disobeyed an order.

He'll want an explanation.

Why risk so much when she was just another shiny new toy to break in, to mold, to reshape and corrupt? She never really knew me. Did she listen to Tommaso's order? Escape while she could? Not that it matters now—what's done is done.

She meant nothing in the grand scheme of things, so what's the point in bringing her up?

A doctor approaches the bed with a clipboard.

I shutter my eyes and buy a few more minutes to prepare myself.

"How is he?" my father demands.

The doctor fumbles nervously, on edge. "He has two broken ribs and a fractured nose, along with severe swelling on his left side. We can't detect any internal bleeding, but there's a strong likelihood he has a concussion."

"Keep him here for the week for further observation."

The doctor makes a strained squeak, clearly unsettled. "We'll do our best. He tore out his tubes, trying to leave, so we've had to restrain him to the bed."

The damn tattletale.

"Free him. He'll do as I say."

"Yes, Mr. Beneventi." The straps pulled tight across my body fall free. Footsteps retreat, leaving my father's tall figure looming over the bed.

"Open your eyes, Sandro. I know you're awake."

Damn it.

I open my good eye and brace for the inquisition.

Predictable isn't a word you'd use to describe my father. "You okay?" His tone's hoarse and brimming with emotion.

Hell, no. This is worse than opening our discussion with "*You disappointed me, you little shit.*" Where is the ambitious capo? The demanding asshole who holds my life by the balls?

I'm unprepared for *him*.

The man who spent every summer fishing with Renzo and me.

The same man who, when I was ten, built me a high-tech fort on our Rhode Island estate. A month later, construction started on Renzo's golf course. I hate golf—loathe it even more after my father's blatant show of favoritism.

But watching him now, something in his behavior makes me question if I had it all wrong.

I get right to the point. "I'm sorry I disappointed you."

"You're alive. That's what matters." He drops into the same chair Renzo vacated. I wait for him to settle before sharing the news.

"Emilio Conti is behind this. He put hits out on both Renzo and me."

I study his reaction—he doesn't seem surprised. Damn, he's been busy. "My men will find him and take care of him," I say, as if dealing with Conti is a mere inconvenience.

"Leave Conti to me."

No way in hell. "Conti's mine," I snarl.

Capo Sebastiano Beneventi leans in, his tone cold and threatening. "You think you can negotiate with me, you little shit?"

I stand my ground. "Fine. Whoever finds him first gets to finish him."

His jaw clenches, and I can see the inevitable question forming on his lips. Finally, he demands, "Who is she?"

"Who?"

In response, he slams his fist into the monitor, sending it crashing to the floor. "Your little fucking sidepiece?"

"I'm too busy with the casino—"

"Don't lie. Who is the woman you risked breaking lockdown for? The reason you were pulled off a Brooklyn street, beaten within an inch of your life and nearly dismembered?"

Madonna, he's been thorough.

I keep my tone neutral. "No one important. Just a fling."

"Let me get this straight. You left your Soho apartment, with security tighter than a supermax prison, during a lockdown, for 'no one'?"

"Correct," I reply, leaning in with a hint of challenge. "A nobody, like sweet little Alessia."

His eyes narrow, warning me not to push too far.

We've clashed for months over Governor Amato's daughter. I might be arrogant, but I'm not blind to his weakness. And my father is stubborn, especially when it comes to his favorite plaything.

He sits back, folding his hands in his lap. I've managed to piss him off again. What's new?

"Tommaso will be questioned."

Motherfucker. "Tommaso follows my orders."

"Your bodyguard's job is to protect you."

"He did what I asked him to do," I grind out.

"That right?"

Do I confess? Admit Tommaso was making a phone call during the most critical time, when we could have escaped?

I purposely shift on the bed so pain shoots through me. To manipulate a master manipulator and trigger more fatherly concern.

He ignores my efforts. "You were snatched off the street. What the hell were you thinking?"

Riley, on her knees.

Riley, struggling against the tie I used to secure her to the bedpost.

Riley, and her sweet smile.

Gone ... possibly dead.

I wasn't careful. I was obsessed.

God, the truth pains me in its own special way. "I fucked up."

"You almost *died.*"

I don't argue. What's the point?

"When you're healed, I'll beat the living crap out of you. Capisci?"

"I understand." My failure. His disappointment.

"You used a goddamn chain saw, huh?"

I blink in surprise. Jesus, he even knows how I escaped? "It was a messy kill," I admit, glancing at my arms. Someone cleaned the blood off me while I was out—probably the tattletale doctor. Can't have Sebastiano Beneventi's son looking like a casualty of war. "They tied me to a wooden chair."

"That right?" His curiosity is piqued. His men gave him the facts; now I fill in the details.

"They left me alone for a coffee break."

"Like attracts like; Conti's a dumb bastard." He pauses, waiting for more. "How'd you get a chain saw?"

"First, I sharpened a chair leg against the cement floor—like you had us do when we were nine." Boy Scout training, Beneventi style. We were taught to be prepared for anything. Chain saws, though, that's a new one. "Then I surprised them when they came back. Sure, I could've gone caveman with the chair leg, but why not use modern tools when they're right there?"

I brace for the tiniest fucking hint of praise—hell, I'll take even a nod.

"Your brother would have bare-knuckled it and used the chair leg."

I flinch.

"But they'd have to catch him first."

There it is—the inevitable comparison. Renzo thumbs his nose at my father, and my father rubs mine in how clever Renzo is.

I stifle my irritation and repeat my warning to Renzo. "I'll hunt him down, then straighten his ass out. I promise you that."

"Start in California. He's still chasing a pipe dream."

By pipe dream, my father means Elia Seraphina Lombardi, our main rival's daughter. Renzo's been fucking around with her for years, since we were kids. If Renzo's a flame, she's a goddamn firecracker. And they aren't the only ones who'll burn in hell if Renzo can't keep his filthy mitts off her.

Except, he just returned from California, didn't he? Now, he's headed to Italy. Maybe rehab did clear his muddled mind?

"Love makes us vulnerable."

My jaw slackens in surprise.

"But vulnerability is a weakness. Capisci?"

Is he talking about my brother's relationship, my feelings, or are we back to Alessia Amato?

"You'll stay here for the week, then take the jet to Sardinia. I've arranged for additional medical care at a trusted facility." He jabs a finger at me. "Don't defy me, or I'll burn your goddamn villa to the ground."

Jesus. "I'll check into the damn facility for a few days," I retort. How many days depends on the doctors and how persuasive I can be.

"Recover in Italy until further notice."

Renzo was right. I'll be hidden away while he does damage

control. "Don Lucchese will consider it disrespectful if I don't visit him."

"I'll handle your godfather."

"Tommaso will accompany me." It's delivered as a statement, not request.

"After I have a *word* with him."

Well, shit. But Tommaso's a big boy. Who fears one man—the great Sebastiano Beneventi. Don't we all?

He stands, having said what he came to say.

"Prima la famiglia," I mutter.

He locks eyes with me. "That's right." Then he repeats my words, and the creed I've been brought up on. "Family first, always."

"I won't let you down again."

Humiliation sinks its claws in deep. I'm disgusted—for breaking lockdown, getting ambushed, disappointing him, and worst of all, by endangering the Beneventi name when the vote for capo di tutti capi looms so close. I'll do whatever it takes to repair the damage, to earn back my father's respect. Starting with cleaning up the mess I made— and putting a bullet in that stranzo Conti.

He nods curtly. "We'll see, won't we?"

"WHO'S EMILIO SMITH?"

I clutch the crumpled fax I found under Ciro's desk, my question reverberating through the office. Hours spent organizing bills, entering invoices into the online ledger for "transparency," as Ciro likes to gripe, balancing C&C Enterprises expenses to ensure contractors get paid, and keeping his desk clear—once again.

I shouldn't care that the CEO of C&C Enterprises dumps paperwork on his desk like a child emptying a backpack. Survive the summer—that's my goal. His crew will be paid on time, so the effort was worth it. Still, who will manage Ciro's sloppy business practices when I'm gone?

Not your problem, Riley. The worst will be behind you.

The fax is a hotel confirmation for a six-month stay in a bungalow suite at the Grand Hotel di Palermo, fully paid for with Monero cryptocurrency. The name on the reservation is Emilio Smith.

It's an unusual bill, and I'm unsure how it should be categorized —travel expenses? Entertainment?

I should leave; Emily and I have a dinner date, and I'll be rushed if I don't hurry. But unlike Ciro, I take pride in my organizational skills and instead set off in search of answers.

C&C Enterprises is housed inside an old garment manufacturing warehouse. Half the space is allotted to construction vehicles and equipment. Dividing the large space is the main entrance, the "Grand Foyer," Ciro calls it, because of the steel beams crisscrossing the pitched ceiling, which gives it a cathedral-like feel. Cubicles have been set up on the other half of the warehouse, with Ciro's office running along the back exterior wall.

I track him down near the cement mixer.

"Glad you're working late, Triple B." He greets me with a smug smirk and his favorite insult. "Can you pick up an envelope at the casino?"

I raise my chin. "Why do you persist in calling me that?"

His twisted grin makes me think he's hiding an enormous secret. "Tell the security guard at the gate you're with C&C."

The paper in my hand crackles beneath my fingers. "Emily and I are having dinner in less than an hour." A girls' night out she insisted on after her meltdown two days ago. I'm hoping over a good meal she'll hear me out about my end-of-summer plans.

"I canceled it."

I frown in confusion. "Excuse me?"

"The reservation. Dining out isn't a good idea right now." He swipes at his nose with the back of his hand and hasn't stopped moving once. Either he's coming down from a high or just getting started.

No. Emily invited him to dinner?

"Does she know you canceled?" I demand.

"Not yet. But things are sketchy at the moment, so I'm ... um ... lying low."

I clench the papers tighter. Lord, he owes a drug dealer money, doesn't he?

He clears his throat. "So, about the envelope? You'd be doing me a huge favor."

I sigh.

"You can walk there and back while I lock up." He glances around nervously, and I follow suit. But the warehouse is quiet, everyone having left for the day. Now his odd behavior has *me* on edge.

He rubs a finger beneath his nose. The cocaine itch, people call it. Often accompanied by a cocaine-induced paranoia—or so the articles I've read have said. Ciro's habit is growing worse, not better. How does Emily not see it?

"Anyway, it's too hot to dine out."

You'll be dining out soon enough with Mema and PopPop. The first dinner you'll treat them to will be at that Italian restaurant they love so much.

"Before I go." I hold up the fax. "This was under your desk in a ball. It's non-construction related, and partially written in Italian. Do I enter it under travel expenses?"

"Give me that."

He lunges for the fax and snatches it from my hand. "Stupid Sicilians needed a freaking phone number for the reservation," he mutters, glaring at the offensive room confirmation.

I frown. "Is Emilio Smith an investor?"

"Jesus Christ." He looks around wildly. "Lower your voice."

My heart sinks. Because his harsh expression says it all—this isn't construction related.

He punches the "on" button on the cement mixer, and it rumbles to life. The cylinder rotates three times before he tosses the paper inside.

I stare in disbelief as the fax disappears into the cement.

"Forget you saw that," he grinds out, in a barely audible tone. With the cement truck churning, I'm sure I misunderstood.

Was that a threat?

Suddenly, I see Ciro in a different light. A mindless ass with a coke habit, and dangerously unpredictable.

"Ask for Tommaso."

I glance from the spinning cement barrel to Ciro and then to the rafters overhead. A few more weeks, and then I'll be gone.

"Wait. And Riley," he says as I turn to leave.

"Be careful."

BROOKLYN'S SIDE streets are less crowded due to an early summer heat wave. Five blocks from the warehouse, and I'm flushed and sweaty. I'd consider hailing a cab if one were available. But instead of slowing, I hurry on, goose bumps prickling my arms.

Because it feels like I'm being followed.

I glance over my shoulder and search the faces of the pedestrians behind me. Nothing outward, no weird expressions or dodgy looks.

I curse the heat and the paranoid man who sent me into it.

Still, when I turn the corner onto a busier avenue, I duck inside my favorite tea shop. An iced lavender Earl Grey tea to cool me, and a few minutes ordering it to shake off my worries, and the imaginary figure who may or may not be following me. Logic says I'm a nobody in this city. Without friends—as Emily so unkindly pointed out. Ciro's erratic behavior must be rubbing off.

Once my racing heart calms, I continue my walk.

Riverview Casino is seven city blocks from the office and overlooks the East River. Pop-up offices fill the parking lot, but after checking in with a guard, I'm informed Tommaso can be found inside the enormous rock star–worthy recreational vehicle that outflanks and outshines the smaller trailers dotting the new asphalt.

With black tar sticking to my heels and the asphalt amplifying the heat, by the time I knock on the door, I'm dizzy and weak.

Which is why I'm slow to process that I recognize the six-foot-five tank of a man who answers the door.

The Uber driver.

What's he doing here?

We stare at each other, both clearly surprised to see the other again. He glances over my shoulder, scanning the parking lot, then frowns and waves me inside.

"You survived," he says, running his fingers through his hair. "And now you're here."

He must know what happened. After all, he dropped me off the night of the casino groundbreaking ceremony. The explosion that destroyed my building made headlines. It's understandable he'd be curious. I'm still in shock I survived. If it hadn't been for that phone call, I wouldn't be standing here, feeling both lightheaded and oddly upbeat—especially since he might know where my mysterious stranger lives.

"Jesus Christ, you look like you're about to pass out. Let me get you some water," he says.

He moves to the refrigerator in the kitchen area while I hover near a cozy kitchen banquette. On the table sits a large manila envelope labeled "C&C Enterprises."

Puzzled by the coincidence that Tommaso is the Uber driver, I glance around.

He returns and hands me a bottle of water. "He's not here."

My pulse quickens. This is the chance I was hoping for. I barely restrain my smile. "Do you know how I can contact him?"

He crosses his massive arms while I drink from the bottle. It takes a moment before I realize he hasn't answered my question. I glance up from his powerful arms to his face; he's scrutinizing me intently.

"You playing me?" he demands.

"Excuse me?"

"All wide eyed and innocent." His brow furrows. "Christ, you came here, so you must know something."

"Know what?" I ask, taking another sip as the fog begins to clear.

"Who ... the Beneventi family ... is."

"Of course. They own the casino."

He stands there, studying me closely, waiting.

"Do you ... does Al ... work for them?" Could it be he's been so close all along?

"You call him Al?" Tommaso asks, incredulous.

Embarrassment washes over me. "Alex? Allen? You know ... him?"

He rubs his jaw, as if weighing his options.

"What's the harm in giving me his contact information?"

"Listen, sweetheart. I'll tell *Al* you stopped by looking for him." Tommaso's lips twitch, and I grimace, disliking being the butt of some inside joke.

"Should I write down my number?"

"Not necessary."

I frown, confused.

Before I can press further, his phone vibrates loudly on the counter by the refrigerator, cutting me off.

He strides over to it, scowling as he checks the caller ID.

"But believe it or not, he's not the reason I'm here," I say, reaching for the envelope.

"You work for Ciro Cigorelli?" His voice reverberates through the trailer.

"Yes, I'm here for the envelope."

His friendly demeanor vanishes instantly. "Fucking hell. Are you in on it?"

We exchange a tense look, then both turn as his phone vibrates angrily again. The caller is persistent.

"In on what? I don't understand ..."

"This explains everything." In a swift motion, he grabs his phone and turns away. Despite his size, he moves with surprising grace, but as he does, his black T-shirt rides up, revealing a gun holstered in his black jeans. "I hate to have to tell you this," he says to whoever is on the line.

I don't wait to hear anything more. My instincts scream danger, and the gun tucked into his jeans is enough to make me heed the warning. While his back is turned, I slip away, leaving behind my one chance to reconnect with my stranger.

CHAPTER 6

Alessandro

IT TAKES persistence on my part and nerve on Tommaso's to get him to answer my call. It'd serve him right if my father knocked on his door without warning.

"I hate to have to tell you this," he begins.

But I cut him off because I'm in the middle of shit. "Hold on."

"Sir. Why are you dressed?" the nurse who just walked into the room exclaims. "You should be in bed."

"Fuck off." I pierce her with a hard look. They sent in a newbie today, all bubble gum and roses. She races from the room quicker than the others did.

"The hospital releasing you early?" Tommaso asks, surprised.

"No. I'm releasing me."

He makes a choking sound.

"Pack your shit. We're going to Italy once my men handle Cigorelli. If you survive."

"What?" he hollers.

"Listen, asshole. He's coming for you. You need to get yourself gone." It's an odd expression Tommaso is fond of using. The drugs I'm on must be getting to me.

73

"Who?" he asks.

"My father."

"Fucking hell."

I smile. For a ballbuster who gets beat up for enjoyment, he's terrified of my father. "Listen, get the story straight because his men fact-checked fucking everything. Tell him you tried to dissuade me from breaking lockdown. Share how you jumped on the van's goddamn hood while attempting to stop Conti's men—he likes heroic bullshit like that."

"Boss ..."

"His men are searching for Conti right now. We've got to find him before they do. Capisci?"

"Yeah, I get it." Pause. "Are the men interviewing Ciro Cigorelli today?"

My fists clench. Shitty food, nervous nurses, and three days confined to a hospital bed make me want to murder someone. But today's my lucky day. "Yeah, but my father isn't aware of his involvement, so keep your trap shut. I need to grab Conti before my old man can. Cigorelli can lead us to him."

He clears his throat. "Sandro ..."

"Conti's not in Atlanta?" I demand, wondering at the odd tone in his voice.

"No. He's gone underground since you diced and sliced his men."

"You hire a tech geek like I asked? One skilled enough to hack Cigorelli's bank account and search his devices?" An average person never disappears without a trace. But mafiosi excel at hiding bodies, dead or alive.

"Won't be an issue. We got a few men on payroll."

I frown. As we talk, Tommaso's voice becomes more and more strained. My father boldly butchered another capo, so I get it. "Calm down. He'll put a beating on you, and that's it. Then we can recover by my pool, bourbon in hand, cocks in a sexy brunette's mouth."

Auburn hair, wound around my fist. Riley, struggling for breath while she swallows me deep down her tiny throat. "Listen, asshole. One more thing. If my old man brings *her* up, don't say a goddamn word. She's a nobody, capisci?"

"About her ..."

I roll my eyes. "You busting my balls right now? While I'm incapacitated, laid up in pain—"

"She's alive. I fucking saw her."

I freeze. "Where?"

"Here. At the trailer ... She was collecting an envelope."

"An envelope?"

"For her boss ... at C&C Enterprises."

The room fucking spins. "What did you say?"

"Sandro. She was in on it."

Riley

WHAT COULD Ciro have possibly done to cause *that* reaction?

Mind racing, I hurry back toward the warehouse and desperately piece together what I know to be true. Tommaso, the Uber driver, works at the Riverview Casino. He despises Ciro—hates him, if I read his expression correctly. Therefore, by association, he now dislikes me. This much I can understand.

But dislike me *how much*? Enough to hurt me? Was he reaching for his gun? If his call hadn't interrupted us, would he have harmed me? Or was it that I was overheated, caught the shift in his expression, saw his gun, and overreacted?

My thoughts circle around to the most heart-wrenching fact of all —I'll never reconnect with Al now.

What's worse? Knowing you'll never again see someone you're obsessed with, or having the opportunity to do so vanish in the blink of a name?

I want to see *him*.

I need to see him again.

Squeezing my eyes shut, I pause in the middle of a city sidewalk. *God, did I make a mistake in running?*

"Are you okay?" someone asks.

No. I was headed toward okay and beyond, until he exited my life. *They all do, don't they?*

"Yes," I lie. "Just hot."

"Well, don't stand there in the sun, honey. Best find a building with AC." She walks off, probably headed toward cool comfort herself.

Sweat coats my forehead, and the envelope sticks to my hand. Deconstructing what transpired inside the trailer right now is counterintuitive. A cold iced tea and twenty-thousand BTUs of air-conditioning will clear my troubled thoughts. I can deal with the fresh dose of heartbreak later.

I reach the back end of our building and, because it'll cut an additional block and a half off my walk, key in the code to the emergency door.

Instead of the cool AC I left behind, I'm greeted by an unwelcome blast of hot air. What is wrong with Ciro? Anyone, with any common sense or consideration, would run the air-conditioning during a heatwave. Everyone knows more energy is used if the AC is shut off then turned back on, and it's more cost effective to leave it running.

Not bothering with the lights, I take a few moments to decompress.

Something crunches beneath my heel, but it doesn't register until I place a hand on Ciro's desk, and touch paper ... papers ... plural.

No. He *didn't*.

I flick on the lights and decide right here and now I'm going to crucify my *ex*-boss, straight after I quit.

Months of organization, and now papers are scattered everywhere. The desk, the floor, even by the door. His office is complete and utter chaos. Did he have to dump every file and cover every surface, floor included? What on earth was he looking for?

"Ciro?" I croak, spitting mad.

No more. I'm *done*.

I head first for the kitchen, and then the garage, crossing the large foyer to get there.

At first, I don't see them. Six men circled together. Chins lifted and eyes focused on something above. I stop in my tracks, my attention immediately lifting to the steel rafters.

I blink.

Ciro hangs by his neck on a rope looped over a beam, his battered body swinging back and forth, back and forth.

Beaten. Dead.

Murdered.

By these six men.

"Oh my God."

The men turn toward me.

A man with a huge scar on the left side of his face shoves the man next to him. "Stupid kid. You said the place was cleared."

"It was," a man my age, about twenty-one but with a goofy, baby-faced expression that makes him appear younger, protests. "She came back ..."

I don't wait to hear the rest. Spinning, I reverse course and take off toward Ciro's office.

I grew up on white bread and bicycle rides, Sunday dinners and county fairs, loving parents and a community where everyone looked out for each other. In a safe world until cancer, and later murder, shattered the illusion. But even so, that could never prepare me for something like this.

A bullet ricochets off the floor. Fight or flight instincts scream "keep running." But logic says I'll be dead if I do. So I stop and freeze, and not knowing what else to do, simply stand there.

"You stupid ciglione." Scarface glares at the gunman, and the shooting stops. "You'll alert the police." His attention swings toward the kid. "Don't stand there, get her."

He charges toward me, then with a death clamp on my arm, drags me into the foyer and pushes me to the floor. I fall backward, my head hitting the cement floor.

Ciro swings like a piñata overhead, blank eyes staring off into nothingness.

As I sit up, my fingers feel tacky like I touched wet chalk. It takes me a moment to process what it is.

Blood. Ciro's blood. I'm covered in it. Bile burns my throat, and my stomach churns, but the agonizing pain within my heart overwhelms everything else. Frantic, I wipe my hands on my shirt. "No, not again. *Please*, not again."

"Shut your trap," Scarface warns.

I swallow a whimper like it's foul medicine. Two men dressed in suits, more suitable for Wall Street than murder, point guns at me. The remaining four wear black sweatpants and hooded sweatshirts. All six are sweating profusely, and a small part of me revels in their discomfort.

Though not enough to ignore the fact they're wound so tight, Saran Wrap would be proud.

"You the girl who left earlier?" Scarface demands.

So, I *was* being followed. The kid answers for me. "I said it's her."

"Shut up." With the barrel of his pistol, Scarface gestures at me. "Answer me."

"Yes."

"Tough luck, then." He grins a twisted, sadistic smile that chills me to the bone. "You should have stayed gone."

Oh God. Am I about to die? Was this my father's last thought when stupid Stephanie welcomed him home with a canceled credit card statement and a bullet?

A cell phone rings.

Scarface turns completely pale as he retrieves it from his jacket. "Fuckin' hell." He tosses it like a hot potato to the kid. "You answer it."

Frantic, the kid swipes to answer. "Boss. They pumping you full of good meds in the hospital?"

Everyone stiffens.

"Che stupido!" Scarface exclaims. "Who does he think he's talking to?"

The kid shuffles nervously as he listens with wide eyes, then stutters, "No. No disrespect. Sorry. It's a goddamn sauna in here and ..."

I study them from beneath my lashes. Dark haired. Speaking Italian mixed with English. Minions to a boss who terrifies them. These men are mafia, for sure.

And the likelihood I'll survive this is less than zero ... in the negatives, really ... I draw in a breath, then gag. The unbearable stench of blood is only magnified by the heat.

Will I be covered in my own blood next?

"Um ... yeah," the kid announces. His eyes skim across the other men before resting on me. "No. No. We locked the building up good and tight like you asked. She must have had a key because she came in through the back." There's a lengthy pause. "No. Nothing on Conti. But we've got some files you'll wanna see."

The kid's eyes bug out of his head as the others exchange worried glances. Soldiers, isn't that the term for lower-ranking mafioso? And the kid did address the man on the phone as "boss."

"Yes. You got it. We won't leave until we've collected every fucking paper. No need for threats ..." Eyes wide, body tense and goofy smile gone, the kid's in full panic mode. By the expression on the other men's faces, they all are freaked out by the phone call. Whoever their boss is, there's no denying his power.

A shudder races up my spine.

"What?" the kid finally exclaims, and abruptly stills. His eyes rake over me. "Brown hair. Short, like five foot three. Really pretty, even with blood all over her."

There's a short pause, before he charges forward and hands me the cell phone. I look at it, and then at them.

All eyes are on me—and everyone is confused.

Slowly I bring the phone to my ear and clear my throat.

"Speak," an impatient voice demands.

"Hello?" I squeak. "Before you ..." ... *kill me* ... Sorrow has me choking on my words as everything hits me at once.

I'll never see my grandparents again.

Or laugh with Emily.

Or fall in love.

So much time wallowing, numb and disinterested in life, a new guest star in *The Walking Dead*, and now I'll be just that—dead.

Like Ciro.

Over something Ciro has *done*.

Tears roll down my cheeks, and I sniffle, trying to get a grip. *Think, Riley. Crying won't help you. A powerful mafioso like him probably gets off on your anguish.*

"Stop fucking sniveling, and tell me where you're from?"

His question confuses me. Where am I from? So he can do what? Hunt down my grandparents? Still he waits, until the silence becomes unbearable.

"Fresno," I blurt. Never been, and never will visit ... now ...

His men scowl at me as I wait for him to speak.

But instead of words, I hear chaos. Things crashing. People screaming. Him shouting profanity.

Until everything falls quiet.

And I wait ... and wait ...

Finally, his muffled voice breaks the silence. "Hand the mother-fucking phone to Guido."

That's it? No more questions? No opportunity to persuade him not to kill me?

"Please," I croak. "I'd like to explain ..."

"And I'd like to pump a bullet into your lying throat."

Oh, hell in a handbasket. Why did I lie about Fresno? Something about his voice may read familiar but his threat completely, utterly terrifies me.

I thrust the phone at the kid. "He wants Guido."

Eyebrows raised, Scarface snatches the cell from my hand and begins speaking before he even raises it to his lips. "I'll toss her ass into the cement truck along with that friggin' traitor's ..." His eyes lock on me, and confusion fills his expression. "Help her up."

The kid grabs my arm and tugs me to my feet.

"The stupid ciglione got it wrong. She's taller, five foot seven. Hair is dark red, a warm Cabernet color." He pauses briefly, his expression more and more perplexed. "More like Pinot Noir? Yeah, that's right—a deep red with blond highlights around her face."

Dread has me stepping backward.

Why the physical description? The highest statistic for female abductions is within my age group, eighteen to twenty-three. Is their boss considering trafficking me?

"Her tits?" The question echoes around the warehouse like an announcement over a bullhorn. They're all looking as I cross my arms across my chest.

"Big, gorgeous knockers, boss."

I'm too frightened to be embarrassed.

"And you work for Ciro Ciglioni?"

"Yes."

"Affirmative, boss."

He jerks his head away from the phone and winces. Like he was on the receiving end of a verbal punch.

"Tell him I keep the books. I'm not part of Ciro's drug deals or money problems, or whatever he's done. I was only staying on through the summer ..." My lips part, words forgotten, as Scarface produces a gun.

Then he shoots.

The kid drops to the floor next to me.

"You killed him?" I cry out, scrambling to put distance between us.

Scarface stalks toward me, and then grabs for me.

I sidestep. Except there's no escape. Fate's wrung me through her wringer until there's nothing left to bleed dry.

His hand clamps on my elbow. "Whatever you do ..." He raises his pistol. "... don't fucking die on me."

His weapon comes barreling down.

Sharp pain.

Before everything fades to black.

CHAPTER 7

I'M HOT, and tired.

So tired.

My brain's foggy, my eyelids heavy. The conversation going on around me cuts through at random.

"She's waking up."

"The dosage was too small."

"He said to inject the bare minimum."

"Give her another shot, or she'll wake up."

My head rolls back as I struggle to do so.

"Porca miseria! She dies, and we die. Look what happened to the kid."

"Give me that." There's a prick in my neck. "Buckle her seat belt. He's boarding right now."

"Wheeere …" I murmur, but the words don't form.

"Shhh, cara mio. Play your cards right, and you might survive."

I fight sleep, but it's no use, and I nod off.

———

"OPEN YOUR MOUTH," *his* voice gruffly says.

He loves ordering me about.

Loves demanding I do dirty, filthy things. Like relaxing into him as he thrusts deep into my throat, submitting to him as I choke and struggle for air.

A dream. I'm dreaming again.

His thumb presses against my bottom lip, then rolled paper touches my tongue. "Drink up."

I tighten my lips around the straw and suck. The water's cold and refreshing. And I'm thirsty, so thirsty.

My head lolls against his chest as he adjusts me on his lap.

After a while, a spoon replaces the straw. I struggle to open my mouth around it.

"A couple spoonfuls. Then you'll sleep off what remains of the sedative."

My eyelids flutter. Sedative? Am I not in my apartment? Isn't *he* the man holding me in his arms? I gasp, and he shoves the spoon into my mouth.

Applesauce.

I swallow it, and that's the last thing I remember.

I'M TRAPPED in a faded memory filled with vague impressions.

Him, in the shower with me. Behind me, with his arm snaked around my waist and chest pressed into my back. I'm pinned against the glass, naked and disoriented.

Shampoo stings my eyes, compounding my confusion. He's washing my hair?

He forks fingers through my locks, making sure to coat each strand before rinsing the suds away. He's meticulous. Businesslike.

Bossy, moving me about like a rag doll. Like I'm his favorite toy to play with.

And punish.

I turn my head slightly to steal a look, but he's not having it. He shoves my face forward, and then winds my hair around his fist until I'm completely immobile.

His heart races against my back.

And mine flutters, because I know what happens next.

His lips on my neck. His cock shoved between my clenched thighs.

"Beg me to fuck you like this."

"Yes. Please ..." I croak.

He tugs my hair. "Say it."

"Please fuck my thighs."

His teeth graze my sensitive skin, then he nuzzles my ear with his nose. "Once more, but this time, say my name. 'Alessandro, fuck my traitorous little body.'"

Wait ... what?

"Let me hear you, Riley."

My heart thumps wildly. "Please ... *Alessandro* ..."

He positions my palms on the glass. "Brace yourself," is all the warning I get before he thrusts forward, violently and without reservation. I still, giving in to the familiar hardness between my thighs. Basking in his possession.

This feels so *real*.

Inch by beautiful inch, he withdraws with agonizing slowness, and then shoves forward hard. My breasts flatten against the glass as he pins me to it, fucking me furiously. He hooks an arm around my waist to prop me in place when my knees give out.

I groan, anxious for the glide of his cock through my slit, ready to go off like a rocket.

Except he doesn't shift higher.

I need him *there*. Why hasn't he shifted higher?

And no comments about my excitement?

No praise for my submission?

The dream begins to fade. No. Please, no. I'm not ready to let it go. I can't lose him all over again.

The warmth against my back disappears, and I slide down the glass, water washing his seed from my bottom.

Stay. Please.

Exhausted, I curl into a ball on the shower floor. Still, words I wish I could have said form.

Don't leave me again.

CHAPTER 8

"ALESSANDRO, STAY."

Sunlight warms my face as imagined words wind through my subconscious. My eyelids are heavy, and it takes my full concentration to open them. Body aches and parched throat register next, but the memories, like a train horn breaking through the fog, have me scrambling into a seated position.

Holy hell.

It all comes back at once. Ciro's murder. The gun crashing against my head. My mafiosi kidnappers. A prick in the arm. A plane ride.

Applesauce.

I'm in an unfamiliar room, in a stranger's bed, naked and disoriented. Sore arm, sore neck and throat … from his fingers …

I frown.

A shower?

My eyes grow wide, and I dip my hand between my thighs. Not tender or swollen—no one abused me while I was drugged.

My therapist used to make me write lists, a repertoire of positive images to draw from during the darker days. At first I found comfort in it, making list after list, even enjoying the process. But with the constant attention—reporters swarming my grandparents' lawn, Mema's friends with their baked casseroles and half-baked smiles—those darks days turned into a waking nightmare. And when the news broke that my father was *engaged* to that monster—a fact he neglected telling me, which I had to learn from the TV—I burned every last one of the lists.

I've subconsciously created a new list, one completely centered around him, haven't I? Memories of our shower sex ranking among the best? A way to cope with witnessing a murder. To deal with the fact I've been kidnapped and possibly trafficked ... though my prison isn't what you'd expect.

Everything in the bedroom is white: the duvet and sheets, the walls and furniture, the crisscrossed beams overhead, even the painted hardwood floor. A table with two chairs sits against a wall, set for dining. My stomach rumbles as the smell of bacon wafts through the air.

I ignore my hunger pangs as I spot the French doors, and then scramble from the bed, dragging the sheet with me. I step onto a small black wrought iron balcony, one of three extending from the sprawling whitewashed villa perched majestically on a mountainside cliff. I stand here, mesmerized, while transported to another world.

An endless sapphire blue sea stretches out before me, with sailboats and yachts scattered across the water like brushstrokes on an impressionist canvas. The serene water, salty breeze, and sunshine offer a welcoming embrace, and for the briefest moment, I forget why I'm here.

Below to my left lies an Olympic-sized pool surrounded by white loungers. A Tiki-style bar with tall stools sits poolside, flanked by striped white and blue canopies and matching daybeds. To the far right, a casita stands as a miniature replica of the villa itself.

Shouting echoes from the opposite direction. Across several football fields and too far for a discreet call for help, a group of teenagers has gathered on a narrow cliff jutting over the sea. One by one, they leap off the edge, vanishing from sight. My heart pounds as I lean forward, only finding relief when I spot the boys minutes later, swimming toward a small beach.

So carefree. So *free*.

Life can be so beautifully cruel, can't it?

The villa is unlike any place I've ever visited, and I've only glimpsed the room and the view. It's the kind of place you bookmark on Vrbo and fantasize about, the sort of dream destination a TikTok travel influencer would kill to showcase.

Italy—must be. My kidnappers spoke Italian.

Far, far away from Marietta.

Far away from anyone who gives two figs about me.

Loud banging causes me to spin and tighten the bedsheet around me. I stare into the room at the door, waiting for Scarface or another mafioso to charge inside.

Several minutes pass, and nothing.

My stomach protests, and my eyes are drawn to the table. Lord, is that a teapot? If they wanted me dead, they wouldn't serve me tea in fine china.

So, what's the plan, Riley? What will you do?

Tea first.

Then bacon.

Followed by whatever else waits for me.

"PUTTANA."

A dark-haired woman in a white uniform with an exceptionally short skirt glares at me from between the French doors. She's beautiful, with a tight, tucked waist and curves men undoubtedly drool over, though her hostile expression ruins the effect.

It's been three days, and different women have been bringing food to the room. They're all exceptionally gorgeous, with dark hair and wide almond-brown eyes, wearing matching white uniforms with skirts so short, I get an eyeful when they bend over.

One thing more they have in common? They hate me.

At least it's clear who keeps pounding on my door.

This morning's brunette jabs her finger toward the tray on the table. "Stai zitta e fai colazione."

If I could bottle her undisguised loathing and sell it, I could buy an expensive yacht like the kind I've spent days watching and sail away. Most of my time is spent in a chair I dragged outside, sunning myself while contemplating life.

And death.

"Please. Telefono." I gesture to my ear like I'm making a call. Repeating the request I've asked the others.

She mimics the gesture, flashing me the finger as she does so. "Non essere patetica!"

Don't these women get I'm a prisoner?

The bedsheet slips, and her gaze flicks over me. What she sees only infuriates her further. "Non sei proprio il suo tipo, sai?"

"I don't understand."

She throws her hands up and charges off, kicking the fluffy white throw rug on her way out of the room.

The door slams behind her.

I return inside to the table. Entertaining myself by tearing bread crust off a slice, sprinkling water on it, then rolling it into a ball to eat.

When I was young, every spring my mother and I'd feed ducks in a park overlooking the Muskingum and Ohio Rivers. We'd dampen bread with water, and then make small dough balls to toss to the less aggressive ducks on the outskirts of the paddling.

My mom was wonderful like that, always kind and fair, always living in the present, always fond of family traditions and openly expressing her love.

Do I even know what love means anymore? Every time I get close to it, it's like reaching for a fallen star. My father. Emily. Al. If only I had more time with each of them.

Voices in Italian float through the French doors, filling the quiet with energy. Do they know I'm here? I don't rush to the balcony or call out—I'd rather remain unnoticed. Being forgotten isn't the worst fate.

My gaze settles on the stale bread. Not entirely forgotten, right? *Be thankful you're still breathing, Riley. Because, despite the idiom, no one ever truly dies of boredom.*

———

Alessandro

THEY SAY RESPECT IS EARNED.

But so is disgrace. Like the pain meds I'm on, it's a bitter pill to swallow.

I was manipulated.

I was *betrayed.*

Humiliation pulses like lava through my bloodstream. Except no amount of drugs will halt the rage from flowing freely.

Mercilessly.

"Signor Beneventi, si prega di mangiare," a nurse pleads, waving a fork full of food in front of my face. A pretty brunette with puffy red lips. She's doing her job, and I'm heavily sedated on Sebastiano Beneventi's orders. But she's got a better chance at my obedience if she first bends over the hospital bed so I can stuff her mouth full of dick. Except an expert blow and poor hospital food are low on my priority list.

At the top of the list is Conti's tortured body. By chain saw? Cement truck? Or do I slowly, methodically slice off small body parts —pinkies, toes, dick—and force him to swallow them whole?

"Da quanti giorni sono qui?" I demand. How many days have I been incapacitated while Conti remains alive?

"Tre giorni. Ma Don Beneventi insiste che lei rimanga ricoverato per una settimana."

Three days?

Fuck.

I struggle to sit up. My old man insisted I accept treatment, and I obeyed. "Was Tommaso Manella admitted?" I ask in English, Italian taking too much effort right now.

"Sì, signor Beneventi."

"Toss his ass in a wheelchair and wheel him in here."

She grins playfully. "If you'll eat just a little..." Her expression changes as my glare cuts her to pieces. I'm seconds from strangling the sweet smiles from her body. But I save that pleasure for someone more deserving.

The nurse drops the fork and plate, and bolts from the hospital room.

I wait, until minutes later Tommaso is pushed in. A male nurse wheels his chair beside my bed, and then flees the room.

"You look like hell," he says as a greeting.

A quick scan confirms my father put a beating on him. The knowledge only adds to my humiliation. He's in a freaking wheelchair because of my shitty judgment. "You survived."

He shrugs. "Don Beneventi was pretty pissed off."

"What did you talk about?" I press on, cold, unsympathetic, and straight to the point. We don't have time for cuddles and fucking hugs.

"Conti. He's got his best men on the hunt."

"Stateside, or elsewhere?" I ask, curious if my father has a lead to his whereabouts.

"The South; Georgia, Tennessee, Alabama, Mississippi. Places Conti has connections." He stretches his legs and folds his hands on his lap, as if he were in a conference room chair instead of wheelchair bound. "And before you ask, I kept my trap shut. No mention of Ciro Cigorelli. Not a single thing said about Riley."

I smash my fist on the standing tray beside the bed and upend it. "Don't say her goddamn name."

He holds up his hands. "Jesus. Fine. We'll decide later when you want me to interrogate her."

"Or kill her."

His expression pinches like he has more to say.

But, like her miserable, lying life, this conversation is over.

"Renzo," I say. "Send men to Rome to see if they can learn anything about where he might be hiding." Because I'll personally drag his ass out of hiding, kick it, and then sort him out. I promised, and I won't disappoint my father again. "My guess is he's holed up in some underground club. They need to be discreet, or he'll disappear."

"Got it." He searches my expression. But whatever softness may have existed is gone. "Anything else?"

"Our time here is done."

CHAPTER 9

Riley

SHOUTING erupts and car doors slam. Footsteps race by my door. The villa is suddenly alive with energy.

Finally, something is happening.

Someone important has arrived. Is it the boss? The mafioso I briefly spoke with?

My elation is tempered with worry. I'm caught up in Ciro's mafia business; this must be why I've been kidnapped. Because of drugs? Money owed? Both?

I wish I could call Emily. She must know by now, right? She must be devastated by Ciro's death and worried about my disappearance.

And my grandparents—I missed my weekly call. They don't deserve any more anguish than what Fate's already dealt them.

You're alive, Riley. Be thankful.

I drape the freshly hand-washed sheet over the balcony railing to dry, and then return to my chair to soak in the morning sun. At this rate, I won't have any tan lines—not that anyone will notice with the sheet blocking the view from below. Not that anyone cares.

I close my eyes and mentally review the plan once more. I'll meet with the man from the phone call, the one everyone refers to as the boss. I'll make it clear I'm not involved in Ciro's illegal activities—that while I knew about his drug habit, I am innocent and uninvolved in his dealings. I'll promise to stay silent, ask to return home, and hope that's enough to earn his trust. The fact I'm still unharmed offers a sliver of hope. The daily pot of tea suggests he might not be entirely merciless; perhaps he's reasonable and I can convince him.

With a glimmer of control, I drift off to sleep.

I don't know how long I'm out for.

What I do know is I wake up to a man shouting less than ten feet away. "Tommaso! Toglila dalla mia vista!"

I straighten, stunned, and my attention snaps to the larger balcony. I jerk as a door slams and violent cursing erupts in the room next to mine. A crash has me retreating inside. It's followed by a renewed round of curses.

Dread sweeps over me, and panic has me pacing. But the name he uses leaves me dumbstruck.

Tommaso.

* * *

Alessandro

I BOUGHT this villa for the view.

And when I needed it most, when I thought the salt in the air and sun on my face might soothe my anger, I see her.

On the adjacent balcony.

Sunbathing nude, her beautiful breasts tan from the sun.

On a vacation in motherfucking paradise.

What. The. Fuck?

I charge inside and then unleash a week of pent-up rage. A lamp, the television, a small armoire, they all take the brunt. By the time I'm done, my lips are busted and ribs are protesting.

I draw in a deep breath. "Tommaso!"

His arrival takes fucking forever. He limps in, takes stock of my bedroom, then turns to leave.

"Are you fucking kidding me?"

"I could say the same," he mutters.

"Do I look like I'm running an Airbnb?" I place a hand on the wall as the room sways. "Why isn't her ass locked in the cellar?"

"You could barely stand the day we arrived, yet you spoon-fed her tea and cleaned the blood off her body. Why would I lock her in the dungeon?"

His words hit me like a blow. It feels like being waterboarded—cloth over my face, gallons of water pouring down, just enough to feel the suffocation. I was utterly out of it when we got to the villa, lost in a familiar addiction—her. My fingers grip the nearest object, an ornate wall sconce the interior designer insisted on. With a savage yank, I wrench it from the wall and throw it, shattering it against the opposite side.

Tommaso ducks, narrowly avoiding the debris.

"She can spend her vacation in hell."

It takes him far too long to respond. "Broken lock."

"What?" I growl.

"The cell door isn't operable."

I glare at him. "Well, call a goddamn locksmith."

"Sandro ... as your friend ..."

"Don't play the friend card, asshole. What the hell, man? You put her in the guest room next to mine? If you think my father wiped your clock clean ..."

He stares at me with that look he gets when he's determined to dig in. My vision blurs, and I'm faced with two obstinate assholes. "Go on," I grunt. "Say it."

"She seemed eager to reconnect with you, not anxious or guilty. Let me interview her, just in case we're wrong ..."

"She worked for Ciro. Lived in his building."

"Yeah," he grunts. "And ..."

"And what?"

He hesitates. "She moved in with him after the explosion."

The whitewashed room turns bloodred. "What?"

"If you'd let me run a background check on your girl earlier ..."

I raise a hand to cut him off. Every moment leading up to the ambush replays in my mind—her empty building, the broken lock she wouldn't fix, her sweet, submissive demeanor. I was blind and predictable. But even with bloodshot eyes, I see more clearly now. My girl—a Broadway-worthy actress. "Find a locksmith today."

"On it." He hesitates, and I brace for more bullshit. "And you'll let me interrogate her?"

Jesus. Guilty or not, the thought of his filthy hands on her ... "I'll handle her."

"You'll kill her, then?"

I shrug.

"Have it your way." He's smart enough to leave it at that. "We have Ciro's girlfriend in a secure place."

"Interrogate the friend but keep her alive for now." Jesus, withdrawal is a bitch. I understand why Renzo can't get clean. Everything hurts, inside and out. What the hell did they pump into me?

He gestures toward the room next door. "Where do you want her?"

Tied up in bed, begging for mercy, fully aware of who I am and why you don't fuck with a Beneventi.

"Leave her there to rot until the cell's ready." I pause, the image of her asleep on the balcony burned into my mind.

"But the motherfucking vacation ends now."

CHAPTER 10

Riley

THE MAN next door's freak-out was the beginning of my situation changing. The relentless banging on my bedroom door, at all hours, day and night, abruptly stopped.

So did my morning tea.

The Michelin-worthy meals are no more—replaced, with glee, by a hostile brunette, who tossed a half loaf of stale bread at me that next morning, then slammed an empty pitcher onto the table.

Fine, I'll pretend it's lasagna and red wine, I thought, hiding my reaction. Her glare turned into a manic smile, then she made a cutting motion with her finger across her throat—complete with gargle—and left.

Jaw falling open, I watched her departure in shock.

But this?

I cover my mouth and hold back a scream. If stale bread and questionable tap water aren't enough reasons, this is why all my energy should be put toward escaping. While I was sunbathing, someone snuck into the room and left a dead canary on my pillow. The poor creature's decapitated body and head are cradled in the indent I left behind.

Don't react, Riley. They're likely listening, gloating over tormenting you using a defenseless bird.

Although I feel sorry for the bird, what these vicious women don't know is this isn't my first encounter with death. This is *far* from the worst tragedy I've stumbled upon.

I hold my breath and take the pillow outside, careful not to upend the bird, then heave everything over the railing. Seconds later, curses burst out. Two guards patrolling the grounds stand directly below and are staring, flabbergasted, at what may or may not have hit them.

Hastily, before they can see me, I back away and retreat inside. Knowing how it feels being in the wrong place at the wrong time.

Lord, I need to find a way out of here.

Pacing gets me nowhere, so I sit on the bed corner, breathe in deep and calm my mind, then consider my options. The housemaids always lock the door behind them when they leave, and if I jump off the balcony, I'll end up like the bird. So I need to be clever if I hope to escape.

I kick my foot, and my toes catch on the shaggy white carpet. And, just like that, an idea forms.

Rearranging the furniture takes more effort than expected. I drag the short bureau to rest against the same wall as the door, then push the table to the opposite side of the bed. The fluffy white rug, surprisingly heavy, resists as I roll it up and lift it upright. I wobble it across the room, steadying its weight as I maneuver it toward the bureau, wedging it tightly between the wall and furniture. The top half leans diagonally across the door, a barrier of soft fabric and stubbornness.

If the canary was a surprise ...

Minutes change into hours as I weigh my next moves. Find a way downstairs and then outside. Get to the water. Hail a sailboat or yacht or follow the shoreline to the beach I saw those teenagers swimming toward.

Or I can search for somewhere on the grounds to hide? The poolside casita?

Also, my chances will improve *greatly* if no one is aware I've escaped ...

Time drags by until the sun sits low on the horizon. With a folded sheet secured around my middle, and legs free, I grasp the pitcher and linger at the right side of the door.

Footsteps approach, and I wait for her to enter. They take turns tormenting me, but I hope tonight's brunette is the gleeful cutthroat and my biggest tormenter. Because I won't feel half as guilty for what I'm about to do.

Keys jingle, then the door's thrust open and she barrels inside. The rolled rug descends with a loud thump in front of her, and before she can process what's happening, she's knocked off balance. Her arms flail, and then over the rug she goes, my dinner—the smallest imaginable loaf of stale bread—sailing across the room.

I rush forward as she stares at me, aghast, then before she can scream, I smash the pitcher into the side of her head.

She instantly goes limp.

Lifeless ... oh no, no, no! I visualized her death a million ways, but I didn't mean it.

I fall to my knees and check her neck for a pulse. Relief washes over me when I feel it racing.

Satisfied, I grab her keys.

Go, Riley. This is happening.

I step over her and the rug, into the hallway, pausing to lock the door behind me. Escaping into unknown territory, though the urgency of the situation is not lost on me.

With a glance around, I realize the villa is even more spectacular than I imagined. I'm in a hallway on a mezzanine floor, with all four sides of the square looking over an open concept living area below. An intricate black wrought iron railing accents the otherwise sparse white space.

My attention pauses on an enormous grand staircase to the left.

I race toward it, not missing a beat, am down the stairs and sprinting across white marble tile, headed toward the kitchen area.

Yes, I think, spotting a single door to the left of an intricately carved wooden pantry and just beyond an island the size of my New York apartment's kitchen.

All that stands between the door and me is another vicious brunette.

She's vacuuming or pretending to. Looking like a Real Housewife, earbuds on as she wiggles and gyrates while pushing the humming machine. Not actually concerned with getting every lick of dirt—although I bet this immaculate floor and these fixtures have never been touched by dust.

When she spins left, I fly by her right side.

Hope pushes through the fright about a third of the way across the sprawling room. I've made it this far. Now exit the kitchen door. Walk, don't run, toward the casita. Pray the guards are looking up for more surprises and not gathered poolside.

A shadow crosses the natural light reflecting off the tile, shifting my attention toward the mezzanine above. I breathe a sigh of relief, not finding anything. Yet something—nerves, incredulousness I've made it this far—has me looking over my shoulder.

I immediately wish I hadn't. Because a man in a suit is descending the staircase, taking two stairs at a time.

Oh no. No. No. No.

My feet can't move quick enough as I pass the island toward the door. *Pull it closed behind you ...*

The sheet tightens around me, and my body jerks to an abrupt stop. I struggle, like a caterpillar inside a cocoon, until my pursuer's full weight slams into me from behind. I land hard on my stomach, the wind knocked out of me as I'm tackled onto the cold tile floor.

His hands bracket my wrists in a bruising grip while his full weight pins me in place. Lord, he's strong, all muscle against my back. My breasts hurt flattened against the floor. And worse, the sheet has risen and is around my waist, his groin flush against my bottom.

I'm completely, utterly at his mercy.

"Please," I pant. "I can't breathe ..."

His fingers find my throat and he squeezes. "Better now?"

Panic washes over me as I attempt to buck him off me.

He waits until I'm exhausted to temporarily pull free. Temporarily, because the next thing I know, he's forced my thighs apart with his knee, spreading them wide, obscenely so, and settled back against me.

I feel his enormous erection immediately.

Oh, God. My struggles turn him on.

I go limp.

He bites my ear, then growls into it. "Your submission is worthless now."

Footsteps echo across the tile until the man racing toward us stands over us. "Fucking hell, Sandro."

The man on top of me ... Sandro ... doesn't budge. My earlobe stings, while his punishing weight crushes me into the floor.

"Clear the room," the other man orders. More footsteps—Lord, how many men are there? And how foolish of me to think I'd escape?

"Listen to me," I croak. "I had nothing to do with—"

"And the lies begin ..."

There's venom in his words, but his voice ... What is it about his voice?

"Boss. I can take over from here."

My heart wedges inside my stomach. Is the man—Sandro—the mafioso I spoke to at the warehouse? The man everyone fears? If I'm right, then I'm a captive inside his beautiful villa, surrounded by the sea, heavily armed men, and cutthroat housekeeping. The villa's quite the juxtaposition to the monster who resides here.

Yet, I'm alive.

Why not kill me? Why drag me across continents, lock me in a resort-worthy room, and then forget I exist?

"Let me deal with her, Sandro," the mob soldier says.

"Don't fucking Sandro me. That lock fixed?"

His voice is oddly familiar. Or is it the discussion about locks, of all things?

"Not yet ... *boss*."

"I'll handle her."

As the soldier's footsteps retreat, I wiggle and try to break free. But the iron pipe thickening against my back halts my actions. "Don't," I cry out. "Don't leave me with him."

"Move that beautiful body, and I'll fuck you into the floor while all my men watch. Capisci?"

His voice.

Can it be?

On the morning my mother passed, I paced the sidewalk outside the hospital, clinging to the promise I made her. "Never give up hope, Riley. You are stronger than you think," she'd had me repeat. Grief-stricken, I wandered aimlessly until, unexpectedly, my toe snagged on a crack and I stumbled. Looking down, I saw a vibrant yellow dandelion pushing through the concrete. Hope in the form of a flower.

Hope, which I abandoned my search for after my father's murder.

No way. It can't be.

"*Fucking beautiful.*" Him, deep inside me.

"*Good girl.*" Me, choking on his massive cock.

Praising me. Corrupting me.

"*Fix the lock, capisci?*"

The scent of his cologne, a fresh, complex mix of lemon and sandalwood, confirms my shocking suspicion. My mind swirls in confusion, leaving me able to utter only a single word.

"Al?"

Alessandro

IF I GOT off on her submission before, I'll get off on her terror now.

"Feel that?" I sink my teeth into her earlobe and thrust my cock into her ass. She relaxes beneath me in a far too familiar way, her every action a lie. "That's the one and only part of me that doesn't despise you."

"Oh my God," she exclaims. "It *is* you." So fucking innocent, Sunset Boulevard should have a billboard with a golden halo circled around her head.

"Shut up." I lift off her, pull her to her feet, and then hiss through my teeth as the sheets pool around her ankles and I get an eyeful of long tan legs and tight ass. She bends to grab the sheet, and a low fucking growl vibrates from my throat. That does it. "Leave it," I snap.

"She's staring ..." she protests.

I look beyond her to the housemaid who has paused her vacuuming to watch the spectacle unfolding. She's one of my favorite fuckdolls I keep at my beck and call. I can whip her ass, and then ride it hard, and it's still not enough. Barbara or Bernadetta—her name eludes me.

As do her eyes right now ... which are glaring daggers at the woman in front of me. I thought Tommaso cleared the room?

"Vattene da qui adesso, cazzo!" I bellow.

She flees, leaving the vacuum behind.

Before the traitor can follow, I grab her by the hips, then spin and toss her over my shoulder. My ribs protest despite her feather-like weight. But my pain's nothing compared to the kind she'll experience.

I charge across the white tile floor then turn down a long hallway to my office.

Once inside, I dump her on the carpet without warning.

With a panicked cry, she lands hard on her hands and knees.

The sound doesn't soothe my rage or please me. Though it doesn't stir my fucking sympathy, either. When it comes to her, I'm twisted—always have been. I'd like to say nothing's changed, but then I'd be the motherfucking liar in the room.

Her first mistake was seducing a monster like me. The second was believing she could betray me and get away with it. The third was not remaining locked up and out of sight. Three strikes, and you're out, right? I should kill her already and be done with it.

"I don't understand ..."

"Shut up." Locked away to rot—she deserves no better.

I stalk across the room and swipe my arm across a table, sending shit flying. A fucking magician, I whip off the tablecloth, and then haul the custom cage collecting dust beneath it to the center of the room.

She's on her knees with her eyes on the floor. The picture of perfect obedience. I pause for a moment to take her in. Long limbs, tight waist, killer breasts, though I avoid looking at her pretty face and fixate on the arms covering her chest. Always hiding what's mine, whether I want it or not. My cock stiffens in agreement.

It's understandable how an average man might be duped by her duplicity.

There are new rules now.

She'll either play or pay.

I move by her to my desk and take out the first lesson to be learned—*obedience.*

I come to stand before her. "Look at me."

Ever so slowly, her eyes rise.

Her fear fades quickly when she finally sees my face.

"Oh my God. What happened?" Her expression becomes wild as she takes in my battered face. Yellow-and-black-ringed eyes.

Bandaged broken nose. Clown lips. Her eyes drop to my body, but the broken ribs and bruising are hidden beneath my suit. "Are you okay?" Her voice quivers as she speaks.

Like I'm some gullible stranzo who might believe her act.

I glare, livid. So livid I'm tempted to pull the knife, instead of a bone, from my desk drawer and carve the word into her skin using all caps. Along with a few other choice words. Liar. Traitor. *Mine*.

Mine, to torment.

Mine, to make pay.

She shakes her head, faking confusion. "Were you in a fight?"

I'm over the hundred-and-fucking-one questions. I want her locked up, and the key thrown away. I tap her beneath the chin with the soft plastic bone. "Fetch."

Her gasp fills the room. "What?"

I hurl the bone across the room. It hits the wall with a loud whack then tumbles to the floor.

"Pick it up with your mouth," I instruct, tone flat and words ice-cold. "Then crawl your ass over here and get inside the cage."

"You can't be serious."

"Dead serious," I growl. "Keep questioning me and you'll end up inside a basement dungeon where no one will remember you long enough to fall for your innocent act."

Where gorgeous green eyes and flushed pink cheeks will get her nowhere.

"Innocent act?" she asks, a vision of innocence.

"You've ten seconds. Fetch the bone like an animal and return with it to your new home ... One ..."

"My new home? You're locking me in a cage?"

"Two, three, four."

Eyes bright with tears, she stares at me like I betrayed *her*.

"You want to live? Be a good dog and do what you're told."

I've reached the point where I hope she'll disobey me. Loyalty and respect—my men, my staff, my fuckdolls, every goddamn person around me exhibits in spades. I'm nothing without it, and God knows

I've earned it. How dare she think I'll tolerate anything else? She should be dead by now. Why prolong the inevitable?

She comes up on all fours, and my eyes narrow. Her body is thinner than the last time I had her naked. Her back arches, breasts swaying as she crawls, tears leaving a trail across my expensive carpet as she crawls to the bone.

Fuck.

I palm my erection, and nearly bust my seams when she turns. Her, with the bone in her mouth. Her, back arched and beautiful. She stops at my feet and looks, first at my hand and then at my face.

Rage resurfaces and blurs my vision as I drop my hand and point. "Welcome home."

She flinches, but then obeys. Crawling inside, turning, and dropping the bone.

I slam the gate shut and click the lock into place. Done. So fucking done.

"Alessandro ..." she pleads. My real name off her lips was all I could think about for weeks.

"Never say my name, capisci?"

She jerks backward like I slapped her.

Unable to look at her any longer, I stalk over to my window and glare at the yachts sailing along on the horizon. I've got shit to do, two men to hunt down, and a father to outsmart. Distractions, especially ones that plead so sweetly, are a mistake I won't make twice.

I risked it all for pussy.

She's a nobody to me now.

CHAPTER 11

Riley

HIS FACE. His handsome face. Bruised yellow and black, and swollen like a monster's.

Which is fitting because he is one.

Al never existed, did he? I invited a violent mob boss home, let him fuck me so hard my teeth rattled, and thought that was it. But it wasn't—he came back. The things we've done, how I gave myself up completely to him, thinking I knew him despite not knowing much about his life outside my bed. How could I be so naive? How could I not worry how dangerous he was? How could I trust a complete stranger?

I was chasing extremes—something, anything to spark life into me.

And he radiated power like a lethal warhead.

Reckless, so reckless.

Because Alessandro Beneventi is exactly why you don't invite strangers home.

Tears wet on my cheeks, I pull my legs into my chest and readjust positions in this cramped cage. I crawled on my knees like an animal for him. Fetched a *bone*. But this wasn't a game to make me submit.

This was an expression of anger ... *loathing*.

He hates me.

"Won't you listen to me?" I call out, throat hoarse.

The soft creak of his office chair is the only sign he's still present.

My throat tightens as I remember Ciro's lifeless body swinging from the rafters. Will that be my fate? How will I survive?

Panic licks up my spine. Ciro *is* the link between us. And Lord knows he has the morals of a hungry pit bull.

Had the morals ... I cover my mouth to block my cry. This is Ciro's fault, and his murderer believes I'm involved.

What did Alessandro say earlier? Stop putting on an innocent act?

Does he not know me at all?

Tears fall without censor, and then I'm full-out bawling.

A door slams, a sign he's left me alone, but caged.

Leaving me to reconcile the man I never truly knew with the monster I don't recognize at all.

A DOOR CRASHES OPEN, followed by laughter, and I'm jolted awake. Pins and needles shoot through my stiff limbs as I unfurl from the ball I curled into hours ago and sit back on my haunches. It takes me a moment to catch on to what's happening. Alessandro enters, but he's not alone. In tow are two brunettes. Their uniforms unzipped to the navel and breasts bouncing, as laughter accompanies them into the room.

Pain catches me off guard like a punch to the stomach. I never imagined him with other women, not even when he disappeared those few weeks. More stupidity on my part, believing our relationship was exclusive. Thinking—naively and with little sexual experience—I could hold his interest. That our souls connected on a deeper level.

Wrong, Riley. He has a staff of vicious brunettes on call. Like he's choosing his favorite popsicle, with each one shaped the same and packaged in white.

The truth crushes me.

We weren't in a relationship. Our souls didn't connect in some deep, profound way. I meant nothing to him. My heart squeezes, and I'm helpless to do anything other than watch.

They stop a few feet away.

He pushes them off him. "Chinarsi sulla gabbia."

"Che cosa?" one asks. I've no idea what's being said, but her expression reads confused. I glance at the second woman, the same one who'd been vacuuming. If looks could kill, I'd escape this nightmare.

"Sandro," she whines, and points to me. "Non con questa stronza che ci guarda!"

He growls her name in warning. "Barbara."

"Non Barbara," she sniffles. "Brigetta."

"Whatever your goddamn name is, bend the fuck over or leave." I hit my head on the top of the cage at his shout.

Both brunettes lean over the cage and flatten their chests against the top.

Lord, this isn't happening.

"On your toes."

No. No. No. No way am I watching this. I grab the bars and rattle the cage. "Let me out of here," I demand.

His belt swings from his hand.

All the aggressive, borderline violent games we played fall short of this kind of pain.

"Don't," I plead. "You're hurting me."

His bruised eyes lock on mine. "Baby, you don't know the definition of hurt. Not yet."

Baby? He decimates the endearment with such a cruel and uncaring tone that my heart pauses with disbelief. And he's wrong ... If he weren't so angry, he'd realize it. Because not only do I know the definition of hurt, I've written books on the topic.

My eyes brighten with tears.

His bruised lips curl, enjoying my distress.

No more. He's not worth it.

"Fate vedere il culo, troie mie."

The women wiggle and claim my attention. A strangling protest escapes my throat as they raise their uniforms. Horrified, I shift my eyes back to Alessandro, only to discover he's looking at me.

"Let's make a deal."

"What?" I gasp.

He snaps the belt in the air.

I stiffen, as do the two brunettes.

"Never blistered your ass, have I?"

Does he actually expect an answer?

"If you want out, I'll grant your request." His eyes flash darkly. "If you join us."

"Join you?" I'm momentarily speechless.

His expression hardens, and I'm slow to acknowledge the monster he truly is.

"How can you be so cruel?"

His knuckles tighten around the belt. "And how can you be such a beautiful liar?"

"I'm not," I say.

"Right."

Our eyes lock.

Energy charges the space between us. Anger mixed with mistrust and rolled up into this undeniable attraction. If only he'd let me explain my troubled relationship with Ciro instead of this torture ...

A woman wiggles her bottom, demanding Alessandro's attention.

God, this shouldn't hurt so much.

"If only you'd listen," I mutter.

He steps closer. "You listen. Either join us or enjoy the show."

I flinch.

"That's what I thought. Now don't speak unless spoken to."

With that, he shifts back and, with the snap of his belt, quickly and efficiently begins whipping the women.

Legs to chest, I curl up into a ball. He warned he'd break me many times in the past. I wanted him to, I eagerly submitted to his power.

But with every smack, pieces of my obsession with the monster fragment.

The women gasp and moan.

And I feel like screaming.

Everything that follows happens as a blur, but I watch it all unfold, barely breathing. The prolonged spanking. His belt hitting the floor. The brunettes touching themselves and each other, an orgy breaking out against the cage. Him, freeing his erection, and then stroking himself aggressively while examining his handiwork. His attention wavering until it fixes on me before snapping back to them. Then back on me, longer this time.

Moans fill the room, and I cover my ears and close my eyes.

My lips move, and words flow silently.

How could you?

I hate you.

I hate you.

A symphony of our hate and their pleasure crescendos. This is torture. Like a soldier losing her mind from sleep deprivation caused by heartbreaking, soul-crushing noises.

I rock back and forth and escape inward. But no matter how deep I go, it's not far enough.

Until his thunderous bellow breaks through. "Leave."

My eyes flash open as two confused women hurry from the room.

"Hate me, is that right?"

Through all that awful moaning, he heard me?

I glare at him as he strokes himself. Unashamed.

Unforgiving.

"Not as much as you will hate me."

I'm close, if not already there. "Whatever you think I've done, you're wrong."

"A week from now, tell me that same lie, and we'll reevaluate where we're at." He moves closer to the cage, his fist quickening the pace. "Squeeze your breasts together."

Confusion washes over me.

"Be a good dog and do it. As a reward, I'll bring you a bowl of water and food. Fuck, I'll even pat your head."

A tear leaks out. But I obey, because it's unclear how long I'll be in here. I cup my breasts and push them together.

"Fuck. Keep looking at me with those big, sorrowful eyes."

"You won't ... You can't be this twisted ..."

"Tell me the truth," he grinds out, his movements borderline frantic. "You miss the taste of me?"

My lips part.

"That's it. Open wide. I could feed you nothing but my come." His warm seed hits lower, missing my lips for my chin, before he unleashes on my breasts.

He always praises me afterward: What a good girl you are, taking a shower in my come. Look at you, decorated with my seed.

I'm frozen in place, his come dripping from my chin and nipples; sticky and vulnerable, so vulnerable. While he tucks himself away and hooks his belt through the loops, like he's ending a business transaction.

Silence echoes loudly in the room.

Finally, he tosses his shirt at me. "I don't want your stench stinking up my office. My man will bring you to a bedroom to shower. You'll have an hour of freedom, then it's back to the cage."

Then he leaves me here.

Dirty.

Degraded.

Destroyed.

CHAPTER 12

Alessandro

SWEAT MINGLES with blood as I heave the heavy barbell overhead. My lip has busted open, and my ribs curse me for my foolishness. From next to the weight bench, Tommaso reprimands me with his eyes.

"What?" I bark once the barbell is back in position.

"I didn't say anything."

"Keep it that way." I roll to my feet.

"Sandro." Tommaso reaches for me as I stagger, but I brush him away. Pain is tolerable. Failure is not.

"You need to give your body time to heal." It takes him less than a minute to begin blabbing, like I asked for his advice. "By recovering in bed and allowing the meds to do their thing."

"Like you're doing?" The asshole was in a wheelchair days ago yet ran a mile last night. Rain, shine, fractured ribs—he never stops.

Behind the towel, I hide my winces while wiping the sweat from my face. The medication might help if I didn't dump it down the toilet. Not that I tell Tommaso I've gone cold turkey. A fighter by nature, he understands a thing or two about recovery, so his advice is solid even if his own actions are contradictory.

Pain management will only dull my senses when I need them sharp. Unlike my brother, I can ignore my inner demons, especially when so much is at stake. The quicker I can show my face again, the less time my father will spend dwelling on what a disappointment I am. Conti sliced and diced—as Tommaso so eloquently put it—with his body parts delivered express mail to Rhode Island should obliterate any lingering thoughts concerning my capabilities.

"I'll say this once, and then I'll drop it," he comments.

"How about you drop it now?" Because I can tell by his bullshit expression, he's about to give me bad news.

"It's okay to be vulnerable."

What. The. Fuck.

"We're best friends. I'd take a bullet for you, Sandro. Hell, I body-surfed a city sidewalk after sailing off a car hood for you. If that isn't proof of my friendship."

"You lose your dick somewhere on that sidewalk?" For fuck's sake, maybe I stopped the drugs too soon? "Am I not holding your hand tight enough when we take a fucking stroll? Or will you surprise me with an unwanted pregnancy?" Vulnerable? Even the word rolls my stomach.

Because vulnerability—Renzo's, not mine—ruined the life I imagined.

"Think about it."

"One, two ..." I count. "Done. No further discussion required."

His sigh fills the gym. "Whatever you say, boss."

"Got something right, today." I change the subject to a more urgent matter. "So there's no sign of Conti?"

"Not since you asked me five minutes ago."

"And the tech experts? Have they hacked into Ciro's bank accounts yet?" I toss the soiled towel into a bin. "Follow the money, isn't that what they say?"

"No word yet."

"For Christ's sake, then get on your phone and demand an update."

"It's three in the fucking morning ..."

"Since when have you become so soft?"

Six foot five and pure muscle, the stone-cold killer has crushed a man's skull with his heel without the slightest flinch. A heartless mafia enforcer, my right hand, and a friend whose reputation with my father is also at stake.

If there's anyone who understands how weak—goddamn *vulnerable*—I truly am, it's Tommaso. Is that what brought this on?

"Fuck."

"Maybe you should. You've house staff on call who are exactly your type." He grins because the fucker likes any filthy brunette who swallows. "Wake them up. Trust me, you'll rest better."

I search his expression. "That why you sleep like the dead?"

His shrug is answer enough. But I don't mind sharing. Tommaso can have his pick of the fuckdoll litter, even Barbara when she's not keeping me occupied.

Occupied. Right. I scowl. Yesterday's session went ass end up. I normally get off on a good, hard scene, but my concentration was shit. My attention kept shifting to the third woman in the room, her shocked expression and pretty pleadings making me harder than anything else.

"And the locksmith? That cell will be operable tomorrow, right?"

"About that ..."

I stiffen.

"On further examination, the door is rusted and needs replacing. It should take a week—"

"A fucking week?" I curse beneath my breath. "The men are assembling for a briefing tomorrow afternoon."

He stares at me, not getting the picture.

Of gorgeous green eyes brimming with tears.

Of my seed decorating her skin.

Of her locked inside a cage I pushed beneath my desk while she was showering.

I curse once more as I place heavier weights on the dumbbell.

"Ciro's girlfriend had a lot of nothing to say."

My full attention shifts his way. "What's her name again?"

"Emily."

"And?" I demand.

"She'll have a few nasty scars, if she lives."

"You think I care about scars?" I scoff. "What'd she say?"

"Bottom line is she knows nothing about Emilio Conti. And before you ask, our men took everything from Ciro's apartment. He was an unorganized prick, so it's taking the men time to cull through his papers. They did uncover the deed to Riley's apartment building. He didn't own the property but had some bogus, handwritten agreement signed by three other men claiming it was his."

I shake my head. "Like that'd hold up in court."

"Didn't stop him from filing an insurance claim the day everything went down." Tommaso's lips tighten. "The piece of shit can rot in hell."

"Shame he wasn't still alive when my men started up the cement truck."

Tommaso snorts. "Now he's just another Jimmy Hoffa."

"See if they can locate banking information. It'll save our tech geeks time."

"They're on it." He pauses for a few seconds too long.

"What?"

"She said a lot of shit about Riley."

I clench my fists, and then bark, "Confirming her involvement?"

"Not sure."

"What the hell does that mean?"

"She blames Riley—her best friend—for stealing her boyfriend. Thinks they ran off together since no one has seen either of them."

Tommaso nods as he polishes off the water from the bottle he's been tossing around in his hand. Drinking like a Neanderthal, water dripping from his lips.

I wait for him to finish.

He takes far too long and forces me to ask. "What else did she say?"

"Told the men your girl is responsible for Ciro's coke habit."

"She's not my girl," I grind out. "Or involved in drugs." It's ludicrous, and I'd laugh if she hadn't betrayed me.

"Ciro had a pet name for her."

I go fucking rigid. "Pet name? Were they fucking?" If that stranzo ran his dirty hands across her body ...

"According to her best friend, they were getting it on like jackrabbits." He studies me closely as my unfettered rage rolls in, then sighs. "It could be a lie. The men said that, when the knives came out, Emily's tune changed. She confessed to never actually seeing them together."

I flex my numb fingers.

"The men said it was like being trapped in a goddamn soap opera. She accused Riley of being a coke-snorting opportunist who seduced her boyfriend and mismanaged his finances—and evidently, the drugs we planted at C&C Enterprises belonged to Riley, not Ciro."

"The police believe it?"

"Not at all. They've had eyes on Ciro for a while. But they do want to question them both."

That's no surprise. "She's a liability. I should get rid of her."

"Whatever you want, boss. But her friend contradicted herself numerous times. Mocked Riley for being weak. Accused her of being antisocial and withdrawn after her father was murdered by his fiancée. Trash-talked her bestie like Riley was her worst enemy."

I scowl.

"Now ask yourself, is your girl a cokehead seductress heavily involved in drug trafficking or an introverted woman recovering from some disturbing personal shit?"

Riley, with her big, sad eyes.

Riley, wrapped up in a bundle of hurt.

Riley, confessing her darkest secret, about herself and her family.

Not everything was a lie.

Tommaso smirks.

I ignore him because I need answers. "What pet name did he call her?"

"That's where things get interesting. Emily confessed Riley positively hated the name. Every time he used it, she'd demand an explanation. Neither woman understood what it meant, but Riley believed he was poking fun at her breasts. Triple B, is what he called her."

I relax. The stupid cazzo would know Riley's a 32DD if they were fucking. Small frame, enormous knockers. My favorite combination.

Tommaso shakes his head. "The nickname has nothing to do with tits. It's an acronym ... that includes your last name."

"You're joking."

"Wish I were. Triple B means Beautiful Beneventi Bait."

"You sure?"

"The interrogation was recorded, so you can listen to it yourself."

I raise the dumbbell, but Tommaso is too quick and grabs it, returning it to the rack before I destroy the place. "Look. It's what we already suspected. Ciro used Riley—knowingly or not—to get to you. Period. End of story."

"Interview her best friend again."

Tommaso arches an eyebrow. "That can be arranged."

"Personally." I wait for him to protest. Ready to shut him down.

He just nods with a knowing smile.

"And Riley. You want me to interrogate her too?"

"I'll handle her."

I'm tired. So fucking tired. Except tomorrow I'm officially back at work. "Be in my office at one o'clock. Then the games will begin."

"Get some rest, Sandro," he says. "You look like hell."

I wait until he's gone before collapsing on the weight bench and relax enough for exhaustion to take over.

MY FATHER IS big into excesses. Power, money, sex ... the Beneventi *honor*. Renzo and I used to joke his pigheaded determination far exceeded everything else.

Neither Renzo nor I are laughing now.

"Everything still set for Tavern on the Green?" It's 6 a.m. in Rhode Island. He's up bright and early and starting off the day with a fresh cup of bullshit. With everything else on my plate, sweet Alessia's been an afterthought.

I'll bet my right arm he's plucked Alessia Amato's cherry and tasted her sweet pie repeatedly. He's a bit of a psycho where she's concerned. If only he'd admit the truth and leave me the hell alone. "Unless you'd like me to cancel?"

But his mind is a steel trap—once it closes on an idea, there's no prying it open again. He vowed to Don Lucchese he'd bring a corrupt politician into the Eleven, and I realized months ago there's no changing his mind. Still, there's a brief pause, likely to prolong the inevitable torment. "Listen, you little shit. I shouldn't have to remind you we're under a goddamn microscope with Don Lucchese's health on the decline. We proceed as planned."

"Fuck." I roll my office chair backward, stand and then move around the office, pacing until a familiar resignation settles in.

Things teeter on the edge of unpredictability right now. When my godfather dies, the Famiglie will choose a new capo di tutti capi from the two candidates Don Lucchese secretly selected. No one knows who the two are—their names are notarized, sealed, and hidden away, only to be revealed after the old man is gone. Then, the Eleven will cast their votes, though it's technically ten votes—since my father eliminated Benny from the equation—that will decide who'll rule with Dante Lucchese at his side.

My father already controls most of their finances, and—ironically—bank accounts have swelled since Bible Belt Benny's demise. "Takes the sting out of Benny's departure," my father confided after manipulating portfolios to crash and soar, timed perfectly with his rival's death. "From ruin to riches with just a click," he boasted, as the

Eleven heaved a sigh of relief, more concerned with their finances than the loss of a fellow capo.

And I nearly ruined everything.

"I'll fly to Rome and pay Don Lucchese a visit." Pay my godfather a visit and remind him I'm my father's son.

"Hell, no. Not while you resemble Freddy fucking Krueger."

I grimace.

"Recover at the villa, that's your orders."

Caged, he means. Like a fucking animal.

"Your current condition will fuel more rumors."

Rumors that suggest we're weak.

Rumors our rivals will latch on to and use to our disadvantage.

He'll never forget I fucked up.

I pace some more, but it's no help, so move to my chair. Before I can sit, my foot collides with a bowl on the floor, and whatever control I have over my temper snaps. I kick the offensive object and send it flying, milk spraying everywhere, all over my desk, my new fucking suit, and even my face, before it crashes and breaks against the wall.

"What in God's teeth was that?" my father demands.

My dignity.

My self-respect.

"Your pride and joy is in Rome," I snap, deflecting.

"That right?" is his immediate reply. Anything to do with Renzo elicits the same eager response.

I flick my wrist and check the time. "I've a meeting in five minutes. I'll offer my men advice on how to proceed and send a team after him."

"If anyone can outwit your brother, it's you."

My shoulders relax at the rare compliment. Even if Renzo and I are twins cut from the same stone.

"I've another matter I'd like you to handle. Discreetly, of course."

"Of course."

"Dante Lucchese is in Italy. Funny thing is, he never mentioned a trip."

Dante Lucchese is my father's right-hand man. He came as a package deal. His father became our godfather, protecting my brother and me from our rivals. And my father agreed to mentor Dante, teaching him book smarts along with street smarts.

"It makes sense he'd be visiting his father ..."

"He was spotted in Catania, not Rome."

I frown. *Sicily?*

"Who do we know in Catania," my father demands, exasperated, "other than the Gallos?"

The Gallos are one of the Eleven and Italy's oldest and most productive famiglia. My father built their stock portfolios and found rich-ass investors for their pistachio farms. Who would have thought a mafiosi could turn a legitimate profit selling nuts? We clean our money through their businesses, just like we do with the casinos. "Maybe Dante likes nuts?"

"You auditioning to be the next Will Ferrell, you little shit?" I can feel him shaking his head. "Can't picture that strutting peacock on a nut farm in a Gucci suit."

I almost grin, but too much is riding on this call. "Give me a week for my men to look into it." I pause but am too impatient not to address the elephant on the line. "And that stranzo Conti?"

"We questioned his great-uncle. Word is he's fled the country."

"Fuck."

"Yeah, fuck. But no one that stupid disappears without a trace. Not unless he's dead and a cleaner is used ... Something to consider for the future. If Conti flew out of Atlanta, we'll know. Same for New York—though that will take time."

I consider my next words, surprised he's sharing this much. "Don't kill Conti's uncle until Tommaso speaks to him."

He snorts. "Like he'll talk to your man but stay silent with mine?"

"Tommaso has a certain charm about him."

"Look, you little shit. Don't play this off like this is for my benefit. You want Conti. Understood."

But does he? Does a man like him understand humiliation? Know how degrading it feels to have been duped by an attractive woman with sad green eyes and a huge motherfucking rack?

There's a knock on the door.

"My men are here. If you have no further orders—"

"I do."

I sigh. Of course the conversation will end on the mighty Sebastiano Beneventi's terms. My fucking life revolves around those same terms. "Yes?"

"Hire a new foreman for Riverview. Seems your man has gone missing."

The call disconnects. And I'm relieved the highly anticipated discussion about Ciro Ciglione's murder was so brief, *I* almost missed it.

I take my seat and then straighten my tie.

A huff filters up from beneath my desk.

"You can't keep me locked inside here all day."

"Not just all day … until fucking infinity."

Why in Christ's name did I secure the cage beneath my desk? Work is impossible with the constant distraction. With her eavesdropping on sensitive conversations.

With her seated at crotch level. With the image of her covered in my come fresh material for my spank bank.

What did she call me yesterday? *Twisted?*

I pull closer to my desk until my knees are touching the cage.

So glad we've broken past the honeymoon stage.

———

CONVERSATIONS COLLIDE as men filter into the office, their footsteps echoing off the floor. The scrape of chairs dragged across the room grows closer, signaling their approach. I shift within the confines of my hiding place, a decorative desk accent shielding me from their view.

It's clear they know exactly who Alessandro is and where they stand in his world. I'm the one who's been slow to catch on.

"Why in God's name does it smell like sour milk in here?" a familiar voice asks. Tommaso. The deep timbre of his tone's recognizable, as is his daring.

The men fall quiet, thinking the same thing.

"How about you interrogate housekeeping? Find out why they can suck a cock clean yet can't clean a room worth shit?"

My gasp is muffled by laughter. Still, Alessandro's comment stings. I had it all wrong, didn't I? The fantasy of who I wanted him to be versus the reality of who he actually is.

Cunning.

Ruthless.

Sadistic.

And proud. So proud, there should be a parade in his honor.

"A warning before we begin. Be careful with what you say because I've a feeling ears are listening in."

I freeze. He means *me*. Because he doesn't trust me. Another wave of hurt washes over me.

"Let's begin. I need the craftiest sons of bitches in Rome. You three ..." He must be pointing at them ... "Hit every kink club, the seedier the better. Make sure he doesn't see you and connect you back to me, or he'll evade capture."

I listen intently, curious who he's searching for. Someone important, as his firm tone suggests.

"Next, get ears out there. I want to know why Dante Lucchese is in Sicily."

"Yes, boss."

His power is difficult to ignore. He demands, and men obey. Yet it isn't so surprising. When I first saw him, he was ordering men about in the club, wasn't he? They kept approaching him and then hurried off, the devil riding their heels. In movies and books, you imagine mafia bosses wearing suits and delivering orders from behind desks, like he is now. Yet I missed it, believing he was a rich investor or stockbroker.

I was so caught up in him I couldn't truly *see* him.

Lord, in retrospect, he could never be a simple Al.

But Alessandro? The name fits him perfectly.

A fist slams onto the desk. I jump, as do his men. "Listen closely," he demands in a low voice that vibrates with rage. "Whoever locates Conti will be set for life. Capisci?"

"Yeah, boss." Their excitement reminds me there's more than one predator in the room.

I bite my lip and listen, curious why Alessandro is hunting these men. Someone who is hiding in Rome. A man named Dante Lucchese. And a third man they call Conti.

Alessandro's seat rolls back behind me. I stiffen, until I realize he's simply shifting positions. "Any suggestions about how to hunt him down?" he asks the group.

"We start by interrogating his relatives," Tommaso says.

"While being a little more persuasive than my father's men." Alessandro chuckles. "My father has given you permission to get your hands dirty. Book a flight to Atlanta. After you're satisfied, head to New York, check in with our men, and reinterview our guest. Confirm everything that's been said but push harder for more."

"You've been busy this morning," Tommaso comments.

Alessandro grunts. "I'll rest when Conti's dead."

Panic sends my heart fluttering. Am I hearing him correctly? His men are hunting to kill? So cold. So cavalier.

So where does that leave me?

"As for the rest of you fucks ..." he continues.

Orders are issued with rapid-fire precision. My eyes widen as men are grouped together by name and then sent across the globe in search of the one man. No man idle. No expense spared.

Having experienced a taste of Alessandro's rage, I almost feel sorry for whoever Conti is.

Except if he's the man who hurt Alessandro ...

I force the thought into a corner of the cage where it belongs. Sympathy, concern, and a deep desire to hurt whoever attacked him aren't feelings I should have for this monster.

"One final request before the hunt begins." There's a long pause, and I wish I could see him to understand why. "Anyone know how this happened?"

The men still, but no one replies.

"An extreme sparring session."

"Understood, boss."

"If anyone says otherwise or spreads unsubstantiated rumors, slice open his tongue. Make sure he understands gossip *hurts*."

Oh. My. God. And I'm caged when he's a violent, twisted animal?

"You have our word, Sandro."

"We won't disappoint you."

"We'll find that asshole Conti."

Alessandro's voice rises above their promises. "Leave."

Within minutes, the office grows quiet.

I sit back on my haunches just as a man, without warning, drops to his knees in front of the desk.

"What the fuck are you doing?" Alessandro snaps.

"Looking for bugs ..." Tommaso's words falter as his gaze falls on me. With a cry, I cover myself.

Alessandro exhales a long breath, and the chair behind me creaks. "Find anything?"

"Fucking hell, Sandro."

"A pretty nuisance, don't you think?"

"This is where you put her?"

"By necessity, not choice." Pause. "Bet she's pink. She blushes so beautifully, doesn't she?"

God, I want to die.

To Tommaso's credit, he looks so perplexed, confusion could be his middle name. He pulls up off the floor and disappears from sight.

"This is your fault," Alessandro accuses. "And now, I'll have to kill her—she's heard too much."

My face pales, and my hands shake.

"Jesus, man."

"He can't save her. No one can."

"I hope you won't regret this."

Alessandro's fist hits the table. "I already do. Why keep her when she's no use to me?"

No use? I want to disappear into the floor and vanish within the cold stone beneath the villa. Yet deep inside me, something uncoils like a snake ready to bite. I'd no control over the cancer that killed my mother. No sway when I pleaded with my father to dump that money-hungry bitch. No defenses in place to deal with the aftermath. And no warning the man I believed might help end my suffering was a control freak with a big dick, vicious tongue, and a heart so cold Death Valley would freeze over.

Do I want my last moments to be filled with heartbreak?

Months of pent-up emotions unfurl.

I snap, and snap hard. "Listen up, you asshole," I shout. "I'm no longer playing your sick and twisted games. You want me dead, then kill me. But know this; whatever you believe I'm guilty of, you're wrong. And I'll curse you from my grave when you realize it."

I'm panting by the time I'm finished.

Both men are silent, which sets me off again.

I rattle the cage. "Are you listening, *stranzo?*" Flavoring my question with an Italian word I don't even understand comes out of nowhere. He's used it several times with good effect, so ...

A throat clears. "Thought you said she was perfectly submissive?" My ears strain to hear Alessandro's response, but only Tommaso speaks. "Let me interview her."

"No."

"Why the hell not? You want answers, and I'll get them."

Alessandro growls low in his throat. "You're on an evening flight to Atlanta, motherfucker. I'll handle her."

Tommaso snorts. "With that knife?"

Fear envelops me. Because I made a mistake. You don't defend yourself against a monster by provoking him. Monsters can only be defeated if you find their soft side.

A fist slams onto the table. "Nothing else to say?"

I blink. Alessandro's addressing *me*. Think, Riley. What's the solution, permanent or temporary? "I *cared* about you," I softly croak.

"Fuck," he curses. "The ankle monitors arrive yet?"

"Yesterday."

"On your way out, send a man to fetch one," Alessandro orders, all business. "He can grab a new uniform while he's at it."

"You certain this is the right call?"

"If I kill her now, I won't get the pleasure of punishing her for disrespecting me."

"You're a sick shit."

"Yeah, isn't that the pot calling the kettle black?"

Tommaso kicks the cage. "Should have kept quiet, sweetheart. And, stronzo ... that's where you really fucked up. Death might have been the better option."

"Any further words for our sweetheart?"

I frown. His tone is downright sinister.

Tommaso laughs. "Nothing more to say, *boss.*" His footsteps cross the room, and I begin to panic. He's leaving me alone ... with him?

"Call me from Atlanta."

The cage door creaks as soon as Tommaso is gone. I spin in place. The cage is open, and Alessandro's pointing to the floor next to his chair. "Out," he bellows.

I crawl from the cage to the desired spot.

"Don't ever disrespect me in front of my men again."

I raise my eyes to his furious ones. Lord, his face. His handsome face. "Would you really kill me?"

He reaches down, then pinches my earlobe.

I wince.

"Good. Now we understand."

The door opens.

I flush and cross my arms over my chest yet keep my eyes on Alessandro. Two packages slide across the desk and tumble to the floor next to me. Then quicker than he appeared, the man disappears.

Picking them up, Alessandro unwraps each item, first the one in the box and then the plastic-wrapped one. "Stand."

I try to rise, but my knees buckle.

With a curse, he catches my elbow and hauls me to my feet.

I grab his shoulder for support, but he brushes my hand off him like my touch offends him.

"Arms to the sides."

I frown at the white uniform in his hands. His cruelty knows no bounds, does it. He's planning on dressing me like *them?*

No.

Absolutely not.

"To the sides. *Now.*"

I calculate how many steps it'd take to reach the door. If my legs were stronger. If I wasn't pursued by a hunter chasing down a wounded animal. We've been down that path before, and he tackled me to the floor so hard I still see stars.

"One," he counts.

I grunt, then do his bidding. *Don't challenge him. Find a soft spot.*

"Put your arms through the sleeves."

I slip my arms into the openings, and he tugs the uniform over my shoulders. All that's left is the long zipper running the length of the front. Slowly, he slides it up my body. His face expressionless and unaffected as, inch by inch, my body's covered.

He's done this *before*, hasn't he?

He disappeared for three weeks. Is this where he was? Being entertained by those bullies?

I close my eyes. My hurt's no longer his reward.

His fingers halt at my chest.

"Fuck," he says. But the groan that follows has me eyes flashing open.

The uniform doesn't fit. Too snug around my breasts, which are disproportionately larger than the rest of me.

His breath quickens.

I try to brush his hand away. "I can zip it ..."

He dips two fingers beneath the material, catching a nipple and catching me by surprise.

A shiver races through me. "What are you doing?"

His entire body stiffens. "Good fucking question." His hand drops. "Leave that zipper exactly where it is, capisci?"

I protest. "My breasts are on full display."

His lips curl, and my heart stops.

There was a time I'd have died and gone to hell to earn a smile. *Now you nearly died and are in hell, Riley. You're one of* them *now.*

"What's inside the other package, a feather duster?"

He blinks, my scorn surprising him.

We stare at each other. Distrust warring with indignation.

"Am I part of your *cleaning* staff now?"

Energy sparks in the air between us. Then he's on me, lifting me by the hips and tossing me across his desk, pushing me down until I'm sprawled across it. The horrid uniform rides up, baring me to him.

Revealing my shame. Confirming that, despite his twisted, wicked soul, my body weeps for him.

"Jesus."

I flush bright red. Because there's no hiding it. He could unzip his pants and drive home, with little resistance.

Physical resistance.

Plastic rattles ... except he's taking too long for it to be a condom. He grabs my ankle, and then locks something else into place. "You're free to move around the villa. Don't stray from the grounds, or my men will shoot you. You'll sleep in the same bedroom as before."

I roll up onto my elbows and jerk the hem lower. I wiggle my leg. "What's that?"

"A tracking device."

I swallow hard. It's better than the cage ... better than death.

"Use the gym, the pool ... library ... Do whatever the hell you want. But at all times know I'll know where to find you."

"Am I supposed to thank you?"

His eyes narrow.

"Be grateful you're still alive."

WATER DRIPS on the white tile floor. Fresh from an after-workout shower, I make my way to the kitchen, my throat parched and body in need of nourishment.

Cursing greets me.

I pat my pockets ... except I'm in a towel. My phone is on the nightstand, charging, and the app I track her movements with inaccessible. The frightened little bunny's been in hiding for days, so I'm surprised to discover her out in the open where dangerous predators lurk.

"Those brunette *bitches* ..."

My eyebrows arch. Aside from her outburst a few days ago, Riley never uses profanity. But how well did I ever fucking know her?

She doesn't notice me as I cross the tile floor, her attention on patting her chest with a wet dishcloth. Muttering beneath her breath, she lifts her hand and reveals a huge red splotch covering her left breast and over her heart.

I charge forward. "What the fuck?"

She jumps, then holds up her hands. Waving the bloodstained dishcloth like that will stop me.

I skim my eyes across the immaculately tidy kitchen. Nothing's out of order except for a plastic container on the floor and red footprints leading toward the nearest door.

Fucking tomato sauce.

My attention shifts to her. Jesus, she's covered in it. Her tit looks like a rindless, overripe watermelon. Juicy and sweet, the kind that takes time to nibble and lick.

She stares at me with alarm.

Surprised to see me? Worried I might pounce or, worse, my towel might slip?

She's not my type, isn't it obvious? Still, my cock always goes rigid at the sight of her. A genuine purity surrounds her that draws me in. She's a fresh breeze on a hellish day, and I'm the devil hell-bent on showing her how it feels to burn.

Fuck, even now my cock stirs.

"Clumsy?" I nod at the mess.

Her lips press tight, confirming my suspicions. This wasn't an accident.

I wait for her explanation, and the silence between us grows.

Grunting, I brush by her. I feel her eyes tracking my movements. I take the pitcher from the fridge and a glass from the cabinet, and then pour myself a water flavored with fresh lemon slices. I finish my drink in a few gulps, and then refresh my glass.

When temptation becomes too unbearable, I finally look at her, only to discover she's eye-fucking me like I'm the finest filet mignon. My glass misses my lips, and water spills all over me.

Fucking hell.

Cheeks darkening, her gaze snaps up. "I'll clean the mess up."

"You do that." I'm tempted to grab her wrist, tug her closer, and order her to start with my wet cock. Instead, I intentionally leave the pitcher and empty glass on the counter and move by her.

"Wait." She touches my arm.

I glare down at her hand until she drops it.

"This stain is stubborn. Is there something else I can wear?"

"Ask a housemaid for a new uniform."

"I can't ... don't want to bother them, being they're so busy *cleaning*." She practically spits out the last word.

"Listen, Cinderella. Either you wear a new uniform or prance around naked." Does she think I've time for standing around chatting about goddamn clothing?

Her lips pull into a thin line.

"Anything else?"

With a sigh, she glances at the stain and then murmurs, "Well, at least now I can go up a size."

"Fuck no," is my firm response.

She frowns, confused.

"Same size."

"But it doesn't *fit*," she protests.

I raise my arms and run my fingers through my hair. The same fire from earlier reappears in her eyes.

Fucking attraction.

"The only reason I'm keeping you around are those tits. Same size or no uniform—your choice. I want to see those beautiful knockers all day and every day. Capisci?"

Her jaw drops, and, issue resolved, I walk away.

Riley

PEOPLE DREAM about escaping to a place like Sardinia, with its white-washed villas, soft sandy beaches, and water as blue as a cloudless sky.

My thoughts are preoccupied with escaping *it*.

I glare at the tracking device anchored around my ankle, a reminder the only way I'm leaving paradise is if he allows it.

A day has passed since he paraded around in a towel, barefoot with damp hair and familiar scowl. I'm still mortified he caught me checking him out. His body battered, bruised, and beautiful in a rugged, manly way.

He seems stronger. But maybe it's because I now know he's a mafioso and have witnessed him in action. Strong? That's an understatement. He leads his men with a sharp bite and an iron fist. They respect him, though. Some men—like the soldier who provided me with a new uniform—even fear him.

Even with a bedsheet wrapped around my waist and concealing more than that horrid uniform, the poor man studied the white rafters overhead while I traded soiled clothes for fresh clothing. His response is familiar. Alessandro's soldiers pretend I don't exist.

And the brunettes are more aggressive. I avoid them but don't always succeed. Like yesterday's incident with the tomato sauce. If a pitcher was within reach inside the refrigerator, I'd have hit her harder this time.

Reluctant to wear the uniform, I toss the new package onto the bed and head outside. Sunshine and time away from a villa full of vipers might ease my mood. I quickly unfurl the sheet and toss it over the balcony balustrade, obstructing the view from below. With a sigh, I settle into a chair and close my eyes, letting the sun's warmth melt away my troubles.

I'm nearly asleep when his punishing voice penetrates deep. "You almost finished in New York?" he demands. A few heartbeats pass. "Good. I'll have a car waiting at the airport ... Miss you? Like a bad case of limp dick."

Who is he talking to? Tommaso? But he's in Atlanta. Is there another soldier Alessandro's on familiar terms with?

"Update me on Atlanta. Was Conti's great-uncle any use?"

Whatever is being relayed takes time.

"Fuck. How can an asshole as stupid as Conti just disappear?" I jump when something crashes against the wall. "And did you find any helpful information in New York? Did she talk?"

I roll up to sit, suddenly chilled to the bone.

"Still believes her boyfriend ran off with Riley?" Pause. "Best friend, my ass."

Oh my God. Is Tommaso with Emily?

"Bleeding like a stuck pig yet still denies knowing anything about that fuckhead's deception?"

I cover my mouth with my hand and stifle a cry. No. No. No.

"If she has nothing more of value to say, then end it. Capisci?"

The room next door grows quiet.

But bells echo through my thoughts like I'm summoned to a Sunday mass.

Emily bleeding.

Emily questioned about Ciro.

Emily ... gone.

I race into the room, and then slide into the uniform. With no plan in mind except to face the monster in the next room and beg him to spare my best friend's life.

CHAPTER 14

AMBUSHED ONCE, call me weak.

Ambushed twice and call me the asshole who didn't learn his lesson.

I'm rinsing off when the bathroom door is thrown open. Years of preparation for a moment like this has me hauling ass from the shower. I slam into my uninvited guest, my hand to their throat and full body weight pinning them to the door. *You dare surprise me in my home, motherfucker?*

Her whimper is what registers first.

Then her big wild eyes.

I ease off her. "How in fuck's name did you get in here?" The bedroom door is locked, as is the hallway entrance to the gym adjacent to my walk-through wardrobe. What I neglected to secure was the bathroom door.

My fingers roll into a ball so tight my knuckles crack. The rage she ignites pumps through me like an IV shot. I'm high with it, edging on borderline psychotic.

Men fear me.

Men respect me.

No one with any self-preservation would interrupt me in my bathroom. Not even my fuckdolls are permitted in my private suite.

"The balcony," she squeaks.

"What?"

"I knocked on the door. You didn't answer, and it was locked. But I knew you were here, and I had to talk to you right away, so I jumped balconies."

"For *Christ's* sake." I grab her shoulders and shake her. "It's a hundred-foot drop."

Tears spring into her eyes. "It's about Emily ..."

I stiffen. "Eavesdropping?"

She draws a breath. "Please, Alessandro."

"What did I tell you? Don't. Say. My. Name." Not so long ago I lost my mind while delirious and high on meds. I gave in to temptation and demanded my name from her lips. Not fucking Al, or Sandro—*Alessandro*.

Weak actions only a weak man would take. It's why I went cold turkey on the meds. It's why I push my body and test my endurance. Al might be a chump, but Alessandro Beneventi is merciless.

"I'm begging you. Spare her."

"Give me one good reason why."

Her big eyes stare at me like I'm not human.

About time she catches on.

"Don't kill her because she's your friend?" I snort. "You've shit luck choosing the company you keep, baby."

She flinches. "Don't call me that."

I get in her face. "You don't tell me what to do."

Our eyes lock, and a familiar stirring hits me like a sledgehammer. I slam it into the ground before I do something I'll regret. "Coke dealer. Seductress. Weak with daddy issues."

She gasps, but I continue on, merciless. "Your best friend had a lot to say about you." I shake my head with pretend disappointment. "Why would she believe you'd run off with her boyfriend?"

"I didn't ... I wouldn't ..." Riley scrunches her face. Disgusted by her friend or Ciro? "Emily doesn't know Ciro's dead?"

Her loyalty's admirable. Shame I wasn't shown the same consideration.

"I saw his body ..." Her face pales as her words sink in. Like it's only just now hit her that I could wrap a rope around her pretty neck and hang her from a balcony, and no one would care.

"No body now. No crime scene. Gone, just like that." I snap my fingers in front of her face, and she jerks back.

Fuck knows why the one and only witness is still alive.

Fear grips her, and her body shakes.

"Get the fuck out." I shove her aside to open the door.

She plants her feet, and I clench my jaw.

"What do you want from me?" Her voice trembles.

"Not a motherfucking thing."

Tension thickens the air between us, yet I see the wheels within her mind spinning.

Then she does the unimaginable, and drops to her knees. Face inches from my erection, she raises beautiful green eyes. "I'll do whatever you demand."

Well, fuck. I wasn't expecting that.

"If you let Emily go." She holds her head high like this bargain she's proposing is the winning numbers on a lottery ticket.

I shrug. "Not anything you can offer that I don't already have."

Hurt washes over her expression, her reaction the equivalent of popping a balloon with a butcher knife. And I want to hurt her.

Almost as much as the desire to flip her onto all fours and drive my way home.

Whatever I want.

Wherever I want.

I take her elbow, tug her onto her feet, and push her out the door. "What I want is you out of my sight," I say, before slamming the door so hard, the crash reverberates louder than my twisted thoughts.

Out of sight.

Now I need to rid her from my mind.

— Riley —

MY EMOTIONS RUN rampant while an alternate plan for saving Emily evades me. I begged Alessandro to spare her. Humiliated myself by getting on my knees. Completely, utterly offered myself to him.

And he slammed the door in my face.

Tears aren't enough to calm my panic. I'm powerless against that unforgiving monster. I press my eyelids tighter, though the worst thought possible pushes through—Emily might be dead by now.

Something rockets by my face, clipping my nose. Startled, my eyes snap open, and I glance around.

There, perched on the wrought iron balcony, is a small bright yellow canary with delicate brown markings. Fearless as it studies me from an arm's breadth away. If its sudden appearance was startling, the perfectly pitched song it begins singing stuns me speechless.

I still and barely breathe for fear of frightening it away.

My mom used to say bird visits have symbolic meaning. A hummingbird brings joy and happiness. A crow represents change. A cardinal's visit is the most precious because it means a loved one who has passed on is thinking of you. *What do you signify, little bird? Because I'm lost as to what to do.*

It's been an hour or two since he didn't simply reject my proposition but literally slammed the door in my face. His room is quiet, and he's likely bossing men about or bending brunettes over to spank them.

Getting what he already has.

I'm a practical person. His harem shouldn't bother me this much. Recklessly falling for a violent mafioso with a short temper and an unforgiving streak a mile long is absurd. Yet logic flies out the door whenever I'm in his company.

That's why you invited him home, Riley. To feel again, remember?

Silent now, the canary bobs its head.

I should warn it. This is no place for beautiful things.

With careful movements, I reach for the stale croissant I brought upstairs from the kitchen earlier. I crush a small piece between my fingers, and then ever so slowly, sprinkle crumbs on the balcony railing behind me.

It immediately hops closer, then closer, then quickly pecks up the pieces.

"Aren't you a brave birdie?" I whisper.

For a long while we study each other. *Hope,* I think. *You're a sign everything will be fine.*

Loud knocking shatters the moment, startling us both. The canary flies off in the direction of the pool as I brace myself for what comes next.

Step by step, I trudge toward the bedroom door, slipping on then zipping up my uniform as I go.

I whisk the door open and am greeted by one of Alessandro's stern-faced soldiers.

"Boss says to get your ass down to the pool, *immediamente.*"

CHAPTER 15

Riley

SURPRISINGLY, the pool is empty except for the figure sprawled on a chair on the far side of the patio. The decorative tile burns my soles as I make my way toward him, apprehension building with each step.

Alessandro's eyes are closed, and he's fast asleep.

So much for *immediamente*.

I hover by his chair and study him. Bruises are fading. Swelling lessening. Muscles are tighter and more sculpted than I remember. His dark beauty is a sight to behold. A man this evil doesn't deserve to be so devilishly handsome.

Unaware of my presence, he breathes softly and deep, while my attention shifts lower onto the distinct bulge beneath his swim trunks. My lips part. Big, beautiful boners are a natural state for this man, aren't they?

Memories flood my mind. Him, pushing into me from behind. Me, riding him, his hands drawing me down hard with each upward thrust. We fit perfectly.

But that was another time, another place. When he was Al, and I was too numb with grief to realize how dangerous he truly is.

Dancing around on my feet, I shake off the burn from stupidly standing here while the man who summoned me sleeps. I search for the man he sent to fetch me, curious if his soldier made a mistake.

"You fuck him?"

I jump, and then turn fully toward him. "You were awake?" And doing what? Studying me beneath his lashes while I drooled over his body?

I stare at him relaxed in the chair, his eyes still closed. Like he's on vacation, and not demanding personal answers like who I've fucked.

"You let that prick touch you?" Flat tone. Not the slightest indication he actually cares how I answer. Still his question catches me off guard.

"What prick?"

My mind races when he doesn't answer and it takes a moment to land on who he's referring to. "Ciro?" My stomach rolls at the thought. "God, no."

"You sure about that?"

I grind my teeth. "Absolutely."

He doesn't react. Doesn't confirm he believes me. Just lies there, while I suffer the heat and his bone-chilling coldness.

Seconds tick by, and I consider retreating inside. Then, his eyes flash open.

"You're blocking my sun."

My lips part. "You should thank me for it."

He waves his hand impatiently for me to step to the side.

I shuffle to his left. If the stubborn fool wants the late afternoon sun to blister him alive, so be it.

"What size bra are you?"

Unbelievable. "My breasts, again?"

"You're a 32DD." He rakes his eyes over me, the one-size-too-small uniform spilling open at the chest—exactly how he demanded I wear it. "But can you explain why that prick nicknamed you Triple B?"

My jaw drops. "Did Emily tell you that?"

"Your best friend had a lot to say about you. None of it was kind."

I flinch.

"Stop acting like a wounded animal and answer me." No compassion, but back to an impatience I've grown accustomed to.

"I never understood the nickname. But ..." I swallow hard. "... your last name is part of it. It's an acronym for Beautiful Beneventi Bait."

"And were you?"

His tone sends a chill through my body. "Bait?" I whisper, dumbstruck.

Our eyes lock as he waits on my answer. And every ounce of me understands on a visceral level that my life depends on my answer.

God help me, what has Ciro done?

"I don't know." My body shakes, in fear and in frustration. "Ciro was a coked-up mess. I never examined why he'd call me that."

Except it's no use, is it? He believes I betrayed him and hates me for it.

"Maybe," I whisper.

The air grows impossibly thick, and the uniform's tight like a wet wool glove. I'm going to faint. I'll pass out on this pool patio at the foot of this man's chair, and he'll either leave me to roast or turn me into toast.

"Here's how this will work. I snap, and you jump. You do exactly as I say, whenever or wherever I want. You'll take everything I demand and beg me to go harder. And, most importantly, this will never be about you."

"Okay." I'm shocked he didn't question me further. Yet relieved, too. What if Ciro did use me to get to him—as bait? Alessandro is a mafioso with enemies—I heard him ordering his men to hunt two people down. But it's impossible to think logically right now, with the bold way he's staring at me. Either he wants to flay me or eat me alive.

Instead, he relaxes and closes his eyes. "There's a shower in the casita. Go cool off."

Emotional whiplash, that's what this is. "Do you believe me or not?"

He pries one eye open. "Still here?"

"I don't need a shower."

He rolls up so fast, I jump. "You don't get to decide what you need—I do. I say jump, you jump, or our arrangement is over. Capisci?"

My heart skips a beat. "What exactly am I agreeing to?"

His smile's pure evil. "Offer accepted, baby. You've just become my personal fuckdoll."

⸺

Alessandro

I GIVE her thirteen minutes *exactly* before charging into the casita after her.

Shock registers when the door's thrown open and I interrupt her naked in the bathroom and drying herself off with a fluffy towel. I crook a finger at her, signaling for her to join me in the living area.

An antique bureau filled with toys sits on one wall. An enormous white sofa with perfectly rounded arms, a glass coffee table, and a decorative rug fill the center of the open space, and a spanking bench completes the unique setup. A small kitchen is on the far-left wall, and a short hallway leading to my fuck room is in the back.

I remove a leather belt from the bureau, and then crack it in the air a few times. Whipping her ass, though, isn't today's appetizer. My cock swells at what I've in store for her, just like it's been doing since I first choked and fucked her against her bathroom door.

Did she know who I was and told Ciro about my visits?

Not sure now.

Does it matter, considering I've decided to use her for my own pleasure?

Not one iota.

My dark side's snapped awake. When you deal with the devil, hell knows no mercy.

I feel her behind me. "Go stand by the sofa."

Her soft footsteps confirm she's obeyed.

"Tell me," I silkily say, not gracing her with a look. "Did you put your uniform back on?"

"Yes," she grumbles.

"What was that?" I get hard at her obedience, especially knowing she hates the uniform. "Louder."

"I. Am. Wearing. It." Each word is pronounced, like she's telling me to fuck off without really telling me.

I smirk at her displeasure.

She clears her throat. "Is Emily okay?"

I flick my wrist, and she flinches as the belt uncoils in the air. "Such concern for Emily, Emily, Emily."

"Will you hurt me?"

"Hurt you? In every way imaginable." I hear her gasp. "But you're asking the wrong questions. Ask me what the right one is, baby."

"What's the right one?" Her voice is barely a whisper.

"How far am I willing to submit to make Alessandro happy?" Because I don't just want her broken. I want her begging me to break her. All the filthy, twisted things I held back from doing to her—denying myself, for the first time in my life, for fear of pushing her too far, for fear of *breaking* her—are on the fucking table now. "Uniform off and kneel."

Rustling behind me tells me she's obeyed.

Temptation takes over, and I finally turn toward her.

Fuck.

Her wide-eyed and kneeling. Beautiful body trembling. A

familiar flush darkening her cheeks, neck, and chest. Is this why I returned to her apartment time and time again?

I whip the leather against my hand. A wake-up call to drive the thought away.

Her gaze fills with dread, even more so as I form the belt into a loop.

"What do you know about birds?"

Her jaw practically hits the floor. "Birds?"

"It's not a difficult question, Riley. Motherfucking *birds*."

"Yes," she says. "As a matter of fact—"

I cut her off. "Chinese fishermen use a special bird to hunt fish."

"Cormorants," she replies. Wicked smart—I'm not surprised. "They can swim underwater and only eat fish and eels."

My lips twist with delight because she's missing the point. "How do the fishermen prevent their pets from swallowing the fish?" Fuck, the anticipation's making me hard.

"They tie rope around their necks."

If I had a fucking camera, I'd take a picture the moment her expression changes. Eyes wide and brilliant, lips parted, her expression oozing innocence.

"You're going to strangle me?"

I shrug. Mindfucks might be my new hobby. "Not if you choked down every fucking drop like an obedient pet."

Every part of her stills, and then she answers with a mindfuck of her own. "Do your worst, then." She drags her tongue across her lips, like she's waving a red flag at a bull. Brave, brave girl.

"Here." I point to my feet.

She shuffles forward on her knees.

I lasso the belt around her neck, and then tighten the soft leather. Ironically, I'm the one who can't breathe, the sight messing with my airways.

Her complete submission's at my fingertips.

"Hands behind your back."

She moves into the desired position.

With my free hand, I tear off my bathing shorts. She gasps as my rock-hard erection greets her, then surprises me again by eye-fucking it like my dick's a just-out-of-reach treat she's dying for a taste of.

She fucking likes this.

"Touch your pussy."

Her cheeks flush, but she dips her hand between her thighs anyway.

"Two fingers inside."

Her eyes brighten at the exact moment of penetration.

"Show me."

If she was pink a second ago, her skin's flushed red now. Shaking, she holds up two fingers. Just as I suspected ... fucking drenched. It takes all my willpower not to flip her onto all fours and fuck her into the floor. Except the bargain was made by a greedy motherfucker. This is about *my* pleasure.

She places her hands behind her back, anticipating the order. Eager to please me? Or is she challenging me?

"Did I say to move?" I scowl. "What if my next direction was to lick the come off your soaking wet fingers?"

Her lips part with a gasp.

I clench my dick. "Beg for it."

"Please."

"No, say Alessandro, please."

"What?" Her entire body goes rigid. "I thought it was a dirty dream augmented by reality. How could you? Say Alessandro please? That was you in the shower?"

Fucking hell. She dares go there? Poke a finger into a festering wound? My shitty judgement, my pitiful desire to get off on her one last time?

"I was drugged. How could you?"

Anger reverberates through me. "How could you?"

Everything stands still.

She shakes her head and stares at the floor. "You still believe I'm lying."

"For your sake"—I give her this much—"you better hope you're not."

Her tearstained eyes rise to lock on mine. "I'll prove it to you."

I harden the itch to give in. "Won't hold my breath … but you can start by holding yours." I tug the belt, driving my words home.

She chokes in the little air I allow her but manages to beg me so prettily. "Alessandro, please."

"I'm shoving the entire length down your little throat. And when I shoot my load, you gobble every last drop down that narrow passage. Capisci?" Her nods cut off when I push my thick crown between her lips.

Her tongue curls beneath my underside and elicits my hiss, before she sucks me in like a goddamn lollipop.

Jesus, her mouth. Her sweet, fuckable mouth.

I tug the belt, and she falls on my dick, getting an unexpected mouthful. It doesn't stop me from viciously thrusting forward until my pelvis is smashed against her face.

She gags and gurgles.

Her throat is perfect, so fucking perfect.

I still. "I own you, capisci? Nod if you hear me?"

Her head nods.

"Remember to use your nose." With that warning, my ruthless assault begins. I flex my hips and push deep, tightening the belt further, testing her limits.

She struggles and I relent for a moment. Loving her shocked expression as she pants in huge gasps of air.

"Enough. Take my dick like a good girl."

She actually tries, bobbing her head and widening her mouth. I cruelly tighten the belt and let loose, quickening the tempo while the rush I'm after grips me by the throat.

"Shit, that's good," I groan.

She drags teeth across my flesh. Stunned, I go rigid.

I withdraw, and then glare at her.

"I no longer want to be a good girl."

What. The. Fuck?

"I want your dick in my throat like a little fuckdoll would take it."

She hopes to tempt the beast and conquer him? I fucking smile.

Without responding, I reposition my rock-hard dick at her mouth. I surprise her by pinching her nostrils closed and tightening the belt on my deep drive home.

Her hands find my thighs.

I hammer into her, counting off in my mind. Milking everything out of her while I reach a high I can easily grow addicted to. Without warning, I drop my hand, the belt, and my load so deep in her throat it's halfway to her stomach.

My heart races as I stagger back.

She falls onto her hands and knees, panting.

"Only a few minutes rest," I warn her. Because even as I'm riding sweet bliss, my appetite isn't satiated.

"Again?" she manages between gasps.

Hell yeah. "Did you think you were done?" I grab my dick. "Now entertain me while I recover."

She rolls back onto her knees, eyebrows raised.

"Grab the belt and mark your breasts."

"What?"

"You heard me. Twenty lashes. Ten each. If you can't, I'll do it."

Her lip trembles, but then, with a fierce crack, the leather crosses her right breast. Tears brighten her eyes, but pure greed forces me to speak. "Gentle your movements. I want them marked pink, not bleeding out."

Her second attempt's much better.

"Keep going," I command.

Over and over, she repeats her actions. Until her tears are replaced by something else—something more dangerous.

If my goal was to break her, I've failed. But do I give two shits right now?

My fingers wrap my dick up in a tight vacuum as I viciously jerk myself. Her beautifully marked breasts are my second target. Her skin's flushed, the marks on her throat a turn-on, and her obedience has me hard again within minutes.

My orgasm hits right on the twentieth stroke.

She drops the belt, her lips *curl*, and then she cups her incredible breasts.

"Aw, fuck," I groan, then pump my seed across her pinkened flesh.

"Please, Alessandro."

I scowl at her speaking out of turn. Not wanting my name on her lips unless I demand it there. I gather the energy to speak, but she mindfucks me again before my blistering reprimand gets out.

"Give me permission to lick it off my fingers."

I'm tempted to say yes. Hell, my dick's stiffening already. "My dirty fuckdoll would enjoy that. But this agreement isn't about you."

Pain crosses her expression. What? I use her body, and she thinks she's earned candy and roses?

I need her out of my sight before I do something stupid. "Get out," I tell her. At her crushed expression, I point to the door. Her, and her wounded look. Her, covered by my seed like it's a second skin.

She grabs her uniform and slides it onto her body as she stumbles to escape.

"Report to my office every day at two." My voice booms.

She stops and spins. "Why?"

I kick my bathing trunks out of the way as I head to clean up in the bathroom, grumbling as I go.

"Just be there."

CHAPTER 16

Riley

TRAPPED IN PARADISE, I walk the grounds, anxiety accompanying every step. A cool ocean breeze tries to offer comfort, but low male voices deep in conversation keep it in check.

I don't hear Alessandro.

But, as I pass his office window, the curtain falls closed.

He was watching me.

He always knows where I am.

His obedient little prisoner is free to wander the grounds. I do so, but walk on eggshells, anticipation building for today's two o'clock appointment and the twisted things he'll demand of me.

Evidence of yesterday is outlined on my body. A red collar around my throat. A bruise on my right breast where I whipped it without mercy. Strokes of light red welts everywhere else.

I should feel horrified. Used. *Dirty.*

Except images burn into my mind and mark it, as well. Deep blue eyes, the color of the sky before a storm. Massive, muscled arms, chest, and thighs, flexing with power. Hard monster cock suited for hammering things with equal force, like nails and women. A face still bruised and battered yet now resembling the man I knew. But my thoughts keep pausing on his wild expression, seconds before release, when his control slipped and I forgot everything, and we were lost in the moment together.

I shake my head. *So reckless, Riley. He could have choked you to death.*

So dangerous.

Beyond thrilling. Did I really offer to lick his seed off my fingers? Did I actually tease him, push his buttons and tempt him?

My face flushes.

You did, Riley. And the twisted part is you got off on it.

I stop at an old stone wall separating the grassy area from a massive drop to the white sandy beach below. The only safe way down is a long, winding staircase accessible from the pool patio.

I head there, but stop short, catching sight of the guards stationed there. They pretend not to see me. All except one, that is.

My eyes lock with Tommaso's.

He nods, and then returns to his discussion.

Emily. He can tell me if she's safe.

Heart in my stomach, I quicken my steps toward him, but my path is cut off by another man hurrying toward me. The same soldier who summoned me to meet Alessandro yesterday.

"Boss says to get your ass into his office now."

I frown, certain I'm not late. I'm keeping my end of our arrangement so long as Alessandro's kept his. "What time is it?" I ask him, flustered.

"Eleven forty-five."

"But he said two o'clock." Lord, I hoped to shower and perhaps drink heavily beforehand.

The man shrugs.

With a sigh, I follow him inside. Butterflies dance in my stomach. I'm anxious, but not necessarily for the right reasons. I'm anxious because I'm excited.

And because I might be as twisted as he is.

HE'S at his desk when I enter, glaring at me ... and my bravery splinters.

"You asked for me?" I breathe.

His suit is neat, without a wrinkle in sight. His blue tie perfectly in place. He's dressed more for a board meeting in a New York high-rise rather than for a luxury villa office fuck.

"You took your time getting here," he says, his voice flat. His eyes rake over me from head to toe, and I'm conscious of my appearance after my lengthy tour of the grounds. "Is that dirt on your uniform?"

My lips part as I glance down.

A black smudge is on the material partially covering my right breast. With a sigh, I brush it off, but it's not budging. What does he expect? His obsession with everything white isn't practical for daily wear. He slapped a monitor on my ankle and offered me more freedom. Dirt happens when you're outside and exploring nature.

But do I say all this?

No. Not a peep.

I stand before his desk, the vision of obedience, the nervous energy buzzing around us holding me in place.

His blue eyes meet mine, and an electric charge zips down my spine and strikes directly between my thighs.

God help me. Forgive me for the sins I'm longing to explore. Because how could I want this? And from the monster who kidnapped me?

Except it's there. This thing. That same sensation I felt when I saw him across the bar. Like I had to get close to him, had to feel his power embrace me, and strike life into me. Chasing extremes after everything else went black.

He licks his lips, feeling it too.

But the second we both realize it, he tenses and looks away. Then ignores me, thumbing through the screen on his phone like he's forgotten me already.

I wait. His stubborn arrogance is unparalleled by anyone else I've met. But it's better this way. I understand my role in his place—and it has nothing to do with emotional connection.

I'll do what I have to do. If the curious facets within me get off on his kinks, so be it.

His impatience is what does it. He abruptly stands and then, still ignoring me, clears his desk. My eyebrows rise, but my lips remain tight.

He rounds the desk, and my pulse kicks up. Only to be disappointed when he disappears into the small bathroom connected to his office.

Curses drift out, then the splash of running water.

When he returns, the hair around his face is damp.

His eyes lock on mine, daring me to comment.

Well, pull out the prize box. Because if this is a test in obedience, I win.

He steps toward me, and I gasp when his fingers brush my breast before he clasps the zipper. Without a word, he tugs it down until the material falls open. His expression's hard, but the familiar hunger within his eyes as they devour me for a few wicked heartbeats before he finishes undressing me.

His movements become more rushed. I'm scooped up, tossed on my ass onto his desk, and then pushed down until I'm sprawled across it. Anticipation building, I stare at the ceiling, not knowing what comes next.

There's the rustling of clothes followed by a whispered curse.

He climbs onto the desk with me and, in all his glorious nakedness, straddles my hips.

"Nothing to say today?"

I blink. "Do I have permission to speak?"

He grunts.

No help there.

He stares at me, then without warning, arches forward and sinks his teeth into my nipple.

"Ahsss," I hiss.

The pain eases as he sucks me in deeper.

Lightning strikes once more at my core.

He releases my nipple with a pop, and dives toward the other. I clench my thighs together, my excitement growing.

My nipples are two stiff peaks caught on fire. His mouth, lips, tongue the firestorm wreaking havoc on my senses.

He sucks harder.

A moan escapes from deep within my throat like a death sentence announced for all to hear. And he does hear it.

"Fuck." His response rolls across my skin, a prelude to the moment ending. He straightens while disappointment bears down on me.

I don't say a word or make a sound, not even when his heavy erection presses against my abdomen.

"You wet?" he demands.

"Yes," I reply. No sense in lying when the proof is the dip of a finger away.

For a long time, he's silent, deep in thought. If only I could read his expression. Understand him better, even if it's on a sexual level rather than an emotional one.

He tenses—a decision's reached.

I bite my bottom lip, prepared for his filthy worst.

"Clasp your fucking tits together."

My lip pops out from between my teeth. I cup each breast from the bottom, and as demanded, hoist and squeeze them into each other.

His irises darken.

I don't dare move as he shuffles forward to straddle my upper abdomen, his steel cock dragging across my body for the ride.

"These perfect fucking tits," he grunts, grabbing and stroking himself.

At first, I believe he'll jerk off on them, like he's done many times before, including yesterday—and the day my world turned upside down. Everything about us has changed except for his freakish obsession with them. At least, he's predictable that way, which is comforting.

But he glides his erection across my skin, and when the fat, bulbous tip nestles between the valley of my breasts, his intent becomes clearer.

"Oh," I gasp.

And nearly mew at the sight of his lips curling.

"Hold them tight, or I'll blister your ass. Capisci?"

I nod.

He sinks his teeth into his lip as he thrusts forward and buries himself between my breasts. I relax yet keep a firm grip like he demanded, not for my efforts at complete obedience but because deep down inside, I'm thrilled at the prospect of watching him get off.

His movements lengthen and pick up speed. So does his breath, until I'm quite certain he's panting.

Lord, he's a sight to see. Lips parted and eyes wild. So untrusting, so unforgiving, yet so handsome it's no wonder my excitement coats my clenched thighs.

I lick my lips.

His eyes narrow. He's well-aware I'm provoking him, and like yesterday, almost seems shocked I'd dare.

And like yesterday, his movements now become more aggressive. His hips flexing as his cock thrusts accelerate.

I recognize the moment he's about to unleash. It's hard to miss, as loud grunts turn into murmured curses.

I part my lips in offering.

His blue eyes turn black, but he shakes his head no. Eyes closing and head angled back, he comes hard and fills the tight tunnel I've created for him.

I hold him in position long afterward, and mentally prepare for the inevitable.

He springs off me, then delivers.

"Get out."

I roll off the desk, and then find my uniform. "Should I report back at two o'clock?"

There's a long silence. "I've got shit to handle."

"Okay."

As I step out, I can't shake the thought: if this was all for his pleasure, why is my body still humming, every inch of me alive, vibrating with the aftershock of what we've just done?

CHAPTER 17

Alessandro

THE SECOND he enters my office, Tommaso's attention swings from my desk to where I'm sitting on the sofa. "Why are you working there?"

"Stop with the inquisition and take a seat." I gesture to a nearby chair. My concentration is shit, my mind on things it shouldn't dwell on. I toss my phone onto the cushion. "You were talking to the men by the pool for a long time. You have updates?"

"The men located Renzo in Rome."

That earns my full attention. "Where did you put him?"

Tommaso grimaces. It's a reaction Renzo frequently inspires.

"Don't tell me he escaped?" I thunder.

"Like goddamn Houdini on speed." He sighs. "The men feared telling you, but then you were busy—"

I cut him off, not giving credence to the comment. My villa, my rules. And if playing with my fuckdoll in the goddamn mid-morning's a problem, my men—even Tommaso—can fuck off.

Wisely, Tommaso drops the subject. "But your brother left you a message."

"Like hell he did."

159

He holds out his hand. Scowling, I take the folded napkin from him. "Let me guess, the message is two letters, *F* and *U*."

"Don't know, Sandro." Tommaso shakes his head. "He sealed the damn thing with chewing gum."

My fist tightens around the napkin. "Yet he had time to do this *and* escape?"

"He locked our soldiers inside a kinky sex dungeon, and then taunted them from a freaking watch tower above. High as hell, half-naked with no shoes, and Renzo still outsmarted them." Tommaso's tone reeks of incredulousness, but I'm not the slightest bit surprised. Renzo lives life like a game, in which he's the chess master.

While I now become the Beneventi heir, filling in for him.

While I deal in reality.

While my life is completely fucked.

Tommaso nods at my hand. "You keep squishing that note, and you won't be able to read it."

I mutter a curse, and then painstakingly unwrap my twin's present. Except the gum sticks tight, and finally all that's decipherable is one word written in bubblegum pink lipstick.

Sicily.

I hand the napkin to Tommaso. "Must be about Dante." It's a logical conclusion. Except nothing about my brother inspires logic. Like my father said days ago, "*Who the fuck's in Sicily?*" "Dante, and Pietro Gallo..."

Tommaso leans forward like he's about to share a secret. "Ready for this? Dante's fucking around with his daughter behind his back."

I've a love/hate relationship with Dante Lucchese, my godfather's only son and my father's long-time protégé. He's a cross between James Bond—with his good looks, charm, and revolving door of women—and Tony Soprano—with a hot temper, crazy-ass psychosis, and passion for violence. I saw him take a butcher knife to some lying stranzo then, as the man's guts spilled onto the floor, pluck the cigarette he'd given the man from his lips and, cool as can be, smoke it. An absolute psycho wrapped in movie-star-themed paper.

And I love him for it.

What I hate is how he assumes Renzo and I are his clean-up crew. Ever pick up a guy's intestines? Pure grunt work—like Dante forgets we're equals. That he and I will lead our famiglie one day.

My lips curl. "Hollywood's asking for drama."

Tommaso eyeballs me, surprised.

"What?" I demand.

"You cracked a joke."

I scowl. "And?"

He thinks twice about answering, and instead turns the discussion back to Dante. "Want to hear the best part?"

Something in his tone says he can't wait to tell me. "No," I fuck with him. "Heard enough."

"She's seventeen."

That's no big deal in Italy if she's consenting. What's mind-blowing is that Dante's kink has always been older women.

"I've developed a taste for pistachios." I grin. A trip to Sicily to visit Pietro Gallo? Can't hurt, right? "Let's investigate further before sharing anything with my father."

Tommaso stares at me with a strange look.

"What now?"

"You're fucking smiling."

I roll my eyes. "Your point?"

"I've not seen you like this for months. You must be feeling better."

He arches an eyebrow, pushing my buttons. But I'm not discussing decisions I made while he was gone. Fuck, I don't even ask him if Riley's lame friend had anything more to say about her before he warned her old-fashioned style—a few cuts here and there, a reminder to keep her trap shut—and set her free. The truth won't change this arrangement. I've got Riley where I want her, and I'm keeping her. *Until you grow bored.*

Until your father's own neat arrangement requires you let her go.

The thought kills any lingering humor, as does my next question. "Any updates on Conti?"

"All bank accounts have been cleared. No trace of Conti. He must be using cash only."

"Crafty fuckhead." My eyes drift to my desk, and I picture her sprawled out across it. I need a stiff drink, and a housemaid to suck me off so fucking good, I'll forget her.

"The doctor change your meds?"

"No, why?" I ask.

"No cursing? No threats? Less evil bastard. You seem *lighter*."

Jesus Christ. I'm tempted to punch his face, then ask him if that felt lighter. Whatever bullshit he's thinking, he's wrong. "Listen, asshole." I roll to my feet, conversation over. "Find Conti, and the evil bastard you think you know will seem like an angel."

———

Riley

HIS, to order about.

His, to play with, on his time and at his beck and call.

His, to sit on a sofa in his office quietly, with my breasts on display while I watch him work.

"Market was down yesterday." Alessandro taps the blunt end of a pen on a paper on his desk. "Good time to purchase gold before it rises."

He listens intently, and then nods. "Yes, *sir*."

Despite how the last word is layered in sarcasm, the honorific signifies respect. He must be on the phone with his father, Sebastiano Beneventi.

I tilt my head, regarding him. Tense shoulders. Tight expression. The tap, tap, tap of the pen because he can't stop moving. He's wound tight, and I feel for him. It's obvious not only does he respect his father, but he's also hungry to please him. The revelation's startling. My perception of him was based on his actions mixed with a handful of conversations. I hardly knew him in New York, and I know less as his captive. Though today, I'm seeing a different side to him. The dutiful and somewhat reluctant son to an important mafioso capo.

Our eyes meet, and his pen halts.

He tosses it aside, then turns away.

Why demand I sit here if he doesn't like me eavesdropping?

I curl my legs beneath me on the cushion, forcing my attention elsewhere. Unfortunately, it drifts to thoughts of my father and our dynamic when I was a little girl.

One Christmas, my parents bought me a plastic four-wheeler. Every day, I'd wait on the corner for him to return from work. As soon as I saw his car turn onto our block, I'd pedal as fast as I could to race him home. We had a front stoop with concrete steps, and I'd ride down the sidewalk at full speed until the wheel crashed into the stoop, stopping me. I did it so many times I wore out the front wheel. We were close. I was loved and protected.

Until he met *her*.

An engagement's supposed to be a happy occasion. What kind of man hides news like that, especially from a loved one?

I frown. Is this the festering wound I keep digging at? Is this why I can forgive him for poor judgement yet hang on to his lie by omission?

I quickly brush aside a random tear before Alessandro notices. My father and I are both victims of monsters. Except mine likes to keep me on hand, caged, bare-breasted, and at his command.

"Less Frankenstein," he cuts in.

I stare at him, wide-eyed—it's almost as if he's read my thoughts.

"More Conor McGregor after a winning fight." He pauses to

listen, before continuing, "Yeah, I understand. Show my face around New York so the vultures can confirm I'm alive and well."

New York—is he leaving?

"Say hello to her?"

My head snaps up at his utterly disgusted tone. His expression's laced with anger. Whoever she is, he wants no part of her. "Hard pass."

The bite of his words are deadly. I don't envy the woman being discussed.

"Fucking hell. Understood."

The phone hits the desk, and he leans back with an annoyed exhale.

I don't know why I comment, but I do. "Your father demands a lot from you?"

He answers me, and I'm just as baffled that he would. "The motherfucking world."

"Is it difficult being a mafia boss's son?"

"It's goddamn la dolce vita when you're *not* the heir."

I do my best not to react. Alessandro's a total control freak. Relinquishing power to anyone, even his father, must frustrate him terribly.

Curious, I push harder, though with a soft, gentle voice. "What would your life be like if you weren't the Beneventi heir?"

"*Mine.*" He shoots me a look filled with such blistering intensity, I feel like I've been struck by lightning. Does he mean his life would be his? Or does he mean ... I'm *his*? Like in his life ... in his future?

But that can't be right. He hates me.

Our eyes lock and hold, and something flashes across his expression. A raw, unguarded vulnerability that makes my heart stop short. Because it reminds me of the morning I nearly died twice—first in his tender arms, and then in a cloud of dust. Why did he keep returning? Why not tell me we were over when I begged him to?

Seconds turn into a minute before a cold steel wall slams back into place.

"How the fuck are you still alive?"

I flinch at his harsh question.

"Six feet under and buried in cement, like your boss. That's where you should be."

Lord. He *didn't*.

"Ciro's a permanent part of my new casino. A fitting death for that asshole, don't you think?"

I rise to my feet.

"Sit your ass back down."

Lord, he's vicious. Vengeful and cruel. I sit down and press my lips together, struggling not to respond.

"Sit there, with your tits out and lips closed. That's your job. Not to pry into my life and fucking psychoanalyze me."

There's no winning when he's like this. He opened up, and I snuck in, and then struck a nerve. Now he's hell-bent on annihilating the tiniest lingering thread that binds us. Like I'm an intolerable weakness that just keeps hanging on.

"I've done *nothing* wrong."

He glares. "Tell me. How much does a gram of coke run?"

"Are you insane?" I gasp. "How would I know that?"

"Ballpark figure. Ten dollars? A thousand?"

"The person who'd know this answer," I sputter, "is buried six feet under."

That seems to appease him and his off-the-cuff questions.

"Come here."

I hesitate, but then do as he bids and walk over to his desk.

He pats the desk before him. "Up."

My eyebrows rise.

Hands on my hips, he hoists me onto his desk. My breasts bounce from landing so hard. Traitors, offering him a reward he doesn't deserve.

Predictably, his eyes track the movement. "Tempting."

I hide my displeasure while I wait him out.

"Go on. Tell me I'm an asshole."

I frown, wondering if I'm hearing him correctly.

"Now's your chance. Alessandro, you're a fucking asshole."

I part my lips, except the words won't come out. My silence fills the room like a thundercloud. There are *so* many names I could call him. But I don't—can't. Because even though he believes I betrayed him, I know otherwise. And one day, he'll hopefully recognize the truth. For now, I'll help him along the way.

"For Christ's sake," he exclaims, hating the silence. "Say something."

"I loved you once."

Oh. My. God. Of all the things to say, why blurt that? Helping him along the way doesn't mean throwing it all out there. I just placed my heart in one of his hands and a knife in the other.

He recoils like I sucker punched him.

Strike one, Alessandro.

Strike two, Riley.

His brows pinch. So distrustful. So ready to believe I'm someone other than a one-night stand turned into an obsession.

"What the fuck?" he mutters. Fuck is his answer to *everything*. It's all we did in New York. Desperately. Recklessly, like the solution to life's problems could be found in my submission. I should have been asking questions. He should have told me his name.

He's deep in thought and impossible to read, as my declaration devours the oxygen in the room until I'm choking for air. His silence is unbearable as it's now my turn waiting for him to speak.

The tiniest shake of his head breaks the spell. "Mouth or finger?"

"What?"

He slides his chair forward, hooks his arms beneath my knees, and tugs me forward. "Your choice, Riley. Mouth or finger?"

I blink at him. My name. He used my name.

Placing his forearms on my inner thighs, he parts my legs. "Answer me."

"You'll lick my ..."

"Mouth it is."

This is how he apologizes?

Yes, I think. *His actions speak louder than his words ever will.*

"Both," I say in a rush.

"Both," he repeats, an evil gleam in his blue eyes. "Greedy girl."

Not *my* greedy girl—he omitted the pronoun and changed a pet name.

"Now beg me for it."

"Lick me." My voice trembles.

"Louder. So my men can hear your sweet pleas."

Confident only he will hear me—because he's sick and twisted, but possessive as hell—I obey. "Lick me, please."

"Good girl. Now beg me to sink a finger in your ass while I do it."

Oh. My. God.

My eyes widen, and his grow impossibly dark. He threatened to break me in months ago. Dirty promises whispered in the heat of the moment. How he'd love watching me struggle. How much he gets off on my submission. But he's six three, muscled, and with a massive appendage. He barely fits in my pussy, so how am I supposed to take him in my backside?

A bead of sweat forms on my brow. Just a finger. "Will it hurt?"

He licks his lips.

Oh, hell. It'll hurt a lot.

"Eyes on me, capisci?"

I nod.

"And what happens if you look away, baby?"

My heart stills. He called me *baby.* "I never do," I whisper. "Or you'll spank me." A rush of lust hits me hard. Combined with *baby,* my entire body is a bundle of need.

He repositions his arms around the back of my knees and spreads me open. "Fuck, I can smell your sweet arousal."

I blush.

His pleasure is as tangible as the wood surface beneath me.

And then, as he dips his head, drags his tongue across my clitoris, and sucks on my nub, I completely give in to my desires. I'm a wet, sobbing mess when he thrusts his tongue inside me, and shaking with need when he does so over and over again.

I don't look away, and brazenly watch him. Half gasping, half moaning as his mouth fucks me toward an orgasm.

And he's loving this. Pleasuring me pleases him.

"Oh God. Please ..."

He abruptly raises his head to scowl at me. Cruel, so cruel. But instead of torture, his mission's to torment me. "I own every inch of you. Say it."

"You own every inch of me, Alessandro," I respond without thinking too deeply about what this actually means for me.

For him.

For us.

Satisfied, he buries his face in my wetness, and quickly, masterfully, works me into a frenzy.

I can't say when his hand shifts but am immediately aware of where his thumb lands. Everything stills: my breath, his tongue, his digit.

"Mine. Capisci?"

"Yours," I breathe.

His teeth graze my clit, surprising me before he drives his wicked tongue inside my wetness. My orgasm builds deep within me, fueled by his handsome face and dirty mouth. Watching this dangerous alpha male pleasuring me is such a rush. My pleasure melding with his until I'm panting. Until I'm seconds from winding my fingers in his hair and forcing him closer ... impossibly closer.

That's when he breaches me.

"Oh Lord." I climax hard, shivering and shaking as my wetness coats his face. Muscles clench around his thumb as he finger-fucks me through it. So dirty and foreign.

Finally, he withdraws and pushes his chair back, distancing himself.

I gaze at him in wonder, until I recognize too late the warmth I'm feeling isn't reciprocated. Experience should have warned me how foolish it'd be to submit.

"Go," he commands, taking a sledgehammer to the moment. None of it ever lasts very long.

Dazed, I blink, not sure I'm hearing him correctly. "But ..." I gasp.

"Run, Riley," he thunders. "Before I hurt you for real."

<hr>

HE SUMMONS me to his office at two o'clock the next day, and much like the previous day, I'm forced to sit on full display and in rapt attention while he goes about business. My courage is on vacation while the prisoner I am waits for the perfect time to add another request to our agreement.

Except as an hour then two passes, his mood worsens. Whoever Conti is, Alessandro is a madman on the hunt for him.

"Keep me posted, motherfuckers," he growls into the phone, and then disconnects. He's thumbing the next call when I interrupt.

"Wait."

"Don't speak unless spoken to."

"Yesterday, I gave you something special." My cheeks heat under his intense scrutiny, but I press on. "I'd like something in return."

"You're not sticking your finger in my ass."

I jerk in surprise. "That's not what ..."

He smirks.

I stare at him, at a loss for words.

"Does my fuckdoll miss my mouth on her pussy?"

"No ... yes." I sigh. "For my submission, I get a reward."

"I'll spank your ass raw for your impertinence. That reward enough?"

"I want to call my grandparents." My eyes lock with his steely blue ones. "Say yes, and you can spank me, and then I'll suck you off afterward."

He snorts. "What you're offering I can easily get elsewhere."

Hurt coils up inside me, and I glance at the carpet. I'm no one to him. Nothing except a doll to be tossed around, and then set aside. Worse still is I'm the only toy made of china. So easy to crack. So easy to ruin. So unlike the thick-skinned rubber dolls with pouty red lips and knives for tongues.

Distress settles over me like a thick fog, so I miss his approach. "You're deliriously in love …" An iPad lands on my lap. "… with your new boyfriend."

I look up at him. "What?"

"He took you to Europe for a dream vacation."

"I can call them?"

He shrugs. "Call, FaceTime."

I seize the device before he can change his mind, and pull up the app.

"Be mindful with what you say. Capisci?"

"Yes," I immediately reply. "Thank you."

"You will. Repeatedly."

Excitement licks up my spine. At his wicked promise? At the prospect of finally speaking with my grandparents? Or both?

With shaky hands, I enter their number.

"Wait."

He hoists me off the sofa, and then zips me up, grunting as he tucks my breasts beneath the material.

I press call, and seconds later, Mema's face appears.

"Riley?"

"Hi, Mema," I croak. God, how I miss them.

"George," she hollers. "Put the paper down and get over here. It's Riley."

"Riley?" he says in the background.

Guilt rolls over me. While in New York, I should have called more often. But I shut down after the Tragedy. A burden of hurt silencing me.

"Thank God you're safe," PopPop exclaims, his anxious face appearing next to Mema's.

"I'm fine. And so, so sorry to have worried you."

"You running off like that? We were about ready to call the police."

The blood drains from my face as I glance at Alessandro, who has returned to his seat but is listening intently. "But you didn't, right?"

"We were about to until Emily called."

Hard to miss his flattening lips. "You spoke with her?"

"A few days ago."

She's alive. He upheld our arrangement?

He shrugs at my unspoken question, but then I turn my attention to my grandparents.

"Listen, honeybunch. If you're in trouble ..." PopPop, always the fixer, begins.

"We raised you better than this," Mema interrupts more harshly. "How could you, Riley?"

Their disappointment could fill a stadium.

"I'm sorry you were worried." I struggle for an excuse. "I lost my bag with my passport, cell phone, and wallet. I'd never willingly cause you such worry."

"And the drugs?"

My eyes grow wide. "Drugs?"

PopPop leans his head toward the phone. "Cat's out of the bag. Emily told us, Riley."

"She told you I'm on drugs?" I exclaim, shocked to my core.

"Not using. Dealing." PopPop shakes his head with a disbelief that matches my own.

"What?" I screech. Unbelievable. "Emily told you I'm a drug dealer?"

I'm hyperventilating by the time I finish. How could Emily be this vindictive? Alessandro alluded she was disloyal. But I was focused on saving her life and didn't believe him. I'm hurt my best friend would lie.

Tears spring into my eyes. "I swear to you, I never touched drugs or sold them. Her boyfriend—my boss—was the cokehead. You warned me about him, remember? And God knows, I regret dismissing you."

"You didn't run off with that horrible man?" Mema asks, confused.

I clench the iPad tighter. "Hell could freeze over twice before I'd date an asshole like Ciro."

Hell is too good a place for him.

They look at each other. "Then why, Riley? Why did you run off?"

"I'm in love with someone." Oh, Lord. Did I have to say it with such conviction? I don't dare look at Alessandro. I loved him once. But then he was a different man. A stranger. "He took me to Europe. Except, like I said, my bag went missing. Cell service here is horrible, but I called as soon as I could." Part truth. Part lie. "He's kind and considerate."

Alessandro makes a choking noise.

"Is he handsome," Mema demands.

My cheeks heat as I answer truthfully. "The most handsome man I've ever met."

"You see that, George. Riley really likes this fella. She's blushing."

Alessandro snorts, while I turn red. But what's a little embarrassment when you can reconnect with the people you love, whether he listens in or not? They believe me. They trust me. Emily can choke on rotten eggs.

If only Alessandro would believe me as well.

"What's his name?"

"His name, honeybunch?" I finally glance at Alessandro, who isn't even hiding he's eavesdropping. He nods.

"Al."

"George, you hear that? Riley's dating an Al."

"Al have a last name?" my grandfather presses.

I squeeze my eyes shut for the briefest moment, then open them wide. "Mema, is that a new refrigerator?" I exclaim, gesturing animatedly. Guilt takes another stab at me. Avoidance is lying, but I don't have a choice.

They turn to look at the same refrigerator that's been in their house since I was a kid. "This old thing?" Mema huffs.

"New isn't always better," PopPop grumbles, the conversation turning to his least favorite—and Mema's favorite—subject. Yet he's a seasoned pro at dodging the refrigerator issue.

"When are you coming home?"

"Soon." I stare over the iPad at Alessandro. "Sooner, after he grows tired of me."

"Tired of you?" PopPop chuckles. "Not a chance. Any man worth a lick of salt can see my girl has a heart of gold."

"He better be worth his weight in salt for stealing you away," Mema chimes in.

"Look, Riley. We've got to get your grandmother to her doctor's appointment. Can you call us tomorrow?"

Is she sick? "Are you okay?" I cautiously ask. When you lose a parent to cancer, a common cold can cause pure panic.

"Don't worry your head, honey. Acid reflux—that's all. They got pills for it." She rolls her eyes, and I relax, knowing she's fine. "But my medication ran out, and the pharmacy won't refill my prescription without a checkup." She continues on and on. If PopPop hates talking about the refrigerator, Mema loves dissing her medical insurance. I mute the mic and lower the iPad. "Can I call them tomorrow?"

"Three o'clock every day unless you're busy pleasuring me."

My lips curve and it feels strange. When was the last time I smiled from the heart?

I unmute the device.

"... and I called them three times. Each time, insurance gave me a different answer. So I hung up—"

"I'll call you every day at three o'clock unless I'm traveling. Is that okay?"

"Call us anytime you want." PopPop waggles his finger at me. "When you're ready, we want to hear more about this guy."

I nod. What else can I say?

Mema fiddles with the phone. "Goodbye for now, honey."

"Wait," I cry out before they disconnect. "I love you so much."

"We love you too, honeybunch. Speak with you tomorrow, okay?"

"Bye," I whisper, and then their faces disappear.

I curl my legs into me, bend my head, and cry. Relief, sorrow, anger, fear—it all comes out.

When I finally lift my head back up, curious why Alessandro's so quiet, he's gone.

Without a snide comment or look, he left me alone with my tears.

CHAPTER 18

Alessandro

THE HEAT COMING off New York City's skyscrapers could roast a turkey. Jet lag doesn't improve my mood. Neither does the bland Italian food I ordered for dinner. Even my luxurious apartment—complete with all the bells and whistles that please me—seems small and empty. One huge fucking pink bow, though, that's wrapped around this shitshow is my visit to Rhode Island has been cancelled. Don Lucchese's health has deteriorated, so while I'm stateside, my father's visiting him in Tuscany. Word is Father left sweet little Alessia behind.

All the more reason to avoid Rhode Island.

"Mr. Beneventi." My new Riverview construction manager races up to me with a fucking helmet in hand. "You need to put this on before we tour the site." He's a churchgoing family man, according to the background check, with a lot of false notions about what I can't do. His concern is noted, and then ignored. I'd rather be hit in the head by a falling object than suffocate beneath this helmet.

I take it from him, and toss it over my shoulder.

He stares at me in horror.

Waving a hand, I gesture toward the newly framed building. "Let's go."

I allow him to lead me inside, and the tour begins. Despite the loss of my former manager, construction's on track. My father will be pleased—isn't that what matters most?

Was it obvious years ago that I'd become the Beneventi heir? One different DNA sequence in the twin gene pool that gave me brass balls and my brother a limp dick in need of medication to get hard? My father would often visit our playroom as kids. He filled it with every toy imaginable, but my favorites were the Lego sets. I'd spend hours assembling them, working out what fits and what doesn't, creating something to its completion, *controlling* every step. Renzo said I played with a stick up my ass. The shithead would steal into the room after I left and wreak havoc on my creations, ruining my hard work.

Even then, I was the son who put things together and Renzo was the son tearing things apart.

Riverview Casino was my father's gift to me, a trade for my sacrifices. Unlike Dante's Atlanta project, I delivered in spades. Riverview will bring in more money than any of our other ventures, and the Eleven will take notice. My reputation as Sebastiano Beneventi's rightful heir will be indisputable. I'll be the son my father can boast about.

"Fuck," I mutter.

My construction manager looks startled. "Something wrong, sir? I'll stop construction—"

"Jet lag, is all." *And a fucked-up psyche I won't dwell long enough on to fix.*

He nods, relieved. "Will you be returning to Italy soon?"

Family man or not, I'd be an idiot to fully trust him. "If we ever get this motherfucking tour over with."

"Oh," he stutters. "Well, then ... over in this area ..." He proceeds to describe in great detail every step in the progress we've made.

While I take half-assed notes to share with my father.

While the honest answer to his question rests on the tip of my tongue.

Not soon enough.

* * *

Riley

FEMININE LAUGHTER FILTERS into the kitchen from the pool deck. I wipe my hands on a towel as the flock of brazen brunettes surrounds a dark-haired man by the bar.

I'm a prisoner here. Unlike them, who leave or stay at will. Unlike Alessandro, who can disappear without warning or explanation.

While the monster's away, the hornets will play.

And I want no part of it.

I recognize Tommaso, as he's feet taller than them. One woman tugs his arm as they shamelessly laugh and flirt.

Even from the door, I can see her red lips pout. Yet he refuses to budge.

Sandro won't like this.

Tommaso ushers them away, probably thinking the same.

I step into the pantry, dodging them as they parade inside.

It's the man outside I've been waiting for an opportunity to speak to.

Tommaso's behind the bar and double-fisting vodka shots when I reach him; an empty glass is in his right hand and a full one raised to his lips in the other. A half-empty vodka bottle sweats on the bar in the summer air.

I slide into a bar seat, and he freezes. "You got to be shitting me," he mutters. "Can't a man find some peace around here?"

"Alessandro won't appreciate that they flirt with you."

His wrist flicks and he shoots back the vodka, and then wipes his mouth with the back of his hand. A bit uncouth, but he is a big brute with huge hands and a neck the size of my thigh. And I confused him for an Uber driver? "Boss doesn't give two shits what they do," he finally says.

"He's possessive," I insist, questioning how well he actually knows his boss. Even I understand playing nice with other men in the same sandbox is not Alessandro's forte.

Tommaso gaze skims over me. "Only about important things."

"Like ...?"

He flips both shot glasses upside down on the bar, then cocks an eyebrow at me. "What he won't like is this. So get yourself gone."

"I waited for him in his office for over an hour." My heart jumping every time footsteps approached, only to sink with disappointment as they passed by. I square myself on the barstool. "He's gone, isn't he?"

He shoots me a hard look.

"But he made me sit there, anyway," I softly add. "So you can report back and communicate what an obedient pet I was."

"Obedient? You're still here, hassling me." He rummages through a cabinet as he speaks, and then places an empty shot glass on the bar top, pours a yellow liquor into it, and pushes it toward me. "If we're doing this, best drink up."

"Limoncello?" I shoot back the shot before he can answer. It's tasty, a refreshing blend of alcohol, lemon, and sugar.

"Describe your relationship with Ciro Cigorelli."

I choke on empty air at his icy tone. "My relationship?" My eyebrows pinch hard enough to give me a headache. "Ciro was my best friend's boyfriend and my boss."

He studies me closely. If I were standing, I'd be shifting on my feet. "You deal coke for him?"

My lips part with a gasp. "You're the second person to accuse me of that, and my answer's the same—no."

"The police discovered a small fortune's worth of coke in his office."

I shake my head. "I promise you it wasn't there the day I met you at the casino. The day Ciro ..."

"Had a date with a cement truck?"

"Yes." A shiver races up my spine. Despising the man is one thing and relishing his murder another. "And he's responsible for Alessandro's injuries?"

He drums his fingers on the bar top. "Partially."

"The other person's Conti? Who has fled?"

"Correct." His fingers still. "And there's one more traitor ... *you.*"

I glance around. A few men stand guard on the lawn beneath the balconies. Otherwise, we're alone.

I wish he were an Uber driver and not a mafiosi. He could dispose of me, and, like Ciro, no one would miss me.

Except my grandparents.

Except Alessandro.

Wrong, Riley. He'd miss tormenting you. That's all.

"I never betrayed him."

"Emily says otherwise."

I need another shot. "She's lying."

"You have shit friends."

My eyes widen. "You believe me?"

"Give me one good reason to, and I just may."

"I loved him."

Tommaso reacts much like Alessandro did. Like I rattled a hornet nest with one switch of a stick, sent the swarm buzzing, and caught him in the middle of it all.

They say the truth sets you free. I hope so, because I'm over being Alessandro's prisoner.

Tommaso stares me down as he weighs my words.

"Ciro discovered our ... *affair*. He used me to get to Alessandro, right?"

"Bing-fucking-go."

"And I'm here because Alessandro believes I was involved."

Tommaso snorts.

"You don't agree?" I demand.

"I'll give you this much. Sandro's proud like his father. Weakness, in any shape or form—even a perceived weakness—is intolerable. Whether you knew or not, no longer matters. It's maintaining the Beneventi name that's important."

Like a pin popping a balloon, any lingering hope of reconciling with the monster disintegrates into air. There is no escape.

Tommaso slides another shot toward me.

I toss it back. "Thanks, I guess."

"Who owned your apartment building?"

Lord, he's relentless. "Ciro claimed he did. But Emily told me the insurance company believed three investors held the deed."

"Why did Ciro call you Triple B?"

"Alessandro asked me this, too." My fingers tighten around the shot glass. "I believed Ciro was poking fun at my bra size. It means Beautiful Beneventi Bait."

He nods. "She said exactly the same thing the second time around."

"The second time? What does that mean?"

He folds his arms across his chest. "I'm curious about one thing? Did you mention your ... *affair* ... to Emily?"

I roll my lip between my teeth. "No."

"You kept it a secret?"

"Yes."

"Why?"

His question stirs up a familiar hurt. "Emily shared her issues, and I listened."

"But you had shit you were dealing with?"

What doesn't this man know about? "Avoiding, not dealing, okay?"

He stares at me, and then flashes me a smile. "You've made some piss-poor relationship choices, you realize that?"

"Piss-poor." I gesture between us. "I liked you better when you were an Uber driver."

His laughter rolls across the pool deck, and heads turn. "Damn it. I'm in trouble now."

"Not as much as the trouble I'm in." My comment begins as a joke and continues as something far more twisted. "Will he kill me?"

Tommaso chokes on his beer. "Listen, Riley. Innocent or not, I can't help you. No one here can. Best advice is to go along with his demands until he figures everything out."

"You mean figures out whether to toss me off this cliff?"

"I'm going to tell you something. If you betray me by repeating it, I'll toss you off the cliff."

My eyes widen. "Okay."

"I sat outside your apartment all those nights."

"You *did?*" It makes sense, now knowing who Alessandro is.

He nods.

"And?"

"You don't fit in with the plan."

I frown. Not fit in ... "What do you mean?"

"Sandro's the Beneventi heir. His will isn't his own anymore—it belongs to his father." He places his forearms on the bar and leans in. "And you, Riley, are Sandro's dirty little secret."

Dirty little secret.

"Did he tell you that?"

Tommaso straightens. "I've said enough, but I'll leave you with this. Play your cards right, and you'll likely survive."

"You mean obey my jailor?"

"We're all prisoners, in one shape or form."

"He's not," I exclaim.

"That's where you're wrong." Tommaso's expression sobers. "Sandro's more trapped than any of us."

———

ALESSANDRO'S SITTING in a chair beside my bed when I wake up. Watching me sleep, like he did the night before the explosion. Looking every bit as troubled as he did then.

My heart leaps. "You're home."

Really, Riley? Home? I sound like a 1950s housewife welcoming her man back from the office. Except, this isn't my home, he isn't returning from a hard day at the office, and I'm not his wife—but hostage.

"What would you do if I removed the tracking device right now?" he silkily asks like he's inquiring about my favorite tea blend.

I blink sleep from my eyes and grumble, "You won't take it off."

He grunts. "You sure?"

I tug the sheet higher, forming a cocoon around my body as if it could protect me. But even if it were steel, studded with pointed blades aimed at him, I'd still be at his mercy. It doesn't help that he's woken me, that I'm naked and exposed. "I'm your pet, right? So why set me free when you enjoy keeping me trapped?"

"What would I do if I set you free?" His eyes darken, and suddenly I'm completely awake.

"What would you do?" I whisper.

His grin's downright sinister. "I'd hunt you down, then spend hours bringing you to climax then denying you release. I won't be satisfied until your skin's pink and your body's bent, straining beneath me. Then, you'd beg me for permission in that fucking sexy, *needy* voice of yours."

Oh my God. He's thought about this. *A lot.* If I didn't know better, it's almost as if he missed me while he was gone.

Impossible. I'm his plaything and a tool for his pleasure.

His face is still slightly bruised, but he's impossibly handsome, gorgeous if you will. "If we had more time ..." His muttered words trail off.

Regret? No, it can't be. The cobwebs in my mind are holding me hostage to ridiculous thoughts. Like our connection's still there. Like he snuck into my room and woke me up because he couldn't wait to see me.

With a soft curse, he abruptly stands.

A familiar loss sweeps over me as our connection slips away on a whisper.

He tosses a satin box onto the night table. "Bring it with you tonight but don't open it."

"Tonight? We're not ... meeting ... at two o'clock?" Lord, I sound eager. Almost as eager as when I was breathlessly waiting for him to appear the day he left.

"I've shit to do." He wipes his fingers across his jaw as he considers me. Whatever this is about, he seems reluctant to share. Finally, he grinds out, "We've dinner reservations at seven."

The sheet drops as I sit up. His gaze falls, then stills, but I'm too excited to fix it. "You're taking me to dinner?"

"If I make it out of this goddamn room."

"In that horrid uniform?"

"I purchased a few things for you while I was in New York."

My eyebrows hit the rafters.

"The women will be bringing in the boxes shortly."

"No," I burst out, not willing to risk another poor canary surprising me inside a box.

He scowls, misunderstanding.

"Did you purchase clothing for any of them?"

"Why the hell would I buy them anything?" he demands, oblivious. "If I wanted Barbara parading around in a red dress and heels, she would be."

"Not Barbara, *Brigetta*."

Despite what he's saying, despite how he can't get her name

straight, jealousy sinks in. The thought that he has a horde of bitchy brunettes on call ...

"You look ready to puke," he comments.

I'm mortified. Because it doesn't take a genius to understand why I'm upset. And he's too smart and knows me too well.

"Put some goddamn clothes on, and I'll have my man bring the boxes in. Report to my office at five in the red dress and fuck-me heels." His tone is flat, yet this is all very specific, like he's been planning this.

I roll my bottom lip between my teeth. *Play your cards right, Riley.* "Is there red lipstick?"

His eyes darken, giving me the courage to test him further.

"You know, to match?"

The energy between us crackles, and I'm absolutely certain he's imagining my red lips wrapped around his cock. My pulse quickens, and beneath his intense scrutiny, my skin flushes pink.

"Find a suitable red on your iPad, and my man will fetch it."

"Are there stores nearby that carry different lipstick shades?"

He shrugs. "Not my problem."

I almost smile. "I'm looking forward to dinner. Thank you."

He pins me with a look that sets me on fire and I wonder what else he has in store for me.

CHAPTER 19

Riley

ALESSANDRO DRIVES LIKE A MADMAN, recklessly accelerating his black Maserati on the flat roadway running along the coastline. Treating it like his own personal racetrack. His security detail must be pulling out their hair in the three trucks that trail us.

The restaurant, Grotta Sardinia, is a small, intimate open-air grotta built into a cliff overlooking the sea and only accessible by a steep stone stairway. The descent is worrisome; I'm wearing a daring red gown with a plunging neckline and expensive five-inch heels. No ankle monitor, though—guess it'd ruin the vibe. Also worrisome is Alessandro's touch; his arm anchors around my waist, and fingers brush places they shouldn't. To his amusement, I gasp and whimper the entire way.

He enjoys showing me off, I think as we reach the bottom step. His arm candy. His fuckdoll. Though, aside from staff, the restaurant's empty. "Did you reserve the entire place?" I ask as he pulls out my chair.

He doesn't respond.

"Isn't that expensive?"

"I can afford it."

My eyebrows arch. "These men must be important."

"Not particularly."

God, could he be any more vague? But even though this unfamiliar situation has me less cautious than curious, the view steals the words off my lips.

It's breathtaking. A U-shaped harbor is below, bustling with yachts, sailboats, and small vessels. A gentle tide rolls in as the sun dips over the open sea. Nature perfectly complemented by man without overtaking it.

Instead of the view, the devil pretending to be an angel by my side watches me like a hawk. Hungry for my reaction? Or worried that if I die and go to heaven at the sight of the beauty surrounding us, he'll need to find another woman who'll fit into this expensive red gown?

"It's spectacular." *Romantic.*

Why am I here?

He takes the seat next to mine, and then tugs me down onto mine. The control freak I know oh so well and love to despise fully reappears. "After they arrive, don't speak unless I say it's okay."

I glance at our large table—set for five—then back at him. Reminded this isn't a date but a business meeting. My excitement deflates like a slowly leaking balloon, but I hide my disappointment by fiddling with the dress's deep V neckline.

"Cover yourself. No one gets to see your beautiful breasts but me."

"Yes, sir," I respond with sass. It's always somewhere between torment and torture with him, isn't it? He dressed me up, took me out, and led me to believe this night was special. Except like the expensive Rolex he's wearing, I'm jewelry.

"I ordered a new chaise for my casita, one particular to my *tastes.*" He unfolds and places his napkin on his lap. "Any further smart-ass responses, and you'll be bent over it for days."

My heart thumps wildly, proof it's as sick and twisted as my mind. "Tastes?"

"Know what? I dare you to mouth off. Because if my finger is a tight fit, my dick will split you in two. And you'll take it all, baby, while handcuffed to the chaise."

My eyes grow wide as his grin confirms his threat.

Instinct presses me to remain quiet. But the promise in what he's clearly been planning is too tempting. In the sexy, pleading tone he likes so much, I ask, "Will it hurt?"

His nostrils flare, and I force back a smile.

"You bring it?"

Whatever power I thought I had vanishes with one abrupt question. "What?"

"The box."

I raise my new leather Louis Vuitton handbag, the satin box tucked inside.

He glances at his watch. "Ten minutes before my guests arrive. There's a bathroom just inside. Go put it on."

Excitement licks up my spine. What's inside the box that has him vibrating with big dick energy?

His wicked eyes track my movements as I rise to my feet. Without a word, I brush by him and head toward the restroom. Inside, I withdraw the box, then open its gold latch, expecting something expensive like my new wardrobe. Must be jewelry, right? A necklace?

Alessandro's surprise has me slamming the lid shut so no one sees.

A vibrator?

Long. Thick. Gold. With dual stimulation, with smaller forked fingers designed to tease a woman's clit.

And I've ten minutes to insert this beast.

I step into a stall, place a heel on the toilet, wiggle and squirm until I fit it inside me. Then, wiping the sweat from my brow, I exit, wash my hands, and return to the table.

The exertion from what I've just been through leaves me breathless. But the hunger in Alessandro's blue eyes makes me lightheaded.

He's like a kid at an ice-cream counter, and I'm his number one flavor. This excites him.

"Good girl."

Pleasure washes over me, his praise a heady thing. It's within my nature to feel this way, isn't it? Though what does this say about me, when the man playing with my emotions has the power to light me up or snuff out my light?

"My guests are here."

I respond to the censure in his tone with a quick nod.

Three men in expensive suits approach the table, and Alessandro stands.

"Buonasera. Stai bene, Alessandro." The older man pulls him into a hug, and unsurprisingly, Alessandro stiffens.

"Come vanno gli affari, Carmine?"

Carmine pulls away and switches to English. "Always so quick with the business questions, Alessandro Magno."

Alessandro offers him a chilly expression, and the other men tense. In fear—they're afraid of him. "Magno? I'm no longer a kid, old man."

"No disrespect, eh? I've known you and your brother since you were tiny bambinos."

Alessandro gestures for me to take my seat.

I do so and release a small squeak, the vibrator pushing deeper.

"Una bella rossa, Alessandro?" Carmine exclaims. "No brunette tonight?"

I flinch.

No. No. No. I'm suddenly buried beneath an avalanche of emotion. Eyes blurry, I look anywhere but at the monster with a penchant for buxom brunettes. He has a type—obviously. Is it boredom that has him switching things up? Or his viciously twisted mind playing games with my heart?

God. I hate him.

"Are you going to introduce us?" Carmine continues, while I

study the horizon. Searching for a life raft to save me from this torture.

"No."

Not even worthy of an introduction, am I?

A waiter sets bottles of red wine on the table and fills our glasses.

"You look like you've fully recovered."

Carmine's comment draws my attention.

"Took a beating, we heard."

Is this man insane? Or does he have a death wish? Beneath my eyelashes, I study Alessandro's reaction. His eyebrows pinch. Otherwise, there's no indication that danger lurks beneath the surface.

"A few taps from a sparring match. My best soldier got carried away. Nothing more worth discussing." Alessandro sips his wine, signaling the end to further discussion.

In on the lie, I do my best to remain passive.

Carmine completely misses the cue. "Tough, like your old man."

So does his younger look-alike. "He still alive? You must be angry?"

Alessandro sips his wine and forces everyone to wait on his response. I brace myself, anticipating the worst.

"Alive?" Alessandro shrugs. "Fuck yeah. Only a stupid stranzo would kill his best man for a small indiscretion." He makes eye contact with all three men. "As for angry? Enough to kill the next fucker who brings it up."

The old man pales.

The other two study the menu.

And Alessandro locks eyes on me.

Proud, to a fault.

Arrogance, in spades.

Borderline sadistic.

Possessing a power to hurt me that goes far beyond my darkest desires or messed-up mind.

I look away, knowing it's safer to hate him.

I take in the harbor, and the small yacht anchored below,

wrapped up so prettily and at the mercy of the tide, yet with nowhere to go.

"Your family's hunting for Conti?"

"What's the word on the street?"

"Just that he angered the Beneventi capo." Carmine grunts. "After your old man chopped Benny Manocchio into fish bait, che palle."

Alessandro nods. "That's right."

I stifle my gasp. Violence is as common as air for these mafiosi. I've witnessed it, firsthand, haven't I? It's a miracle I'm alive, considering.

"Spread the word. A million euros to anyone who has information on Conti."

The men look startled.

"And they contact me directly, capisci?"

Euros light up in their eyes. Money's a great motivator.

Satisfied, Alessandro reclines in his chair, and his attention shifts back to me.

I swiftly look elsewhere, angry at him yet anxiously wondering when he'll activate the vibrator. It's wrong, so wrong to yearn for such a thing. To give him power over my pleasure and pain, especially with an audience who might notice my discomfort.

A waiter appears with plates of food for the table. No one comments on how Alessandro preordered, though idle conversation continues while we eat. I tune them out and relax enough to eat my first meal out in Italy.

I'm spiraling fettuccine around my fork when Alessandro places a hand on my arm, and then leans in. "You're doing it wrong," he murmurs. My skin pricks with awareness at his proximity. I'm offered a spoon before his big hand clamps down on my other hand. "The proper way is to wind the fork against a spoon. Like this." He gently turns my hand while pushing fettuccine into the spoon and creating a neat, bite-size nest.

"Good girl," he softly praises me.

Twice today, he's done so. With equally devastating effect. Because my fork hand is shaking so hard, I'm afraid to raise it to my mouth.

The men notice I'm flustered. The weight of their regard heavy—though Alessandro could care less.

I don't look at him ... how can I when he's like this? *Now,* I think, and breathlessly wait for the vibrator to hum to life.

He draws closer, his breath warm on my ear. "As much as I'd love getting you off right now, my greedy girl will have to wait until business is over."

I gasp, and he withdraws. Then, to my immense disappointment, he graces them once more with his attention.

We finish our meal, and the table's cleared. Carmine Jr. clears his throat. "You speak with your stepbrother these days?"

"Stepbrother?" The question's tossed in the air like a grenade.

Alessandro has a brother—he shared this with me in New York. But a stepbrother?

"Dante Lucchese?" Carmine Jr. clarifies.

"You mean the son of Don Lucchese, our capo di tutti capi's son?"

The man squirms in his chair.

"True, my father treats Dante Lucchese like a son. True that Lucchese runs Atlanta now. As for being my stepbrother ..."

The men exchange looks.

"Tell me," Alessandro snaps.

"Just a rumor."

"Just like the knife I carry in my pocket's a rumor."

"Two months ago, Dante Lucchese met with Conti in Rome."

Alessandro drums his fingers on the table. "That right?"

"Yes."

"You said it was a rumor yet you're stating it like a fact."

The mafiosi quiet.

"A fact I'm only hearing about now." Alessandro studies each man with a blank expression.

As the dynamics play out, my admiration grows. He's pure alpha, no question. And I crave security, something lacking in my life for a long time. A familiar ache presses against my heart. If he'd only believe me. If he'd only trust me.

"Dante represents the Atlanta casinos, but Conti controls everything else," he casually explains. "We Beneventi would never negotiate with that worm. It makes sense Dante would."

Stepbrother by proxy or not, he's protecting his father's man.

Carmine Jr. lowers his voice. "Rumor has it that Lucchese resents your father's position. That he'd prefer to be named capo di tutti capi and not share responsibilities."

It happens so fast, no one's prepared.

Alessandro jumps to his feet, gun drawn. "Rumors like this bear consequences." He shoots both younger men in the thigh while the third man scrambles to his feet, hands up in surrender.

I freeze, pulse pounding.

"That's for not sharing this petty gossip sooner, Carmine *Magno*." Alessandro thrusts his fingers into the man's mouth, snatches his tongue and runs the knife across it, cutting it like he's fileting a fish. "But this is for insulting me earlier." Alessandro raises an eyebrow, completely unaffected by their blood and panic. "Any more subtle references about Beneventi weaknesses?"

"Mr. Beneventi," Carmine Jr. blusters. "Apologies for offending you."

"The only goddamn rumors I'm interested in revolve around Conti's location. Capisci?"

Carmine nods vigorously.

Alessandro pulls out his wallet and tosses a wad of money onto the table. "For the food and hospital bills. When we meet next time, I'll bring a suitcase with the reward money. The deal's still on. Find that motherfucker."

Alessandro curls his fingers around my biceps and hauls me out of the restaurant.

"YOU SHOT THEM."

He fastens my seat belt, then rounds the car and climbs in.

"Clean shots. They'll be out of the hospital in no time. They should be thankful they're alive."

"But did you have to cut his tongue?"

His eyebrows pinch in annoyance at my shaky tone. Like my fear upsets him ... like his brutality is justified. "He'll think twice about running it now."

"How can you be so cavalier?"

"It's what monsters do."

I flinch.

He leans toward me, and I immediately sink back in the seat. With a vicious tug, he rips my gown wide open. My breasts spill out, but I don't dare cover them. Not with him wound tighter than a spring inside a loaded shotgun.

The Maserati purrs to life and he accelerates out of the parking lot like a madman.

With a cry, I tumble back in the seat.

"Keep pushing me with those hurt-filled looks. It's not like I took a knife to you, though fuck knows I should have a long time ago."

I shrink away, even though I recognize what's become a pattern of idle threats.

"What? Did you anticipate a fun night out?" he grinds out. "You think Alessandro Beneventi gets to do fun nights out?" He slams his palm against the steering wheel. "I'm only a pawn in a bigger game, baby. It's play or pay. And if you think what happened back there was horrifying, my father's payment for the insults would be ten times more brutal."

He falls silent.

And I don't utter a word, but Tommaso's admission plays on repeat in my mind. *Alessandro's more trapped than any of us.*

Maybe I have it wrong.

Maybe he doesn't enjoy being a heartless monster.

Maybe this is the "play" his father expects from him?

"I want to hear you say it," he growls. "I hate you, Alessandro."

"What?" I cry out.

"You need a hearing aid? Say it. I hate you, Alessandro."

I press my lips together, refusing to give in. Yes, I've thought it before—whispered it in my mind, chanting it, when he was spanking those bullies—but I didn't mean it. How could I? Anyone would snap under the pressure he's put me through. But now, even with everything he's done, with the promise of an easier life if I just give him the words he craves, I can't summon a hatred that isn't there.

He tilts his head, a dark smirk playing on his lips. "Disobey me?" he sneers. "Seems like I've neglected you."

And then I feel it. The vibrator's sudden quake.

No. No. No. This is *so* wrong. *So* cruel. Why now, with so much anger behind it?

I will my body not to respond, and he amps up the vibrations. "Say it, and I'll stop."

My lips part with a gasp, but no words accompany it. Why not obey? Why not give in to his command and be done with this misery? This isn't a game. This is torture. His will against mine. I'm at a serious disadvantage here.

"One press of a button is the difference between agony and peace."

By agony, he means the vibrator. But, for whatever reason, saying those words is worse. "You go first," I blurt out. "And then I'll obey. Go on: I hate you, Riley."

I brace for his response.

"You invited me in."

"What?"

"With your pretty green eyes, tight fucking pussy, and sweet words. But the best part was your submission. Remember what you told me?"

I'm shocked to my core. "What did I say?" I ask in a rush.

"You're the best kind of hurt."

Oh my God. He remembers? Our last morning was the most intimate moment in my life. I felt cared for. Protected. *In love*. Yet time has a funny way of altering the truth. I told myself it wasn't real. My feelings, maybe. But his emotional involvement, not a chance, especially considering he smashed my heart with the breakup that followed.

"Why did you go and ruin it?" he continues, relentless. "A dirty fuck and some laughs, that's what I was after."

"I trusted you." There, I said it.

"I never asked for your trust."

"No," I whisper. "You were too busy demanding my heart and soul."

"You came alive beneath my touch."

"I've been making love to a heartless killer."

He snorts. "Fucking a heartless killer."

I spin on him. "No. We made love that morning."

"Love?" he repeats like it's a dirty word.

His jaw tics, and the vibration stops.

I watch and wait. But then he cranks up the radio and ends all conversation.

We reach the villa, and he pulls into the garage like a bat out of hell, nearly hitting the wall before the brakes lock.

What in God's teeth? Is he completely, utterly deranged?

"Fuck." He pounds the steering wheel.

Wide-eyed, I stare at him.

He glares at me and then, in the next blink, exits the car.

"Where are you going?" I ask, concerned. We were so close ... so blissfully close to reconciling. I want the time back ... want our discussion to continue ...

"To find an obedient distraction."

He disappears inside.

Pain, deep and profound, grips me. How can he be so callous? How can he be so cruel?

I was wrong that morning.

He's the *worst* kind of hurt.

CHAPTER 20

MY FAVORITE PAIN-slut licks her lips. She's exactly what I need whenever the responsibilities of being the Beneventi heir become too much.

Except I don't want her.

I don't want any of them.

Carmine Bartolucci and his son's insinuations eat at me like a festering wound. The second they mentioned my injuries, my self-control became a battle between "Do I knife him?" and "How long do I wait before doing so?" Hunting Conti took precedence over my pride. So I waited, said what needed to be said, then corrected the mafioso's perception of me. Weak? For the insult, he'll now curse me every time he licks a gelato.

And I need to get to Sicily immediamente. Dante meeting secretly with Conti? Is his future, albeit lackluster, role beside my father in the Eleven not enough for his refined Hollywood tastes? What in God's name is Dante up to?

I tuck my cock inside my silk boxers. Fuck, a drink or two should take the edge off. Or the joint I stashed in my office drawer. Since my brother's self-medicating issues, I avoid the heavier shit, though often wonder if I got it all wrong. That fucker's free as a bird, isn't he? Living life and doing whatever the hell he pleases. While my father proudly boasts how crafty he is for breaking out of rehab.

His responsibilities. *His* bullshit. *My* future not of my making.

"Vattene!" I shout, and the trio on their knees by my feet haul ass from the casita.

I need to get rid of Riley just as fast.

Before I *can't.*

Tommaso can handle her ... Though, the thought of his dirty hands on her ...

I stalk from the casita and bypass the bar, heading straight for my office.

The famiglie live by strict rules.

Sacrifices are necessary. I can't have more Carmine Bartoluccis running their mouths and questioning my capabilities. If I had a choice, then things would be different.

I curl my fingers into a fist.

As the saying goes—out of sight, out of my mind.

One order and she'll be gone.

Tomorrow. Or maybe even the next day.

After I've had one final taste of her.

Riley

THEIR LAUGHTER'S UNBEARABLE.

Their behavior horrible. The hisses. The eye rolls. The dead mouse on the balcony chair. I'm an uninvited prisoner in the spank-me squad. Surrounded by mafiosi, I wish things were different, that we'd support each other without all this animosity. Girl power, and all that. It's the man they're hovering around and watching swimming laps who's the true villain.

Back and forth with fluid strokes, he completes multiple laps.

While they laugh and point.

It's ridiculous.

Beyond annoying.

Pathetic.

I bite my lip as he pulls himself up to sit on the pool ledge. His beautiful physique is bigger now, though he's too far away to savor his eight-pack abs or the deep V dive toward his massive cock. His body's branded in my mind from that morning, when my fingers explored every inch of him in the afterglow of our lovemaking.

How I wish he'd left when he threatened to and that what followed never happened.

He lifts his head and looks toward me.

Why mention that morning—and in vivid detail?

Why bring up the past when I'm clearly not part of the future?

A brunette approaches, distracting him.

I grit my teeth as her uniform drops.

Then retreat back inside my gilded cage.

I'm not special. Or the object of his affection.

I am just a plaything he loves to hate on.

"WHAT DOES FIDANZATA MEAN?"

Tommaso stops in his tracks as I catch up to him. Four days have passed since the disastrous dinner. The weather's beautiful even if my mood's sour, and my time's spent strolling the beach and avoiding the monster. Not that he notices or cares.

Except his best soldier always seems in a hurry whenever I'm near.

"For shit's sake, why ask me that?"

I shrug a shoulder. "I keep hearing it, is all." Heard, as in hissed, snarled, taunted, and gloated. If my iPad hadn't disappeared, I'd translate the word. I'd be better prepared for them if I understood what they're saying.

Alessandro's horde keep saying it like it's a huge secret I'm not privy to.

"Heard where?" With forked eyebrows, Tommaso scans the patio until his attention halts on the horde sunning themselves by the casita. "What exactly are they saying?"

Four days spent hearing it, and despite the limited Italian, I'm confident in my pronunciation. "Sandro odia la sua fidanzata."

"You tell Sandro?"

"We're not speaking."

Tommaso looks pained. "That explains everything."

"So, what does it mean?"

"It means ..." He shakes his head. "... You should ignore it."

I glance at the women, wishing them sunburns on their bared breasts, then mutter, "I wish I could."

"That bad?" he asks like he genuinely cares. Alessandro called him his "best man," so it's strange my only friend is this hulking brute.

"Bad. I can't call my grandparents today. Seems my iPad's disappeared."

His scowl's fierce. "Fuck that. I'll handle it."

I flash him a smile. "Thank you."

"In exchange for something else."

That gives me pause. "We bargaining now?"

"Life's a bargain, Riley. Don't you know that by now?" He leans in and brings his mouth near my ear. "And for all our sakes, work things out with him."

I pull back. "He's forgotten me."

Tommaso snorts.

"His villa's overflowing with obedient women."

He folds his arms across his big body and cocks his head. "Then why are you here?"

I laugh, except it's bitter, not sweet. "He kidnapped me."

"If his father learned of your involvement, you'd be dead without questions asked. Believe it or not, this is the best place for you."

I swallow hard. I never considered his father as a threat. "I'm innocent."

"Doesn't matter, Riley. You're disposable."

"And Alessandro?" I can't hide my desperation. "Will he dispose of me, now that he's moved on?"

"Been waiting for his order."

Oh, sweet hell. I view Tommaso in an entirely new light. Not only as a fighter, but Alessandro's problem-solver.

"Four days, right?"

"Yes," I squeak.

"And he hasn't said a goddamn word." His grin catches me off guard. "My advice? Stop hiding and get in his miserable face."

With that, he stalks off.

Whistling as he leaves me standing here, flabbergasted.

MY LIFE HAS BECOME a game of dodge-and-evade, with one glaring exception.

Conti's dodged every attempt to locate him.

Renzo slipped past my men again, this time giving them a scenic tour of the Roman Colosseum.

My father's been ignoring my calls, which means he's avoiding the one topic on both our minds—Alessia Amato.

Even Don Lucchese, my godfather and the toughest old bastard I know, is hanging on by a thread, defying every prediction, ghosting death, and prolonging my inevitable fate.

The exception is my right-hand man, deadly enforcer, and occasional best friend, who's been getting in my face and demanding if I've got any specific orders regarding Riley. Like the asshole's read my mind and is daring me to finally do what needs to be done.

Passing on a hard scene or a good blow job, from a litter of willing women eager to get me off at this late hour, I instead head to the pool to burn off steam. Only to discover it occupied by the woman behind all my recent mindfucks.

I stop dead in my tracks.

She's drifting in my pool, eyes closed, lounging on a pink flamingo float. The ridiculously tiny black bikini she's wearing is doing a shit job of covering her luscious curves, and there's a drink lazily balanced in her hand.

Jesus, the sight of her gets under my skin.

I resist the urge to shout for Tommaso. This is fucking unacceptable. She's fair game right now. An open invitation to any man passing by—not that my men would dare touch what's mine. But her gorgeous body ... those tits ... could tempt even the most devoted man to sin.

The beast inside me both terrifies and excites her—just as I intended. But she needs to be broken in. I won't tolerate her looking at me with those wounded eyes, as if I committed a crime against her delicate sensibilities. She's been doing it since dinner. I warned her I'd corrupt her. What did she expect, rainbows and roses?

Time she learned I am who I am.

And the thrill to be had from a good fucking hunt.

I drain my whiskey, the glass cool against my lips, before hurling it over my shoulder. Kicking off my shoes, I tuck my Rolex into one and toss them aside.

Fuck it.

I dive into the pool, sacrificing an expensive suit and four days of pretending she doesn't drive me insane.

The flamingo floatie is less than an arm's stretch away when I surface.

She starts paddling frantically, trying to escape, but the float flips, sending her crashing into the pool. She kicks out, hitting me in the thigh, then thrusts her other leg into my chest to push herself away. Wide-eyed, she treads water, staring at me, realizing the fun is over—yet completely unaware the real game is just beginning.

I throw out a hand, snatch her bikini bottom, and draw her in, then anchor an arm around her waist and haul her toward the shallow end of the pool.

"You dove in to get me."

I ignore the unspoken question in her tone—the one that questions my sanity. With one arm beneath her knees, I lift her out of the water, carrying her across the pool patio into the casita.

"You ruined your suit."

"That isn't what should concern you right now." I abruptly set her on her feet, and she throws out a hand, catching my arm for balance.

"But I guess you're good at ruining things," she continues, bitterness lacing her words.

My tone is low and threatening. "That's right. And in a few minutes, my suit won't be the only thing I ruin."

"Why don't you snap a finger and beckon a woman more willing to be bossed around?" She draws to her full height and glares at me. Not yet understanding the rules of the game, or even that it's begun. The anticipation makes my dick hard, despite how I find myself wanting to play with *her*, when my needs can easily be fulfilled elsewhere.

It's the question of the fucking decade. And I have to say, this self-imposed monogamy bullshit frustrates me. "A snap of my finger is how I like things," I sneer. "You just need to accept who's in charge." She tenses further, so I lean in to slam the issue home. "I fuck who I want to fuck. Tonight, you'll do."

She chokes on her own breath, her shock palpable. "Excuse me?"

"You heard me."

"I'll do," she repeats, disbelief in her tone.

"That's right."

A heavy silence falls between us, her chest heaving as anger vibrates through her body. I almost smirk, enjoying the fire in her eyes. Fucking hell, why does she have to be this gorgeous? Her wet hair curls against her cheekbones, the unruly mess giving her a just-been-screwed vibe. Her tan emphasizes those hypnotic green eyes— which now sparkle with an irresistible challenge. The sadistic part of me wants to squash her anger and remind her she'll do as I command because that's how our arrangement works. But the truth is, I crave her sweet submission.

I've fucking missed it.

Goddamn her.

Grinding my teeth, I force out the words, "You'll more than do."

"I don't understand."

Statement of the fucking century.

"What happened? Did you grow tired of *them?*"

I scowl. Have I?

Jesus.

The night air's interrupted by her sigh. "Alessandro, why won't you let me go? Don't you know by now you can trust me? I won't say a word. Living here with them is ..."

Her voice trails off as I stalk over to the bureau and retrieve a key, before returning to where she's standing, intently watching me. Dropping to my knee, I remove her ankle monitor and toss it aside. I make a mental note to replace it, now that it's likely ruined.

"You actually listened to me?" Her tone is incredulous. "You're releasing me?"

I straighten. "You get a one-minute head start."

Her jaw practically hits the floor as she struggles to process that the game is fucking on.

I lean in, brush my lips against her ear, and enlighten her. "You better fucking run, Riley. But know, when I catch you—because I'll always catch you—you'll give it up like a good, obedient girl. I want to pound that pussy so hard, you won't be able to run again."

She shivers.

I begin counting off in my head.

Then, with a soft gasp, she's off.

Let the hunt begin.

———

I HIT the pool deck at a dead run.

One minute to escape him, and then a lifetime to look back over the troublesome choices I've made.

If he doesn't catch me.

If I can thwart his promise to do so.

Fear licks up my spine, but it's tangled up with something else— exhilaration. He made love to me the last time he was inside me. Who's to say this won't lead to a more meaningful connection again?

No, Riley. Wrong. Wrong. Wrong. *He promised a pounding. A domination of your body, not your heart.*

I glance over my shoulder and spy him in the door. His wet suit molded to his muscular body. His expression firm with intent. He licks his lips like a hungry beast, and I nearly stumble. How can a man be this electric? How many times do I allow myself to get burned before nothing remains but ash?

Tonight, I'll *do*.

My sprint takes on a new urgency. I'm not a housemaid, waiting on his beck and call. If he wants me, he can work for it.

I burst through the kitchen door. Cross the tile floor, bare feet sliding to a stop at the staircase. I won't outrun him, but maybe I can outsmart him. He'll expect me to head outside where freedom can be found through the gardens or at the beach. It's a risky choice not to hide right away—or to put as much distance between us as humanly possible. But I make it upstairs, push into the last place he'll search— his private suite of rooms—and then keep running, ignoring the closet and bathroom for the exercise room next door.

It's dark inside, which works to my advantage. Pulse pounding, I duck behind a punching bag, and then try to rein in my thoughts and fail.

Will he punish me if he catches me? Take me over his knee like he's always threatening to do and spank me? Or will he command me to press my tits together and offer my body up as a canvas for his seed? I bite my lip as excitement shivers through my body. God, why him? Why do I crave his darkness like it's a naughty treat?

It's so quiet I can hear my heart beating, and as a few more minutes pass, I'm convinced I've evaded capture.

But what now? Because if I wait too long and don't escape the villa, he'll return to his ...

His voice cuts through the silence. "You can run and hide, baby ..." I muffle my gasp because he's close, like a few feet away. "... but I'm never fucking letting you go."

Suddenly, the exercise room is flooded with light and my surprised reaction's reflected from various angles in the mirrors lining the back wall.

Flashing me a sinister smile, he enters the exercise room.

I bolt for the door.

His footsteps quicken behind me.

I reach it but not fast enough, and as a shriek escapes me, he slams into my back and pins me against it. Bucking wildly, I attempt to dislodge his massive weight.

"Keep rubbing your ass against my dick like that and your pussy will weep when I fuck you." He thrusts forward, and I feel every inch of his massive erection.

And then, spurred on by some inner demon, I slowly roll my bottom against him in response.

His hiss is music. Hard rock.

I almost smile because clearly insanity's taken hold. But then I'm plucked off my feet, dropped facedown onto a long padded bench, and positioned to his liking before he straddles my hips, and with very little effort, pins my arms overhead.

Water from his suit drips onto the curve of my ass, and the bench beneath me vibrates from my pounding heart.

"How did you find me?"

He wiggles something in front of my face for me to see—my black bikini top. Oh, sweet hell. I'm so worked up, and because it weighs practically nothing, I wasn't even aware it'd fallen off.

Given his breast obsession, why didn't he roll me out on my back? I'm still beneath him, cognizant these aren't the kind of thoughts I should be having right now.

"The beach would have been a better choice." His voice rumbles. "More space to chase you down like a wild gazelle."

My breath hitches, and I'm suddenly lightheaded.

"Ask me what I'd do next," he murmurs darkly in my ear.

My voice quivers as I reply, "What would you do next?"

"Mark you. Claim you. Show you in every damn way imaginable that you're mine."

Everything around me pauses. My mind drifts, leaving my body to float in a sea of what-ifs. What if he really means it? What if our undeniable connection leads to something deeper, something lasting? What if he actually cares about me?

"Don't fucking move, capisci?"

I nod.

He lifts off me, and movement rustles behind me. Anticipation tingles up my spine. "What will you do?"

His tone is downright sinister. "Toughen you up."

Alarmed, I glance over my shoulder.

Oh God. His jaw's tight with intent. His white shirt clings to his muscles and outlines every inch of his powerful frame as he rolls up his sleeves. The belt he's holding sways in the air between us.

"Are you about to spank me?"

"Fuck yeah."

The idea excites him. "Will it hurt?" Because my skin stung when I marked my breasts with the same leather belt, though his reaction to the sight was worth it.

"You need to be broken in."

My eyes widen. "What does that mean?"

"I've been too fucking careful with you, and it's time I stop holding back."

My throat goes dry. He whipped those brunettes while I watched. Forced his cock down my throat. Choked me. And that was him holding back?

"Violence is who I am. I can't have you casting doe eyes at me every time I knife some stranzo or worse. Tonight, you'll dance the fine line between pain and pleasure."

"And if I say no?" Because I should. Violence *is* who he is, and who's to say he won't actually harm me?

He stares at me blankly, his expression unreadable. So in control. So dominant. So beautiful, it hurts. And then, his lips lift into a maddening grin, and I'm thunderstruck.

It takes another minute to realize why he's smiling.

He was waiting for me to say no.

Right here and now, my decision's made.

"Mark me. Claim me. Show me in every possible way you're *mine* as much as I'm yours."

His smile vanishes. "Fuck."

I grin, then turn away. "Go on. Punish me, then."

The first lash makes me jump, and it stings a lot more than I anticipated. As do the next few lashes. I grit my teeth and brace for more, willing myself not to cry.

He surprises me by placing a palm over the burn. "You're so fucking beautiful, you know that?"

The reverence in his tone quickens my heart.

"Goddamn it." He wraps his fingers around my ankles and tugs me backward until I'm hanging over the bench. "I hate how much I want you."

"What?" His words sting in a way that's ten times more powerful than his belt. A compliment followed by a low blow is like receiving roses only to discover nothing but thorns in the bouquet.

"I fucking hate how I can't get enough of you. How I can't follow through on one simple act and punish you the way I do the others."

The *others*.

I kick him in the knee and, as he falls back with a muttered curse, spring from the bench. All my what-ifs crescendo into no-more.

"What the fuck?" he demands.

"You hate me?"

"That's not what I said."

We glare at each other. The tension between us grows thick enough that you can cut a slice of it.

"Get your ass back on the bench."

"Let me go."

He frowns in confusion, then steps closer and mutters my name in warning. "Riley."

Before I can stop myself, the words spill out. "You hurt me."

Alarm flashes in his eyes as he spins me around, and my heart skips a beat. He cares.

"Which blow?" he demands.

For someone so clever and controlling, he's utterly clueless, isn't he? I face him, take his hand and press it against my heart. "Here."

He snatches his hand away like I doused it with gasoline and set it on fire. "What the fuck?"

If he truly wants me on a deeper level, he needs to toughen up. "You, with those *others*, hurts me."

I brace myself, expecting him to throw his hired harem in my face.

"Go. Get out of here."

I blink in surprise. "You'll allow me to leave?"

"Leave?" He laughs, a harsh, bitter sound. "Not on your life."

I hesitate, drawn to the wildness in his manner, like my honest confession has shaken him.

"Go," he roars, loud enough to wake the entire villa. "Get out of my sight before I destroy my goddamn destiny."

Perplexed, I follow his command and flee, wondering why—of all reasons to push me away—he chose destiny.

* * *

Alessandro

PARADISE IN HELL is what this trip to Italy's become.

I designed this villa to my exact liking—clean white accents, immaculately groomed grounds, and a staff handpicked to suit my every preference. It's supposed to be my sanctuary, an escape from a world I've no control over.

But ever since Riley dropped her hurt bomb, I'm suffocating here.

I push Barbara off my lap and, once more, curse Riley beneath my breath. For two days, I've reverted to old habits. Women parade in and out of the casita, a sight any man would give his right nut for, yet none of them hold any appeal. A few favorites have tried—Barbara being the wickedest, touching me and even climbing onto my lap uninvited—but they've only confirmed my suspicions.

I'm completely, utterly fucked.

A change of scenery will clear my head. That, and catching Dante red-handed, doing whatever nefarious bullshit he's up to in Sicily.

The hunt for Conti continues. Capturing Renzo is proving to be challenging, to say the least. Something's got to give, sooner than later.

Barbara pouts as I sidestep her and exit the casita. I cross the pool deck and enter the villa, then find my way upstairs. Tense and troubled, I forget to fix myself a whiskey to help me sleep off my frustrations. It's not until I reach the mezzanine level that I see Riley's door is partially open.

Tommaso was told to lock her up tonight.

Not to keep her in, but me out.

I pause in indecision, and then stalk toward her room and push inside.

She's asleep on a bare mattress, naked and exposed, completely defenseless against any stronzo who might stroll into her bedroom and take advantage of her.

This is inexcusable. "Tommaso!" I bellow.

Riley jolts up, mouth open and eyes wide like a woman possessed. "What's happening?" she exclaims, looking around wildly, her gorgeous body on full fucking display.

I rip my dress shirt off and toss it at her. "Cover yourself."

She frowns but obeys.

Tommaso appears a few minutes later, dragging ass like I woke him up.

Probably did.

I point to Riley, who's curled into a ball, and is staring at us with sad kitten eyes.

"Locked up," I grind out. "That's what I said."

Brow wrinkling, he wiggles the door handle. "It's unlocked."

"No shit."

We turn to Riley for an explanation.

She shrugs a shoulder, nonchalant. "Your staff enjoy keeping me entertained."

With a frown, I search the room. It's completely bare. No chairs. No lamp. No goddamn bedding.

"Jesus," Tommaso exclaims. "You said bad, not viciously bullied."

"The service here sucks." Her eyes narrow on me. "But you like that, don't you?"

"Bullied?" I charge across the room to the closet, throw the door open, and find it completely empty. "Where are the clothes I bought you?"

"Did you think your fuckdolls didn't notice?" Her voice is calm, her tone cold, and I almost don't recognize it. "You favored me temporarily. They didn't like it. And this is what I've been reduced to. While you were fucking them, they were fucking me over."

"I wasn't fucking anyone," I grind out. Should have been. Every. Goddamn. Day.

She comes up on her knees, spitting fire. "Fucking, spanking, testing out your new chaise."

"Easy," Tommaso warns her.

Her attention snaps toward him. "Hard to get in his face ..." She jabs a finger in the air at me. "... when it's buried between another woman's thighs."

"Christ's sake," Tommaso mutters.

"If I want to eat pussy, I eat pussy," I thunder. "If I want to fuck, I fuck. If I want my women crawling and begging for my dick, that's what they do." And like some limp dick stronzo, I've gone days without any of it.

"Must be lucky to have that freedom," she sasses back. Her cheeks are flushed. Her gorgeous green eyes a shade darker in anger. Without an ounce of fear. No longer afraid of me, is she?

"Sandro ..."

"Freedom," I proclaim. "You believe you're trapped? Join the fucking club, baby. If I had a choice, this ..." I mimic her gesture and jab a finger between us. "... would be different."

"Don't," she chokes out. She's shaking, and I don't like it. Not. At. All.

"Riley..."

"I should have answered you during the car ride home."

"But you didn't."

She glances down at her folded hands. "No."

"Go on. Say it now," I push. Except do I want her hatred? Or do I crave the opposite? That thought eases my anger better than yesterday's joint.

"You're cruel."

"You're goddamn beautiful."

Tommaso clears his throat. "On that note ..."

"Wait," I demand. Calmer. "Staff meeting. Get *them*."

"Now? It's close to 1 a.m."

"Just do it."

"Yes, boss." Except he doesn't immediately leave. "Tell him what they've been saying to you, sweetheart."

I go rigid. "Sweetheart ..."

He grins at me. "I love it when you prove me right."

I wait for him to leave, and then for her to speak.

She rolls her lip between her teeth in that innocent way that makes me immediately hard, and she quietly studies me.

"What have they been saying, Riley?"

"I don't know what it means ... and perhaps it's nothing ..."

"Nothing, like the bullying? Nothing, like your feelings toward me?"

She draws a breath. "Sandro odia la sua fidanzata."

The truth blindsides me, and I see red. This is my villa. My sanctuary. And they've soiled it with bullshit I can't seem to escape.

"Alessandro, please," she pleads, reading my reaction perfectly. "Don't hurt them. They're jealous, is all."

"I'll have my man pack a bag after he returns with your wardrobe. You're coming to Sicily with me tomorrow."

"If that's what you want ..."

I pin her with a look.

"Okay," she squeaks, but then curiosity creeps in. "What does the expression mean?"

"Sandro hates his girlfriend," I say, and feeling my night turning ass end up, shift the conversation. "Nine a.m. Be ready."

She looks relieved, and I escape the room.

Italians use the same word with different meanings. Sandro *odia la sua fidanzata?*

Even if Riley were my girlfriend, I couldn't hate her. My feelings are not even close to hatred.

But what is fucking true?
Alessandro *odia la sua fidanzata*.
Alessandro hates his *fiancée*.

CHAPTER 22

Riley

IT'S impossible to remain angry with a man who ravages your body with his eyes as you bare your soul to him beneath the full brunt of his attention. I'm dining on an expensive yacht's deck on a twelve-hour cruise to Sicily, and—aside from the small crew tending to us—am highly unsettled by the thought of spending so much alone time with such an unpredictable man.

Out on open water, the world seems vast, and we're simply two tiny figures frantically navigating life. Fate's brought us together, ripped us apart, and now is having a good laugh at my expense. It's much easier being angry than emotionally sabotaged this way.

He licks the red wine stain from his lips, and my breath hitches in my throat. He has no business looking like a CEO anticipating the glory of a hostile takeover.

And I'm the target in his sights.

"Did you wear the bathing suit like I asked?"

I reply with a simple nod. The white crochet bikini is tiny, with two triangles covering my areolas and a third my sex. Over top, I'm wearing a sheer white cover-up.

There's no hiding from this man.

His shining blue eyes say he knows it, too.

"Nothing to say?"

A soft sigh escapes me. "Not really."

With a pensive stare, he pulls a joint from his pocket, places it between his lips, lights it, and reclining in his chair, inhales.

My jaw goes slack.

He watches my reaction with amusement, and then blows out smoke. "I've been neglecting our arrangement."

Sometimes, like now, it feels like we're so close. Other times, far, far away. "You've been *busy*."

"I fired them."

Everything within me stills. "Because they touched the clothing you purchased me?"

His expression gives nothing away, but his next words ring loud and clear. "No one hurts you but me."

I duck my head to hide the ridiculous flush flooding my cheeks. He might be smoking a blunt, but I'm suddenly high, dizzying so. Caution has me asking, "What happens when you grow bored with me?"

He crosses his ankles, his gaze steady. "That's the crux of the problem, isn't it?"

Seconds turn into minutes as I wait for him to elaborate. Then he curls a finger at me, gesturing me closer.

I stand and round the table.

Without warning, he tugs me onto his lap. "Better."

"Is it?"

"Twelve hours is all I ask." He leans his head back and takes another drag, the sweet, woodsy scent tickling my nose.

"Right. Twelve hours is *all* you *ask*?" To do what, exactly? Dine on deck? Get stoned? Play with me, make me hope for more, then toss me aside on the shelf of forgotten toys?

He chuckles.

My eyebrows prop up the sky.

"Hyperbole."

Insanity. That he's offering me an English lesson along with twelve hours of God knows what.

"Smoke?"

"Um ... I never ..."

His face is close, so close, then he blows smoke over my head. "Always so perfectly corruptible."

Everything about this situation is unfamiliar. I fully expected to be seated silently on an airplane and watching him work.

"And you enjoy corrupting me?"

"Press your lips to mine, and I'll remind you that I do."

I arch up, like a fool, and after taking another hit, he presses his mouth to mine. My lips part on his exhale, then he withdraws with a smile. "Close your mouth and suck the smoke into your lungs."

I do, then cough.

He waits for me to recover before his lips crash against mine. Our tongues tangle, and his earthy taste hits my taste buds.

Everything about this is mind-blowing.

I like this side of him.

He breaks the kiss. "One more hit, and then I'll lay you out across the front deck and fuck away days of getting off only with my hand."

My hand shakes from his admission as I pluck the joint from his fingers and place it between my lips. He told me last night that he hadn't gone through with his threat and touched any of those bitches. But I didn't believe him, until now.

His eyes brighten as he watches me smoke.

Butterflies erupt in my stomach—I'm more attracted to him now than I ever was. I inhale sharply, and my throat suddenly burns. Gasping, I drop the joint, and then erupt into a coughing fit.

"Easy, baby." He caresses my shoulders and back of my neck, and I calm beneath his touch.

"I dropped it."

"Doesn't matter." He rolls to stand with me in his arms. "I'm in the mood for something sweeter."

Alessandro

I'M FEELING MORE content than I have in years as she settles onto a blanket I've rolled out on deck. Tommaso's receiving a huge fat raise for booking the yacht instead of the plane ticket I asked for. Yeah, it'll take longer to get to Sicily, but the anticipation of sinking into Riley's sweet body and fucking her until the sun sets on the horizon has me tearing off my dress shirt and kicking off my pants in a rush.

She lifts onto her knees to slip off the white cover-up. Her body strains against that tiny bikini. My girl's so fucking gorgeous, it hurts.

My girl.

Mine.

For as long as I can keep her.

"You look funny," she murmurs.

"You look sexy as fuck."

It's not lost on me I've wasted precious time denying I want her. My sore fingers from days spent jerking off are proof. A warning label should be attached to this woman; highly addictive and may cause lunacy, chaos, and ruin.

"Why do you keep looking at me that way?"

"What way?" I deny it, still.

"Like you can't decide whether to hurt me or fuck me."

When did she become this brazen?

To prove my point, her greedy gaze drops to my dick, and then my girl licks her lips. A rush of blood has me hard within seconds. Does a more perfect woman exist? A man will never grow tired of her reaction to his dick.

My dick.

My girl.

Jesus, what's wrong with me? Next, I'll be reciting Shakespearean sonnets or some other shit. I cup my dick crudely to ruin the effect she has on me. "Ask me to fuck you," I command in a hard voice.

"Don't tell me you don't feel it too?"

Fuck you, Shakespeare.

I'll keep her as my sidepiece. Locked inside my villa, out of sight and harm's way. Toss away the key so she'll never escape. Because she'll want to. If my girl—with her fucked-up past, daddy issues, and eagerness to submit to me, who's offered herself up with such astonishing trust that I demand but don't deserve—discovers the truth, she'll say the three words she's reluctant to utter.

I hate you.

My father won't change his mind. Alessia Amato is back in Rhode Island, waiting for the church bells to ring. Trapped in a hate-love triangle—with me on one end and my stubborn father on the other. Don Lucchese is happy. They are counting Benjamins at the financial benefits of bringing the daughter of a prominent politician into the *famiglie.* Governor Amato's new business tax breaks in New York are just the start.

And Renzo, the shithead who should be in my shoes, runs amok while giving two middle fingers to the world. He thinks he's so clever. Yet no one understands him better than his twin. If I'm made to suffer, so will he. The difference is it's what's best for him.

Just like being the Beneventi heir suits me better.

Why make it more difficult than it already is?

"Alessandro." Her voice cuts through.

I draw on a rage simmering like lava beneath the surface.

Except I'm stoned.

And she's staring at me with soft kitten eyes. "Are you having weird side effects from the pot?"

"What?"

"You disappeared for a moment."

And I'll disappear inside her warm pussy for twelve hours more. "You hungry for my cock, baby?"

"Yes."

All thought goes straight to my dick.

We lock eyes.

Without shying away, she slowly, ever so slowly, tugs her bikini top aside.

Fuck. I'll never get over the sight.

"Lick me."

My ears perk up ... Did she ...

"I want your filthy mouth on my pussy."

"Either I'm never letting you smoke again or buying a fucking dispensary." I grin like a madman. If my goal was to corrupt her, holy fuck have I succeeded.

"Please, Alessandro." She rolls back onto her elbows and parts her thighs. My eyes shift from her face to her breasts to the tiny stretch of material barely covering her pussy.

Something inside me snaps.

I drop to my knees then, as she gasps, shove my face into her waiting warmth. I suck at the material and shake my head like an animal, ripping the bikini off her body with my teeth, then spitting it to the side.

"Oh my God," she exclaims.

I hook my elbows beneath her knees and raise her hips. Her arousal fills my nostrils, sweet, musky, and all mine. Hell yeah. I can feel her tightness milking my cock already, and I have barely touched her.

It won't kill me to be gentle, right? Ironic how I threatened to prolong her gratification if she ran, yet I'm the one who's been running. Denying myself her addictive pussy and instead distancing myself, keeping her on her knees and always an arm's length away. A fool who preferred not to believe her for fear of losing her.

"Is this your idea of delayed gratification?"

I tear my eyes away from her sweet pussy. And then I fucking grin. "You've been thinking about it, baby?"

"Yes." Her simple admission is music to my ears. Except there's one problem—the beast within me who won't be delayed, denied, forgotten.

"No."

Her glossy green eyes widen.

I lick her from the bottom landing strip to her clit, and then raise my head. "I want you coming hard, repeatedly." I do it again, with more force, and she wiggles and squirms in my arms. So responsive. So eager.

So exquisitely perfect.

I dive in and go to town, licking her and fucking her like a man possessed. And I am ... Why deny it any longer?

She grips my hair and gently tugs me closer. I let her. If my girl deludes herself into believing she has any control, so be it. Though I do go harder and faster, plunging mercilessly into her while pressing my thumb against her clit.

She moans my name, and I still. "Alessandro. Please, Alessandro."

How many orgasms will it take to make her forget that fucker Al?

I tilt her up, drive my tongue deep, and grin like a fool as she goes off like a rocket. Withdrawing, I suck on her clit until she can't take any more.

But we're far from done.

I crawl over her limp body and, with an unsteady hand, drag my raging erection across her excitement. Whatever control I still have slips. I need inside like fucking yesterday.

"Look at me."

Her eyes flash open.

I thrust deep.

It's hard to say what gets me off more, her wide-eyed bewilderment or her greedy pussy squeezing around me, missing me almost as much as I missed her. "I've failed."

"Failed?"

"At breaking you in." I withdraw, and then slam home. "All the fucking back in New York, and you still fit snug as a glove."

She reaches up to cup my face. "There's really only ever been you."

Fuck. Her admission makes me want to howl. I'm a possessive fucker, yet something about her brings it out in extremes.

I'll figure out a way to keep her.

Mine.

I lean in and kiss her, catching her surprised gasp in my throat. And then with great control, I move, pulling back and sinking deep with slow, methodic movements.

Sweet Riley's tongue matches the rhythm. Fucking my mouth as my cock fills her up. I'm rarely slow and never soft, and always after my own filthy pleasures. This is different. And as her beautiful breasts bounce beneath me, her warm body surrounds me, and her heart races against mine, like a man in uncharted territory who knows when he's landed a good thing, I give in to the intense pleasure.

Our lips never part. Not when she's moaning. Not when I'm struggling not to release my load into her like a randy teen. Prolonged gratification, my ass.

Her thighs clench my hips tighter, seconds before my girl breaks our kiss with a scream.

I slam home deep, and then shake with pleasure as I pump her full of seed.

Cock still buried inside her, I lie part on her, part off.

Stealing time, like a thief.

Holding her, as if I'll never let her go.

CHAPTER 23

Riley

COMPARED to Alessandro's stoic white villa surrounded by lush green landscapes and the blue waters of Sardinia ... Catania, Sicily is grey. It's because the buildings are made of Mount Etna's lava rock, the active volcano spitting steam off in the distance.

We travel in silence, Alessandro deep in thought while I'm unwilling to interrupt it, fearful of breaking the fragile bond between us. The moody scenery mirrors our relationship, doesn't it? A constant navigation through shades of grey, where the soul-crushing darkness is balanced by beautiful blinding light? Alessandro and I walk an endless tightrope between the two, don't we?

But as we travel Sicily's roads in a black rented Ferrari, heading out of the city into the rolling hills surrounding it, life bustles around us. Giving me hope that we, too, can break through tumultuous times.

And holy hell was yesterday a strong step forward.

I touch the hickey on my neck. A second one marks my right breast. A third, my inner thigh. "Reminders of who owns you," he growled against my breast in a sleepy, satisfied tone. As if making love to me over and over again wasn't enough to convince me.

He was relentless.

Gentle.

Everything I've ever wanted him to be.

For twelve hours on a yacht, in his arms, him *inside me*, we lived in a bubble.

Is it better not knowing he could be a tender lover?

Is it better not imagining he might care?

My thoughts might be loud, but I dread the moment things go pop, so I keep quiet and wait for him to speak.

Nearly a half hour later, we turn off the road and down a gravel driveway flanked by cypresses. Alessandro drives around a large ornate fountain set before an old yet charming farmhouse. An older man waits on the porch to greet us.

I hesitate, unsure what to do.

"You like pistachios?" Alessandro demands.

"Yes."

"Then you're in fucking luck. Come on, let's go. Speak when he addresses you, capisci?" His eyes meet mine, and then rake over me. Hungrily, and not for nuts.

A familiar warmth settles over me.

"Don Gallo's a business associate."

"Mafiosi?" I blurt out.

He arches an eyebrow. "You're part of my world now, baby."

My heart climbs into my throat. *Part of his world?*

He exits the car before I fully recover, paralyzed by hope. Does he see a future with me? Because it sounds like he does.

He embraces the older man, and then turns and waves at me. The second I draw near, he grabs my hand and tugs me along as we enter the farmhouse.

Don Gallo was expecting us, evident in the farm-size table set with enough food to feed an army.

"La tua fidanzata è bellissima, Alessandro."

Alessandro's hand tightens around mine, while I string together the Italian words I know. *"Beautiful girlfriend."* I flash Don Gallo a smile for the compliment, then wait for Alessandro to correct the assumption.

"È stupenda, vero?" he smoothly replies. "She's gorgeous."

I tremble beneath his scorching look.

"Only English?" Don Gallo interrupts, before I combust into ashes.

"Yes, Don Gallo."

"So polite. She's a keeper, Alessandro." He spins toward the stealer of hearts. "I hope you brought your appetite."

"Always, Don Gallo. Along with my checkbook. My father would like us to discuss expanding our profit margins on green gold."

The man laughs.

Alessandro must read the confusion on my face. "The pistachio market's exploded worldwide. Who would have thought fucking nuts could be worth over four billion US dollars with a four percent growth estimate?"

Yes, I knew Alessandro was intelligent. But watching him in real time makes my lady parts hum.

Our eyes meet, and my knees wobble.

Don Gallo clears his throat. "If you'd like to clean up before we eat, il bagno is down the hallway." He gestures in the desired direction, but Alessandro already has me by the hand and is dragging me along.

We enter.

He pushes my back into the door and shuts it.

And then his lips slam into mine.

His kiss is aggressive. I come up onto my toes and give myself over to it, as our tongues mash together. Fire reignites between us, and then consumes us until we break away, panting with need. "I want to take your virgin ass right here against the bathroom door while the old man waits."

Oh my God. Is he serious?

And how can I want that? How will I sit through lunch?

The devil grins.

Teasing me, and he knows I was about to submit, too.

He presses a gentle kiss on my lips. "I fucking want to in the worst way. But I can't disrespect Don Gallo, capisci?"

"Yes," I grumble. I need to be careful around this version of Alessandro Beneventi, or I'll lose my heart fast.

He unzips his trousers.

"I thought..."

He steps up to the toilet.

Lord, men can be so wickedly coarse.

"Your turn," he tosses over his shoulder after finishing, flushing the toilet and then moving to the sink to wash his hands.

I will *not* pee in front of him.

"Not keen on showing me your tender little pussy right now?" Another laugh fills the air. Who is this man?

"Very well. But don't be too long. I'm fucking famished."

He exits and closes the door behind him.

I lean back on it, completely unhinged.

A few minutes pass, and I use the modern amenities and freshen up.

Exiting, I follow the hallway to the dining room, only to end up in a large living area. Wrong direction, Riley.

I'm about to retrace my steps when the window across the room is flung open. I freeze, then watch a girl a few years younger than me hoist herself over the frame and inside. Her dress slides up, and I immediately look away. Because she's not wearing underwear.

"Oh, shit," she exclaims. "You frightened the hell out of me."

I turn back toward her as she closes the window behind her. Her black hair is wild, her cheeks flushed, and if I'm not mistaken, she has a nearly identical hickey on her neck. I'm too stunned to respond.

"Please tell me I didn't miss lunch?"

I blink. "No."

"Thank you, sweet Jesus." She strides across the room. "That your car outside?"

"My ..." Boyfriend? Lover? Kidnapper?

"Let me guess. Dante's fratello rented it?"

I recognize the word fratello, as well as the name associated with it—Dante. But don't correct her, not that she's giving me the opportunity, as I track her quick progress across the floor.

"Do me a favor, girl to girl. Don't share that you saw me."

"My lips are sealed," I reply. What would I say, anyway? That I encountered a barely dressed wild child with a hickey on her neck sneaking into the farmhouse through a window?

"See you in a few minutes."

I hurry back down the hallway and reenter the dining room.

Both men are standing, politely waiting for me.

Alessandro pulls out my chair, and I sit.

They follow suit.

A server comes to pour us wine. "White," Don Gallo says. "To complement the dishes."

The aroma of pistachios fills the air. It takes me a moment to realize every dish on the table includes them, even the pasta.

"Catania specials," the proud man informs us. It's hard to believe a man this enthusiastic about farming is a mafioso.

We wait, and although no explanation is offered, I'm well aware who is late to lunch.

She comes racing in a few minutes later with a flurry of rapid Italian excuses. "Mi scuso, padre. Mi sono addormentato nella mia stanza e ho perso la cognizione del tempo. Spero di non aver fatto aspettare troppo i tuoi ospiti?" She abruptly stops, her eyes sweeping over Alessandro. She recovers, and then offers him a polite nod, the picture of innocence in her somber, high-collared dress more fitting for winter than the dead heat of summer. "Don Beneventi."

"Alessandro," he corrects. "And you must be Luna Cecilia Gallo?"

I watch her closely as she looks confused and turns to her father for help. Curious how she doesn't recognize her own name, especially since Alessandro pronounced it in Italian.

"Failed her English classes, I'm sorry to admit. My principessa only speaks Italian."

My lips part. What?

The wild child's eyes meet mine, almost daring me to rat her out.

Except I don't. I've my own worries to contend with without causing more trouble by ruining her fun. With Dante? I'd bet ten sacks of pistachios I'm right.

Lunch begins, and the men talk business in Italian.

Not that I'm completely ignored, not with the principessa's curious glances. Not when Alessandro places his palm on my lap, his fingers dangling precariously close to my already sensitive nerves.

"Cos'è questa storia che Dante Lucchese ha acquistato il terreno accanto al tuo?" Alessandro asks. I catch Dante Lucchese's name, but so does Luna as she sits up a little straighter in her chair.

Dante Lucchese gave her that hickey, didn't he?

Except, Alessandro is also staring at her. Like he *knows*.

"Don Lucchese sent his son to secure the land. We were held up at gunpoint a few months ago, and the thieves stole thousands of handpicked pistachios. They pushed around my baby and threatened her life if I didn't put down my weapon. Dante Lucchese bought the land next door days later."

"At his father's request?" Alessandro repeats.

Don Gallo seems confused. "That's what he claims. We haven't had a problem since."

If her father looked closer, he'd realize the loss of pistachio nuts are the least of his problems.

My gaze locks on Alessandro. He doesn't believe that's why Dante is here either, does he?

"Emilio Conti visit my fratello?" The last word is said with clear sarcasm, except I'm more interested in the man's first name. Until now, Alessandro and his men only referred to him as Conti. But Emilio ... Something about his name nags at me, but I can't quite work it out.

"No. Dante met him in Rome months ago. Something about repositioning Atlanta. My men inform me Conti left the meeting furious."

Alessandro seems satisfied. "Lucky he left at all. Hollywood isn't one to take shit."

"Hollywood?" Luna bursts out, her English accent perfect. Realizing her mistake, she begins speaking in rapid Italian. "Ho sempre desiderato visitare la Hollywood Walk of Fame. Sai, dove tutte le famose star del cinema mettono le loro impronte digitali nel cemento? Padre, dovrai portarmi con te un giorno, presto ..."

"Quiet, principessa. Alessandro and Riley aren't here to listen to you ramble on."

She nods, the picture of obedience.

The men turn back to business.

We finish our meal and say our goodbyes. My heart is in my stomach because our trip to Sicily's ending. Will things now be different back in Sardinia?

The brunettes are gone, I reassure myself.

He's holding my hand.

He seems lighter ... happy, even.

We pause outside as Don Gallo waves his hands and enthusiastically describes the new pistachio crop about to be harvested after a two-year wait.

I feel a tug on my elbow.

Luna.

She pulls me out of earshot of the men. "Thank you. I owe you a huge favor."

"Just be careful." I feel obligated as an older woman to warn her.

Instead of being worried, she rolls her eyes. "Your boyfriend's Alessandro Beneventi. You be careful."

CHAPTER 24

Alessandro

"CHANGE IN PLANS. The yacht's been directed to Salerno."

There's a long pause on the other end of the call. We've shit to do, and prolonging this trip upends the meetings I've scheduled tomorrow. I wait for Tommaso to ask why, but he doesn't.

Next to me in the passenger seat of the Maserati, Miss Ears quietly listens. I should make her take her tits out and get us back into familiar territory. "I'm taking this baby for a test drive and am considering purchasing one. The car's fucking sweet."

"You're shitting me, right?"

I scowl.

Riley studies me. Probably preparing for me to lash out, as I'm notorious for doing.

"Because of the car, my ass," Tommaso comments. Perceptive motherfucker.

"Keep talking to me like that and I'll be handing you yours."

Time isn't on my side.

Yet that's exactly what I'm doing—stealing time.

Was it foolish presenting her to Don Gallo as my girl? He might mention it to my father, but the check I wrote to extend nut sales into

231

the US market will more likely be at the heart of any conversation. If my sidepiece accompanies me to the meeting, so fucking what? What, does my father expect celibacy before the vows are read? Which would be rich considering he's likely screwing my fiancée.

Anyway, news that Hollywood still has his star on the Beneventi Walk of Shame is a more interesting topic than who I'm fucking.

She glances up from beneath her lashes and offers me a shy smile.

My dick stirs. Christ, I can't keep my hands off her. I was seconds from taking her virgin ass against Don Gallo's bathroom door. But like the obedient son I am, I refrained from disrespecting a good business associate.

"And Hollywood?" Tommaso asks.

"All clear. Met Conti in Rome to handle an issue with the Atlanta casino expansion. Heard it was ugly."

"It always is with that worm."

I place my arm on the back of her seat and coil a lock of her hair around my finger.

"Your weekly call's tomorrow with Don Beneventi." Dread fills his tone. You'd think he spent his formative years picking daisies in a fucking field instead of burying bodies beneath the soil.

I weigh my answer. But if I call my father from the yacht, it'll raise questions. Fucking pass on that. "Tell him business with Don Gallo went better than expected and I'll review our new arrangement in two days, that something's come up."

"Like your dick."

Jesus. Am I that fucking obvious?

Dusk spills across the horizon, the sun's golden warmth fading into a cool wash of silver. I'm not one for sentiment, but when I catch sight of the lone billboard rising in the distance, I see it for what it is—and opportunity. I'll fuck her right there, driving her into the sunset and back again.

"Gotta go," I tell Tommaso.

"Wait."

I pull off the road and park. "Be quick. I've shit to do."

"I've a present waiting for you." His excitement says our men have done the impossible. But I'm done with business and focused now on pleasure.

"Call you from the yacht." I disconnect, then turn to Riley. "Out, and on the hood."

She turns pink, glances around to be sure no cars are around, and then scrambles out.

By the time I'm in front of the car, she's seated on it.

"On your stomach."

She obeys.

"Should I spank your pretty bottom for your disobedience?" I ask in a silky voice.

She looks over her shoulder at me in confusion. "I thought ..."

"Thought you were a good girl?"

"Yes?"

She was, perfectly so. Even Don Gallo was smitten. "Luna Gallo have something to say that you're not sharing?"

"You knew?"

"That the Don Gallo's principessa is full of shit? Or that my so-called fratello is knee deep in it?"

"She's a girl with a crush."

Riley's gaze softens. And suddenly, my collar burns my neck. Hot, I quickly unbutton my shirt.

"Fuck."

"Alessandro?"

"What?"

She stares at me unflinching. "I'm going to say it."

I still. "That's in the past."

"Not that—this. I love you, Alessandro."

My shirt shreds beneath my fingers, and buttons fly everywhere.

"Show me, then, if you can't say it."

"Riley ..."

My girl flips her skirt. If I wasn't a tit man, I'd be an ass man. Her tight ass is spank bank material. The stuff of wet dreams.

I'm back in control within seconds.

Hands on her hips, I tug her forward until her legs hang over the chrome grill. For a long time, I just look at her.

She wiggles her bottom, teasing me.

I simply stare.

"What are you doing?"

"Taking a mental picture of the beautiful sight."

She groans. "Someone might drive by ..."

I run a palm across her tight ass. "You want it quick and hard, baby?"

"Please."

Music to my fucking ears.

Zipper down, I palm my erection, giving my dick a few firm strokes. Anticipation makes my hand shake—it better be anticipation and nothing to do with her earnest declaration. Stepping closer, I bend her knee, getting a better look at her wet pussy.

Once again, my control slips.

I push inside her so fast, I see stars. Instincts take over, and I flex my hips and sink deeper. "So tight, baby." Then my pace turns frantic, like I can't get deep enough. Inside her warmth is my favorite place to be.

Problem is, my lips are moving quickly, too, and I unleash a litany of love bombs in rapid succession. "Love your tight pussy." "Love how perfect you are." "Love how you were made for me."

"Harder," she demands over the bullshit noise I'm making.

I anchor an arm around her waist and pull her flush against me, fucking her mercilessly now. The car shaking beneath us.

Perfect.

Special.

"Riley." My release tears through me, and my seed jets into her womb. Beneath me—thank fuck—her body shivers as she climaxes hard.

We stay like that for a while, until I withdraw. I roll onto the hood next to her.

She flips onto her back and stretches, a smug smile hugging her lips.

She doesn't bring it up again.

I'll protect her as long as I can—even from myself.

Abruptly, she sits up. "Oh my God."

I follow her gaze up to the billboard. A decaying sign advertising the Grand Hotel di Palermo.

"Alessandro, please tell me you trust me."

My eyes narrow on her. She looks ready to puke.

"I swear, I didn't know until now. Even during your conversation with Tommaso, everyone refers to him as Conti. The first time I heard his first name was at lunch."

What. The. Fuck?

Wide-eyed, she pleads for mercy.

My gaze cuts back to the cause of her abrupt freak-out. Then she delivers a motherfucking bombshell.

"Emilio Smith ... Conti ... is hiding at that resort."

Riley

TWENTY-FOUR HOURS of bliss blows up in my face within seconds. If there was ever a time to be afraid, it's now.

I hang on to the door handle as he drives like a madman, making repeated calls while navigating the roads. Darkness descends long before we reach Salerno. He hasn't uttered a word to me since I made the Conti connection. Does he believe me? Or does he think I withheld information on the man who hurt him?

I can't ask. My attentive lover's turned to dust, and out of the ash the monster's resurfaced.

He makes two stops. Each time, I'm ordered to wait in the car.

I don't protest.

I don't say a peep.

The back door swings open, and a rectangular black bag is flung onto the backseat along with ... "Is that a ...?"

Chain saw.

He glares me back into silence.

The car pulls away from the curb, and then we're winding through a series of alleyways. A few times, the GPS directions lead us astray, which has him cursing and smashing his fist into the steering wheel before recklessly reversing the car down the narrow roads.

When we arrive at the Grand Hotel di Palermo, he parks on a dark side street, and then turns his blistering attention my way. "Listen to me. This is the life, Riley. We mafiosi live in a violent world. An eye for an eye, that's how we deal with issues. Conti knows this, yet still moved to sabotage my famiglia. If Tommaso hadn't warned you, you'd be buried beneath rubble, dead." He punches the steering wheel. "I'll murder that stranzo, and it won't be pretty. I need to know if you're in?"

I consider what he's said. Is he asking if I'm in ... like in love the monster? But there's something else within his words that gives me pause. "Tommaso warned me?" Memories of that morning rush through me. "You had Tommaso call my cell to warn me to get out?"

"You're fucking alive, aren't you?"

He broke up with me that morning. Crushed my soul so it matched my empty heart.

The gunshots. The explosion. "What were you doing while he called me?"

His lips pull into a line. "Fucking up."

I wait, sensing there's more. And I get it, in spades.

"You want the truth? Conti paid Ciro to spy on me, and then sent his men to murder me. They sealed the apartment beneath yours, filled it with fucking gas, set a detonator, and then waited. But I didn't show for three weeks, and the stupid stronzos were too busy drinking lattes and missed me by minutes. But when I spied them outside your building, I went back."

I watch him closely, his frustration with his actions obvious.

"They grabbed me, beat me, and thought they'd chop me up with a chain saw. Turns out, I'm the motherfucking chef. It's Conti's turn now." He turns off the car. "You in?"

After Stephanie's murder sentencing for killing my father, I wanted her dead. Is it evil to feel this way? Yes. But her punishment ended up being a slap on the hand in the form of reduced jail time due to mental issues. The legal system is about whose lawyer knows whom. An eye for an eye ... Yeah, I can see the merit in it.

"Yes. I'm with you, always."

He leans in, and I blink, thinking he's about to kiss me. Instead, he tugs at my dress, parting the neckline. "Go to the reception desk and ask what room Conti's staying in."

"They'll think ..."

"Exactly." He reaches out and presses a roll of euros into my palm. "Just in case."

"Okay." I exit the car, then pick my way along a pebbled road and round the corner toward the main entrance. I smooth my dress but don't fix the collar, entering without hesitation.

The foyer is spectacular, the floor covered in decorative Italian tile and tall white columns dividing the sprawling space. Reception is straight ahead, and I line up for the younger male receptionist to assist me.

When my turn arrives, I swallow back my nerves and lean in. "I have an appointment with Emilio Smith. Where can I find him?"

The man blushes, and I immediately sympathize with him. "Mr. Smith is in a private bungalow, suite number 1235." He plucks a resort map from a stand, then circles the building. "The bungalows are at the back of the property. Follow the winding path from the pool area to reach them."

Alessandro will be pleased. "Thank you."

He rubs his fingers together. The universal sign for "pay up." He's done this before?

Oh my God. He has. And Alessandro knew ...

I peel off a few euro.

He quirks a brow, prompting me to continue.

I hand him a small fortune then wait off to the side until he's occupied before retracing my steps to the car.

A dark figure dressed in black sweats, a black t-shirt, and baseball cap waits by the car. The bag's over his shoulder, and I've no idea where the chain saw is. "Did you know Conti has paid visitors?"

"What do you think?"

I pass him the resort map. "The bungalow he's in is circled."

He studies it intently. "Let's go. I'll park around back."

We circle the car behind the resort and park. Then we're moving. We push through hedges, and he lifts me over a grey stone wall, then creates a path until we draw up behind the bungalows.

He glances at his watch. "Head around front and locate his bungalow. Keep your chin down in case there are cameras."

"Okay," I whisper.

It takes a few seconds to locate Conti's bungalow. It's off to the side and larger than the others. I walk back toward Alessandro, who is talking on the phone. Quickly, I relay the information.

"Stupid *stranzo* is making this easy." His face hardens, and a shiver races up my spine. It's a terrifying sight to see him like this. But this is him, Alessandro Beneventi. An important mafioso's son.

"Stay here, *capisci?*"

I nod.

He flicks his wrist once more to check his watch. "Time to secure my motherfucking legacy," he grinds out, and charges off.

Every sound is magnified. Birds rustling in a nearby bush. Conversations drifting from the bungalow patios or the path out front. Robust laughter from guests in much more pleasant circumstances.

But my thoughts keep returning to the chain saw. Is it still in the backseat of the car? Did he place it in the bag?

What in God's teeth will he do with it? And if that horrible thought isn't enough, how about this one: If he cuts Conti up like he did his men, how will no one hear?

Lord, I'm unprepared for what's about to unfold.

I jump out of my skin when, out of nowhere, a siren goes off. It's louder than ten church bells and more obnoxious than the tornado siren local officials had installed in Marietta. It's so loud, I swear the ground shakes.

I hurry back to the pathway, and find people flooding out of the buildings, coming from every which way. In panicked voices, they talk over the siren, and as an English-speaking couple passes, I learn what's going on.

"Is Mount Etna erupting?"

"No, dear. It's too far away from Salerno. Must be an earthquake's imminent."

An announcement comes over a speaker, which then repeats in English. "Please keep away from the buildings and exit onto the main street."

This isn't really happening, right?

I wait as the bungalow area clears. But the only thing shaking is my nerves. I head in the opposite way from the crowd, toward Conti's location.

Outside, I pause. Because even with the ruckus around me, I can hear the chain saw's hum inside.

Then it all seems to happen in slow motion.

Everything inside goes quiet.

The door swings open.

And Alessandro appears ... covered in blood, chain saw in one hand and the decapitated head of Emilio Conti in the other.

Everything quickly fades to black as my legs buckle and I faint.

CHAPTER 25

Alessandro

I REMAIN in Sicily for two more days while my men clean up the bungalow. Not even Riley's horrified expression as she caught sight of the stranzo's head in my hand can ruin my glory.

I got the fucker.

Alone and barehanded.

My father will love the chain saw twist, and the Eleven will be sitting straighter in their chairs.

As for our enemies, they'll shudder every time they hear one purr to life.

Don Gallo has been managing the local police for me, and the worms on his farm received something rotten to nibble on.

But I'm anxious to get home. Tommaso's informed me Riley hasn't come out of her bedroom in two days. "Traumatized," was how he described her.

"Adjusting," was my response. Because it's not every day you view the man you love in full villain mode. My girl's been through a lot of shit and recovered fine. She'll get over this.

We all do.

There's also a present waiting for me at the villa. The final feather for my cap. Given all my success, maybe my father will be more reasonable? I'm running out of time for him to realize what a huge mistake he's making.

Because only one issue remains.

My upcoming fucking nuptials.

Riley

THE WAILING BEGINS at two in the morning.

Coming from a man in a room nearby, who's in complete and utter agony and making terrifying noises mixed with incoherent words, all except for one.

"Motherfucker!"

He bellows it with such a gut-wrenching emotion, I shoot out of bed.

Alessandro warned me this world is violent. I witnessed it with Ciro's lifeless body swinging from the warehouse rafters. Nothing, though, can erase the image burned into my memory banks of the man I love splattered in blood after viciously beheading his enemy.

It's been a few days since he dropped me off with his man, who escorted me back to the villa. Unnerved, I've kept to my room and balcony in Alessandro's absence.

He arrived home yesterday but has left me alone.

I'm both disappointed and thankful.

I pace back and forth. Is this prisoner a Conti associate? Or is Alessandro eradicating all his enemies in one sweep?

"Aahh. Ohhh." And then a thump.

The silence afterward is positively ominous.

I wait, listening. God, I'm delusional for loving a coldhearted monster.

"Help. I'll die if someone doesn't help me."

Before I lose my nerve, I'm out the door and heading to Alessandro's bedroom. It's locked, so I knock and wait.

Either he's in a deep sleep or elsewhere.

With leaden legs, I trudge back to my room. Except downstairs in the living area, all the lights are on.

I pause as Alessandro's men cross the room, deep in discussion. I sense a shift in the air as bits of conversation drift through. "Funeral." "The Eleven decide." "New capo di tutti capi."

A few more men appear. Strangers I've never seen. The villa walls can barely contain the undeniable tension building.

What's happening?

I pull my new robe closed, and head downstairs to Alessandro's office.

A man stops me outside. "He's busy."

"We need to speak."

"Not tonight, you don't."

I bite my lip. "Ask him."

"His orders are not to be interrupted."

My stomach drops. "Who's in there with him?" On instinct, I act, feigning to the left, surprising his man by brushing by him on the right. Halfway inside, he snatches my elbow.

The office is dark, but I spy Alessandro immediately.

Behind his desk.

His head in his hands.

Alone.

"Alessandro."

The guard's grip is firm, and I struggle to free myself. "What's wrong?"

I'm pulled backward, out into the hallway.

There's no way he didn't hear me.

Yet he never looked up.

CHAPTER 26

Riley

THE NEXT MORNING, I discover Alessandro's big body slumped in the hallway in front of the prisoner's room. Head bowed, like the weight on his shoulders has become unbearable.

I fall onto my knees beside him, then place the back of my hand on his forehead, worried he's ill.

In a blink, I'm pitched sideways and pinned to the floor.

"What the fuck, Riley?" He glares down at me for a few heart-beats, and then rolls off and tugs me up to a seated position. "Go back to your room."

I flinch but hold my ground. "What's happening?"

"Fucking time, that's what's happening."

"Who's in there?"

"Not your business."

"You're wrong," I murmur. "It's my business because you're my business."

"That why you were hiding like a frightened little bunny in your room?"

"I'm still here, aren't I?"

His eyes drop to the ankle monitor his man snapped back in place upon my return. Even now, my freedom isn't a choice.

"Just leave me alone and let me deal with my shit."

My eyes narrow on the scratch on his neck. "He hurt you."

"Fucker fought me as I tied him to the bed."

My eyes go wide. "He's tied to the bed?"

He gives me this look, like I should know by now who is in charge.

"Sicily. Now. It's a lot to *absorb*," I admit.

"You said you were in, baby."

"You're not a monster."

His laugh's a horrible, terrifying sound.

"You think this is funny, asshole?" the man inside screeches.

Alessandro sends a fist over his head into the door. "Don't make me come back in there."

My eyes pop out of my head.

He sighs. "One last chance. Go."

"What happened last night? I went to your office ..."

"Riley," he warns, then grumbles. "Fuck it. My godfather died."

"Don Lucchese?"

"Yes."

"I'm sorry."

"Everyone anticipated it. My father's headed to Rome. The famiglie will meet and vote on our new capo di tutti capi before the funeral service. I've a few days, then I'll be gone for a week."

I touch his face.

"I'll be here."

"You better," he growls, then pulls me to my feet and hoists me over his shoulder.

"I can walk," I cry out. "Let me go."

"Let. Me. Go." The prisoner echoes my words, followed by a few more, which accompany us down the hallway as Alessandro carries me away.

"Let me go," the man screeches, "and *I'll* marry her."

Alessandro

"WAIT," she gasps, totally unprepared for my onslaught.

"I'm done waiting ..." I thrust a hand between her thighs and drag two fingers across her slick folds, gathering enough moisture to draw a wet line across her flushed cheek. "... and ready to play." I set her on her feet, and she scurries away toward the door.

Like I won't catch her.

I'll always catch her.

I slam against her back and pin her to the wooden frame. "Good girl." I nip her earlobe. "Feel how hard you make me."

Freeing my erection, I glide it between her ass cheeks, and then press the thick head against her tight bud.

"Oh," she utters, suddenly keyed in on what I'm about.

I shift my hips, poking at her, teasing her, daring her to say no, but never breaching her. Not yet.

"Should I come all over this luscious ass and mark you as mine?" I cup a breast, and my dick hardens as if by magic. "Or spread my seed over your breasts?" I love seeing her covered in my come.

I love a lot of things about Riley.

She arches back toward me, and my tip connects with her dripping pussy.

"Your choice, baby. But I'm taking your ass first."

Her body trembles beneath mine, then that needy little voice I love so much rings out. "Please, Alessandro."

I smack her ass. Once. Twice. A third time. For hiding from me. For making me regret involving her in my business. For looking at me with large, horrified eyes. I warned her this world's vicious. Now, there's no going back.

I carry her to my bed and toss her onto the mattress. She bounces three times, then scurries backward.

Still running.

The idea makes me even harder.

I grab her ankles and yank her forward. Her eyes widen as I drop to my knees, part her thighs with my shoulders, and push my face into her pussy. She cries out as my tongue penetrates deep. I eat her out like a man obsessed. In and out, long licks followed by short, my nose brushing her clitoris and sending shivers up her entire body.

The things I want to do to her. The lessons I'd get off on teaching her. Every day, she becomes more addictive. I'll never grow bored of her taste.

She told me she was in.

And today, she'll kiss the last of her innocence goodbye.

I raise her bottom and run my tongue along her landing strip to rest at her backside.

Her skin warms beneath me.

"Tell me what you need," I grind out.

"Your tongue inside my pussy and your finger ..."

My girl's completely, utterly corrupted.

"I'll give you what you need, greedy girl. Don't worry."

I go to town on her pussy and offer her encouragement as her orgasm builds. "You'll come so hard. Let me feel your juices all over my face."

She cries out as she peaks. "Alessandro!"

While she's still shaking, I pluck her up and roll her back flat, and then straddle her chest. "Suck."

Her lips wrap around me, and I hiss. I let her suck me off until I'm ready to explode but push her off me, anticipating my next move. "My greedy girl gets a reward. You're in charge of your pussy."

She searches my face, disbelieving a control freak like me would give her this. Then I hit her with part two. "But I'm in charge of your tight ass. Capisci?"

"Not completely."

"You will. That I can promise you." I roll, then position her on top. "Now, straddle me, wrap your fingers around my cock, and bring me to you."

She hesitates, then jumps when my palm connects with her ass. I curve my palm over it, feeling the heat.

With a grunt, she folds her fingers around my girth and strokes me a few times before positioning me at her entrance.

"Don't move until I say so."

I slap her once on one cheek, a second time on the other, and then without warning, thrust my cock inside as I sink a finger into her ass. "Ride me while I kiss you."

I raise my head and claim her lips. She jerks in surprise, and then groans, my cock and finger going deeper.

She sets the tempo, until my control slips and I begin bucking into her, my finger penetrating deeper and deeper and her movements growing more frantic.

I feel her *everywhere*. Lips, pussy, ass.

With care, I insert a second digit, and she hisses, clenching around me.

"You're beautiful even here," I murmur. "Look at how sweetly your body accepts mine. Do you feel what you do to me, baby? You and you alone? I'll never tire of you, will I?"

And I'm never fucking letting you go.

I thrust into her, and her eyes gloss over. "That's my girl. Come for me, now, Riley."

And she does, shattering into pieces as she grinds down hard onto me.

I'm shaking as I flip her onto her stomach and sink into her ass with such force, she pushes forward on the mattress. I hesitate a few seconds, letting her catch her breath. But my breaking point's quickly approaching.

I rub her clit as I pound into her, cursing as I go, my cock swelling larger than life inside her. "Goddamn it. Jesus. Holy fuck."

The moment she surrenders is the moment my world shifts. "Mine, mine, mine," I chant like an asshole. "Every fucking part of you."

I shout her name as I come. "Riley."

She falls limp beneath me, breathing raggedly.

I withdraw, and then half walk, half stagger to the bathroom. Returning, I wipe a warm washcloth across her before cleaning myself off.

"What now," she whispers when I return from disposing of it.

I gather her into my arms and pull her into me. "Now, we take a break from the world for a while."

CHAPTER 27

SHOUTING WAKES ME.

I sit up in bed, immediately aware I'm alone.

"Get your ugly mug out of my face," a man bellows.

I hurry into the hallway and peer down into the living area. Two guards lay immobile on the floor as Alessandro and another man fight in a full-on brawl.

"I'll kill you," the prisoner cries out, body-slamming Alessandro and taking him to the floor.

"Not if I kill you first, you son of a bitch."

I race for the stairs and drum down them. By the time I reach the living room, both men are on their feet. Alessandro faces me, his expression furious. He punches the man, sending his head pitching sideways. Blood splatters across the tile.

There's a brief pause as the intruder recovers. And then the battle's on.

My fingers clench into a fist as I hover helplessly nearby.

"Your men tied me to a hotel bed for days, you control freak."

So, he *does* know Alessandro.

"What else would you have me do?" Alessandro snarls. "Hold

your hand while the shit you snorted leaves your system? Allow you to bring down the Beneventi empire?"

"I'm not the one who was ambushed."

Oh no. Wound, meet poking finger. The man is either a fool or the bravest soul on earth.

Alessandro launches at him. After several brutal punches, the boxing match turns into a grappling session as they take it to the floor.

I snatch a vase off a table, dump the contents on the floor, and creep forward until I'm a few feet away. They're about the same size. Same dark hair. Same tenacity. Alessandro is more muscular, more strategic. His attacker is wild and unpredictable.

"Thank fuck I caught you." Alessandro flips the man onto his back and pins his arms overhead. "He's dead."

"Like you'll be if you don't get off me."

"You listening? Don Lucchese's dead. Funeral and the vote is in less than a week."

I can't see the man's face or read his reaction. But within seconds he goes completely feral. "You can't keep me from going." His fist connects with Alessandro's side.

Alessandro gets in his face. "Watch me."

It happens so fast, and I'm completely caught off guard. The man crashes his head into Alessandro's in a vicious headbutt and flips positions.

Then he produces a gun.

"You fucking froze before," Alessandro taunts. "Now you're going to shoot *me?*"

"You hold a grudge like nobody else."

"You ruined my life," Alessandro snarls. "Go on. Shoot me. Then you'll be stepping up instead of shooting up."

The man's hand shakes.

"Pussy," Alessandro gloats.

"You controlling prick. I'm this close to putting you out of your misery."

Fear moves me closer. Love has me raising the vase to strike.

Alessandro's eyes snap to mine as I swing. But sensing danger, the man shifts, and I hit him in his upper arm.

The man's up and on me before the vase crashes to the ground. I'm tackled, my head hitting the tile floor. Gun to my temple, I can only stare up at him.

What? Am I seeing double?

He looks like Alessandro.

"Don't you fucking hurt her, Renzo." Never, in all this time, have I heard Alessandro so desperate. So vulnerable. "Hurt her, and I will kill you."

The stranger and I lock eyes. He's a mess, a beautiful, wild mess. "Who the hell are you?"

"You're Alessandro's twin."

"Get your filthy hands off her."

His twin—Renzo—relaxes but keeps the gun to my temple. "Well, this is worth the unexpected brotherly visit. You've a pretty sidepiece."

Alessandro rolls to his feet, his panic subsiding, then shoves Renzo off me.

His brother, twisted and delirious, falls on his back, laughing.

"Keep your trap shut."

"Father doesn't know," Renzo laughs harder. "Sandro Beneventi, the next Beneventi capo, obedient heir and sacrificial lamb, has been keeping a secret."

"Shut up."

"Make me."

"I love her."

I gasp.

Renzo's laughter abruptly stops. He sits up, giving Alessandro a steady look, weighing his words, while my heart nearly leaps out of my chest.

My lips part. I can barely breathe.

Renzo smirks.

And Alessandro punches him in the side of the head, knocking him out cold.

Alessandro

"GLAD YOU INVITED me over for this Hallmark moment." Renzo's got a knot on his head the size of a fist, a tracking device secured around his ankle, and a shit-eating grin permanently etched on his lips. He keeps eyeing Riley like she's the eighth Wonder of the World.

The three of us are eating leftover gnocchi at the kitchen island and pretending a bomb didn't just detonate in the living area.

"What's your name?" he asks, mouth half-full. He's skinnier than when I last saw him, although I only had one functional eye, so I could be wrong.

"Her name's Riley," I mutter.

Renzo laughs. "Won't even let you answer, huh? If you're in it for the long haul"—he glances at her ankle monitor, then at me—"best get used to it."

My girl shrugs her shoulder. "He's not that bad."

Renzo chokes on his gnocchi, and it's my turn to laugh.

"How could he be?" Her eyes collide with mine. "When he *loves* me."

"Fuck."

"I *like* her," Renzo exclaims. "Sure, her aim sucks. But she went after me ... *me*, the eldest son of Sebastiano Beneventi."

"By five minutes, idiot."

Riley glances between me and my twin.

Renzo flashes his trademark smirk at her. "He's an asshole. Always has been, always will be. And now, he's an asshole in love. Glad I went cold turkey and currently am sober enough to witness this."

"Christ's sake. Will you shut up?"

Renzo draws a zipping line across his lips.

"Come here, baby," I order in a low, gravelly voice.

Riley climbs off the stool and steps between my thighs. I wrap my arms around her and pull her in, then kiss the top of her head. I need to give her something. Raising her chin with my finger, I gaze into her eyes. "I love you. Capisci?"

"Yes."

"Good girl." I pause, waiting. "Anything you'd like to say to me?"

Renzo nearly pisses his pants.

But I realize love's made me stronger, not weaker.

Not yet.

My gaze connects with Renzo's. And for the first time since I stepped into his shoes, I read regret in his eyes.

CHAPTER 28

Riley

"DO YOU LOVE HIM BACK?"

My omelet falls off my fork. "What?"

Renzo stretches his big body on the barstool, as if his question were as casual as asking me about the weather. I've become fast friends with Alessandro's twin. I can't help comparing the two. Alessandro's bossy and unhinged in a controlled way, if that makes sense. He can be a wild lunatic one moment and rigidly recentered the other. Renzo's unhinged in the way free spirits are, full of life, charming and charismatic, easy to be around, yet deeply, deeply troubled. Alessandro's the overbearing protector. His brother the lost soul.

And, if I'm reading his expression correctly, I'm the fish out of water.

Alessandro stalked off a few moments ago to take an urgent call, leaving us alone.

I bite my lip, wondering why Renzo doubts me.

"You're wearing one, too." He kicks out his foot, drawing my attention to the tracking device hooked around his ankle.

"What does a tracking device have to do with love?" *Why am I wearing this device?*

"When we were kids, Sandro had a pet turtle named Gelato."

I laugh. "Like the ice cream?"

"Your Italian is impressive."

I roll my eyes.

"He was so freaking protective of it, and I was never allowed to play with it."

"Because you were a hot mess even then?"

"No. That happened afterward." Renzo sobers, and then shrugs off the abrupt flash of sadness. "I asked him why, of all animals, he chose a turtle. And you know what he said?"

"Let me guess. Slow and steady won the race?" Except Alessandro's bossy and not into delayed gratification—not his own, anyway.

His brother rakes his eyes over me.

"Tell me."

"It will never run away without me catching it."

I blink.

"He likes to trap the things he loves."

My stomach flutters as I murmur, "But what if I like being trapped."

That catches Renzo's attention, and he offers me a long look.

"What if I feel secure and safe, knowing he'll always be there."

His face pinches, then he leans back and runs his fingers through his hair. "How are you so certain he will be?"

I shrug. "Experience."

"Ah, I get it now."

A flush creeps up my neck. "Do you?"

"You like submitting to him?"

"Yes." I don't elaborate, the conversation too raw, too intimate. But I can't deny the dynamic I have with his brother. It is what it is.

"We Beneventi all have our vices. Enough said."

He gets it, doesn't he?

Renzo's expression sobers yet again. "Just ... be careful."

"He won't hurt me."

"You're too sweet for that asshole." He shakes his head. "But I'm rooting for you, Riley. I really, truly am."

"I'm rooting for you, too. To get clean. It wasn't easy for him to see you like that?"

He grunts. "I'll get clean on my own terms."

"Promise?" I offer him an encouraging smile.

"Promise."

We eat breakfast in a comfortable silence until I break it. "How many years did Alessandro take care of Gelato?" I don't know where the question comes from or why I ask it. But the answer suddenly feels important.

"He hired some turtle expert to look after it when he's away. They live like fucking forever."

Oh. My. God. All this time?

Renzo turns his attention to his breakfast.

While my mind races with the possibilities.

Of a lifetime.

With Alessandro.

PEACE IS a fragile tightrope the twins walk. I'm outside Alessandro's office and about to enter, craving my dose of wickedness before he leaves tomorrow, when the bickering begins.

"You can't even keep your dick in your pants," Renzo exclaims with a short laugh. "What makes you think you can keep me here?"

"Little pricks like yourself are easily contained."

A pissing contest over dicks? I roll my eyes. Men can be so crass.

"Let me ask you this: when he snaps his fingers, do you ask, 'How high do I jump?'"

I flinch as something crashes against a wall.

"That's the spirit," Renzo continues, laughing wildly. "You've no problem raging at everyone else, why not the great Sebastiano Beneventi?"

"You don't get it, do you? This has been years in the making. It's *time*."

"What if the Eleven don't vote him in?"

"You ever hear of the French artist, Vincent Van Gogh?"

Renzo sighs. "Here we go with the anecdotes."

"Never guess what he mailed to his brother."

"The key to his ankle monitor?"

Renzo's like being trapped inside a champagne glass, surrounded by his effervescent personality and drunk right along with him on life. Alessandro thrives on control and his twin on being out-of-control. I feel sorry for Renzo and for how the Beneventis aim to put a cork in his life. It could ruin a spirit to contain such passion.

His voice interrupts the thought. "I give in. What did he send him?"

"His ear."

My smile drops.

"I swear to God, Sandro, if I get home to find a fucking ear—"

"I mailed each famiglia a piece of that stranzo along with a personalized note."

I place my hand on the wall to steady myself. What?

"Now that's fucked up." Renzo's reaction is so calm. Maybe he's not quite as fragile as I believe. Because my stomach rolls at the savagery. I'm part of his world now, but that doesn't mean I'm heartless. Like Renzo, I'll adapt with time. I hope.

"You used a chain saw on Conti?"

"No," Alessandro sarcastically replies. "I used a butter knife, asshole."

"Chain saws will now be the Beneventi trademark. We'll be feared for this."

"Not if they vote Father in."

There's a long pause.

"You clever bastard." The reverence in his twin's reaction's undeniable. "What did the note say?"

"Prima la famiglia."

"Family first."

I've always seen Alessandro as a lone wolf type. Independent. Proud. A powerful, driven man others flock to. Hearing the strength in his tone, the love and commitment he's made to his family paints a broader picture. Yes, he's driven to impress his father and secure his legacy. Yet there's a bigger, much more complicated world out there, a mafioso world in which the Beneventis rule.

"I'm attending the funeral tomorrow."

"You're going nowhere, capisci? Enjoy the amenities, detox, and get your shit together."

"And cast aside all the fun?"

"You want to ruin us?" Alessandro grinds out.

"You really willing to ruin your life by going through with this?"

I still, listening intently. Surprised by Renzo's comment.

The deafening silence descends on the other side of the door.

"I couldn't shoot him. And for that, I'm sorry."

Alessandro grunts.

"And Riley? You keeping her locked away forever?"

"Not your business."

"She loves you. And you love her."

"Will you shut your trap, already," Alessandro exclaims. "Love has nothing to do with it."

"So your plan is to keep her here, tucked away and ignorant?"

My pulse quickens, kicking the air within my lungs from my body. The monitor around my ankle suddenly feels heavier. My freedom, an intangible object flickering through my fingertips as I attempt to grasp it. But that's a lie, isn't it? Ankle monitor or not, I've been at the villa of my own will. Because he loves me, and I love him.

What is Alessandro protecting me from? And why am I suddenly filled with dread?

Footsteps sound, and I retreat.

But Alessandro's final words carry with me down the hallway. "I'll do what's necessary, capisci?"

* * *

Alessandro

"ALESSANDRO."

Her sleepy murmur makes me hard, and I'm anxious to fuck her one last time before I leave. I deposit her in my bed, tear off her nightgown, and wetting my thumb with saliva, roll it across her clit a few times before I sink inside her warmth with a hiss.

Her falling asleep in her room rather than my bed was an inconvenience. Time is the enemy, after all. But I push that aside as she sweetly arches up to meet my thrusts.

"We need to talk," she pants at one point.

"My cock is doing the talking. It'll fill you with enough seed," I grind out, "my come will be dripping from your sweet pussy all week."

That shuts her up.

And then, proving I can be soft and tender with her and only her, I make love to her.

CHAPTER 29

Riley

SEX APPEAL MUST BE a Beneventi trait. I blush as Renzo unwinds his body in the seat next to mine, shirtless, with messy bedhead and a winsome smile. He picks up the cup of coffee I have waiting for him—to butter him up, because I've a question only he can answer now that Alessandro is gone.

"You're too sweet for the likes of him."

"Is that why I'm in this ankle monitor?"

He sputters on the sip of coffee. "Damn, you waste no time. I'm barely awake."

"Am I another Gelato?"

"Riley, don't ask questions you won't like hearing the answers to."

My eyes narrow on him. "So I am?"

"What do you think?" he tries to deflect.

"I think Alessandro's keeping a secret from me." He glances away, and my stomach knots. Still, I press on. "But is he protecting me or making certain I'll be here when he returns?"

He sips his coffee and contemplates my question. Or rather, contemplates how to answer. "My brother's married to this life, first and foremost. He won't leave it—can't, as the heir. Family first—that's what we say."

"So Alessandro will do what, break up with me?"

Renzo gives me a somber look. "Trust me, that'd be the best scenario."

My heart drops, and the kitchen spins. "I don't understand."

"He doesn't want you to."

I stand, needing to feel the ground beneath my feet. "So explain it to me."

For a long while, Renzo stares at me with sad eyes. He reaches into his pocket, places something shiny on the kitchen island, and pushes it toward me.

My eyebrows arch. "A key?"

"Finish the question, Riley."

"A key to ..." It's then that I glance down. His ankle monitor's missing.

"They never learn you can't keep a free spirit caged."

"Where did you get that?"

He chuckles. "My wallet. I had the key made years ago, yet they always use the same monitors. I smash the device up really good so they think I broke free. Once, I left it locked to really fuck with them, so they'd believe I either broke my ankle escaping it or suddenly became a world-class contortionist."

My lips part in disbelief.

"Look. You don't deserve to be caged, either. So here's what I'm proposing. We crash Don Lucchese's funeral this afternoon, and you can see for yourself the sacrificial bullshit Alessandro's agreed to."

I glance from the key to Renzo.

They say love will set you free. Only they never fell for a twisted control freak like Alessandro Beneventi.

"Good." Renzo jumps off his stool, takes the key, unlocks and slips off my monitor, and then places it and the key in his pocket. "He took that big goon with him—"

"Tommaso?"

"You met him, of course."

"Besides Alessandro, he's the only person I talk to. He's been nice."

Renzo jerks back. "Nice? You know he's Sandro's enforcer, right?"

I grin. "For the longest time, I thought he was an Uber driver." If I could bottle up Renzo's shock, I could cause a small earthquake.

"We need to get moving to make it to Rome in time. We'll escape separately, and then meet up. Gather your things and in a half hour, be on your balcony and waiting for my signal. Then head down into the cellar. Pass the cell to the wall at the end and feel around for the lever that opens the hidden door leading into the tunnel. It's unlikely Alessandro's been down there, and even less likely any of his men have been in the tunnel. To the right on the floor should be the suitcase I placed there a few months ago, after I escaped rehab. Make sure you grab that before you leave. Wait for me at the end of the tunnel."

My jaw touches the floor by the time he finishes. Because there was so much to absorb in what he's said.

"A cell?" I manage. A suitcase. A tunnel.

"You think you were vacationing at the Hyatt?"

"How will I avoid the guards?"

He grins like a madman, and my heart hurts. In the moment, I can see so much of Alessandro in him. Cocky. Confident. Bent. "I'll draw their attention away from you. That I can promise you." Once again, he pins his gaze on me. "Your choice, Riley. Freedom to decide or blind trust?"

I swallow hard.

Because, really, there is no choice.

Whatever Alessandro is keeping from me, I'll discover for myself.

A HALF HOUR LATER, I wait on the balcony for Renzo's signal. I stuffed a small bag with clothing, heart in my throat, wondering if I'll see the wardrobe Alessandro purchased for me again.

Will he be angry I escaped? Yes. But I'm no longer his prisoner. Renzo's right, it's my decision whether to stay or go. He can't just lock me away, even to protect me.

From what, is what I'll soon find out.

I lean over the balcony and search for Renzo. Alessandro's men mill about, relaxed and unaware of our imminent departure.

All of a sudden, shouting and chaos erupt. "Get him." "Sandro will kill us if he escapes." "That clever motherfucker."

The men below spin and point to my right before they start running.

I follow their gestures, scanning the villa grounds. At first, I don't see him—until my gaze sweeps further out ... toward the cliff.

"Oh my God," I exclaim.

Renzo stands there, waving his arms, drawing Alessandro's soldiers.

No. Please don't tell me jumping is his escape plan.

Men are in a dead run and swarming like angry bees from everywhere.

I offer Renzo a quick prayer for a safe landing, and quietly slip out of my room.

RAIN DRIZZLES over the Roman cemetery, and the grey tombstones darken to black. Don Lucchese's open grave sits below the small hill Renzo and I stand on, waiting for the procession to arrive. Renzo keeps the banter light by jokingly recapping highlights from "our brave escape."

"You should have seen their dumbstruck expressions when I jumped," he proclaims, then contorts his features in a ridiculous way. I appreciate the distraction yet only half engage in his fun. Worried I made a mistake coming here. Wishing I were the type of person who embraced ignorance, especially when it's accompanied by bliss.

I remind myself how far we've come. My relationship with Alessandro Beneventi's survived insurmountable challenges. If I can still love the man after witnessing the monster within murder a man, whatever else comes our way will feel like child's play, right?

"I'll take you back, if that's what you want."

"You'll miss the funeral."

He pauses pacing, always in a constant state of movement, and rubs his fingers across his jaw. Looking so much like Alessandro in this moment that it hurts. "Given any thought to where you'd go if you flee?"

I frown. "Flee?"

"Shit, Riley."

Dread coils around my windpipes. "Why would I do that?" I murmur. *What aren't you telling me?*

"Alessandro will dismember me and send my pieces to all the hearts I've broken. I shouldn't have brought you here."

"We're here now." I bite my lip to stop it from quivering, and then answer his question. "Home to Marietta, I suppose."

"Bad move. It's the first place he'll look, and his men will turn your town upside down or risk his wrath. My advice is to stay close yet out of sight instead of running far away, which is so predictable. Do you have anyone to help you who he'd never suspect?"

"Luna Gallo."

Renzo grins. "Perfect."

Disturbed, I can't find it in me to smile back.

"Don't look at me like I'm breaking your heart." Something lands at my feet. I blink in surprise at the thick bundle of euros.

"Take it."

"But ..."

He stills and looks past me. "Shit, they're coming."

A procession of black cars wind along the pathway leading toward us. Quickly, I scoop up the money and join Renzo behind a huge tree.

"Look at that *stranzo* driving his red Maserati to a fucking funeral."

I don't dare look. "Who is he?"

"Matteo Lombardi. A family friend."

I catch the sarcasm in his voice. "You say it like he's your enemy."

"Yeah, well, I survived three murder attempts, so I wouldn't exactly say we're BFFs."

My eyes widen. Will the Beneventi brothers ever cease in shocking me?

"Is there a dark-haired bombshell in the passenger seat?"

The answer is no, because Renzo's done so again. I look from him —eyes closed with his back pressed to the tree protecting us from sight and in what I guess is some state of instantaneous agony—to the Maserati below. Bombshell suddenly takes on greater significance. "Only one person is inside, and he's driving."

Renzo pulls away from the tree with a fresh burst of adrenaline. "Just as well."

"It's not what you're running from but *who*," I exclaim. It's likely Mr. Lombardi has good reason to murder Renzo.

Sunlight peeks between the clouds, and the quiet is interrupted from its nap as men exit their cars and somberly gather around the grave. My heart dips when I spy Alessandro carrying the casket.

"Lucky shit's a pallbearer," Renzo grumbles beside me.

An extremely attractive man bearing a strong resemblance to the twins is across from him. This must be Don Beneventi—the air of power around him is undeniable.

Don Lucchese's coffin is set in the grave, and men take their positions around it.

"Look at them pay my father respect." Renzo points to a large group gathered around his father. "The sly bastard succeeded."

"He's in charge now, right?"

Renzo snorts. "He's always been in charge. But formally, yes. The vote went his way. He's now capo di tutti capi."

Sadness and excitement mix in the air, and conversations drift on the wind. My focus shifts to Alessandro standing across the grave and encircled by more men. Unlike with his father, men get in, say their piece, and hurry away. Reminding me of the first time I saw him, terrorizing men from across the bar.

Oddly, the thought soothes me. Because we're not strangers meeting for the first time. We're two people in love and navigating every day the best we can.

"I'm going down for a closer look," Renzo murmurs. "You coming?"

I swallow hard. "I'd rather stay here."

"Suit yourself." He pauses, and then kicks at a stone, sending it flying. "Look, Riley. Whatever you decide, keep this in mind. My brother's an asshole who doesn't deserve you. But if he obeys my father's wishes and goes through with this bullshit, you still should know his heart will only belong to you."

"What?" I gasp, but he disappears down the hillside.

Alessandro's heart?

No. No. No.

A long sermon begins as my world splinters. Because I know before I see her what this is about. Heart in my throat, I watch and wait, never taking my eyes off him.

Then the group surrounding him parts.

And there she is. A beautiful blond woman at Alessandro's side. He dips his head to say something to her. A short conversation follows, and I cling to the last threads of hope.

He's being polite.

She's no one.

But then her voice rises like she wants the world to hear her, and she exclaims, "Soon-to-be husband."

I place a hand on the tree to steady myself.

Seconds before Alessandro's reply knocks my feet from beneath me.

"Wife."

He clasps her hand, and together they approach the grave.

I tumble against the tree and cling to it.

Alessandro's engaged. He touched her and took her palm in his hand.

How? When?

Vibrating with anger, I sink to the ground. He betrayed me.

I confided in him and shared my soul with the asshole. Did he miss the part where my father was secretly engaged? How that lie nearly destroyed me? How it twisted the grieving process and turned my emotions black? Months after his murder, I was a ghostly shell.

Now, to discover, Alessandro's engaged? Did he think I'd never find out? Was he hoping to marry her and keep me on the side?

Yes. That's exactly what he was doing. Selfishly locking me away, his fuckdoll to play with when the mood strikes.

I curl up into a ball and try to make sense of it. I remain this way, and then somehow manage to get back on my feet.

I spot her, halfway up the hill. His blonde, who waves at me. She's gorgeous, with long hair and a full figure. "I'm hoping there's a breeze up here," she softly says as she approaches me.

Friendly and *sweet*.

Oh my God.

My eyes drop to the ring on her hand. Huge and ridiculous. Staring at it feels like pieces of diamond shard come at me to pierce my heart. "You're engaged to Alessandro?" I cry out.

"Excuse me?"

"Or are you already married? He called you *wife*."

"Not yet. I'm his fiancée."

My knees give out, and I drop to them.

She falls to the ground beside me and lightly touches my arm. "Are you okay?"

I shake my head. "For how long?" I choke out.

"Months."

"This summer?"

"Yes."

That lying *stronzo*. I rise, as Renzo's earlier advice resonates. He knew and correctly predicted my reaction. I want to cry on his shoulder, shake him, and thank him for the money and reasoning with me.

The woman stands beside me. "He's an asshole for not telling you."

"Yes, he is."

"I dislike him. And he loathes me, if it makes you feel better ..."

Right. That's why he was holding her hand. "It doesn't. What I feel is ..." I stare off into the distance. I feel everything at once. Despair, sadness, anger, and hurt, all bundled up in a ball of betrayal.

"Lost?" I hear her say.

"Yes."

"I'm sorry," she whispers.

There's nothing left to say, so I excuse myself. "I'll be going now."

To collect on a promise.

To, once and for all, escape the monster I fell in love with.

CHAPTER 31

Alessandro

"TAKE HER TO YOUR HOTEL."

It's my first official order from the new capo di tutti capi, which comes after the last of the Eleven leave the cemetery. I hesitate, three seconds shy of telling my father to get his head out of his ass, but Alessia pleads with me to keep quiet.

I had an epiphany this afternoon while staring into my godfather's grave. Fuck this arrangement with Alessia Amato. Not only am I not going through with this marriage but it's time the great Sebastiano Beneventi sees the light.

Alessia's quiet as she slides into the backseat of the limousine next to me. I take out my phone, which I turned off for the vote and funeral service, and turn it on. Message after message pop up on the screen, all saying the same thing: Renzo and Riley are gone.

I call Tommaso.

"Tried reaching you, Sandro. They escaped."

"How?"

"That crazy motherfucker jumped off the cliff."

My fingers tighten around the phone. "And Riley?"

Alessia makes a face, blatantly eavesdropping on my conversation. I glare at her until she looks away. My love life isn't her business, and it never will be.

"Escaped through the cellar tunnel. Renzo must have discovered it existed and told her."

"They can run, but we'll get them." I pull up the monitor app, then grind my teeth. "Either they never left or returned home." *Or my asshole brother wiggled them free of the devices.*

"Search the entire fucking island."

"I'm headed there to do so myself."

She told me she loved me. Why wouldn't she wait for me?

The answer comes at me like a hammer to the head. What did Renzo tell her?

"Call me with an update." I disconnect, toss my cell onto the seat, and then lean back and close my eyes.

So this is what it feels like to be dumped.

Alessia clears her throat.

"Not now."

"I saw her."

I shoot up in the seat and swing toward her.

"Your girlfriend. The gorgeous redhead."

"Where?"

"On the hill overlooking the funeral."

Rolling my fingers into a ball, I slam my fist into the driver's seat. "Stop the motherfucking car."

The driver pulls over, and I'm out and running.

"Sandro," Alessia shouts after me.

I race down the city street, mindless of the puddles soaking my expensive shoes or the suit jacket and tie I've tossed aside. In a dead run, I turn into the cemetery and follow the driveway to the midway mark, where I then cut between tombstones to reach the hill. Panting, I push on, hiking to the top and charging forward, searching everywhere for signs of her.

But Riley's nowhere to be found.

My asshole brother couldn't leave well enough alone, could he?

I punch a tree. There's a panoramic view of the gravesite below. Knowing what she saw and the presumptions she made ... Hell, I only decided an hour ago to bail on my obligation.

"Fuck."

The limousine is waiting for me when I reach flat ground. Alessia doesn't say a word when I climb back in beside her.

My chest hurts like I'm having a heart attack. *Riley left me.*

"Sandro?"

"Let's get drunk."

I CALL for an update on the hour, every hour.

And every goddamn second, my despair grows.

But I can't hunt my girl down while this marriage bullshit has yet to be resolved. It's nearly eleven at night, and I'm so shitfaced I'm not just seeing double, but Renzo's smug face hovering over me. I punch the air, trying to nail him in the head with my fist and wipe that fucking "I told you so" expression from his ugly mug.

Beside me on the floor, Alessia laughs at my antics.

I tap my whiskey glass to her empty wine bottle. "Here's to Renzo, running wild and free."

We drink more, and I call for another update.

Alessia watches the clock. She's worried my father won't return, but, although I'm anxious to get this bullshit over with, I know my father won't be long. He'll entertain the Eleven like they're celebrities while establishing his authority and making them believe their say is important. Then he'll return to pull the same shit on us, minus the Hollywood treatment.

I rub my chin and try to see things from his perspective. "He's never committed to a woman before," I mutter. "Having two heirs to carry on the Beneventi name without marrying allowed him the freedom to do whatever the fuck he wants."

Like break her heart.

Jesus. It's the whiskey bringing out the human side in me. Since when do I care about Alessia Amato's tender heart?

Alessia stares at her wine like it's suddenly been poisoned.

But the fact is my father's obsessed with her. What he needs is a slap in the face and a wake-up call. "If you love him, really love him, then you'll need to teach him how to love a woman. Because I'm not sure he's capable of it."

She looks pale.

"I said too much." I mutter. She's as much a victim of my father's ambition as I am, and as fucking annoying as it's been seeing her underfoot at the Beneventi estate, I might have been a dick but I never actually hated her.

Her eyes light up with an idea. "Next time he mentions the wedding, we tell him no. What's the worst he'll do? Lock us in the dungeon?"

Yeah, she's likeable, and a perfect match for *him*.

My perfect woman, despite my slapping a goddamn ankle monitor on her and expecting her to stay put, has escaped me.

I take another deep drink, and Alessia follows suit. Until we're two drunk assholes acting out situations that'd piss off my father.

Fierce pounding on the hotel room door interrupts us.

I brace myself as the door swings open and my father staggers in. "You didn't book her a room."

Thumb, meet button I'm about to press. Because we Beneventi loathe sharing our toys, and women. I toss an arm around her shoulder. "She's spending the evening with her fiancé."

Dumbfounded—there's no better word for his reaction. It's understandable, considering how my relationship with Alessia has been like navigating a minefield, with his future wife cautiously stepping around the explosives I set to go off.

He scowls.

And then his gaze descends on her.

I hold my breath as *stubborn pride* battles it out with *possessive asshole*. I squeeze her shoulder, and if I wasn't his son—wasn't his only reliable heir—I'd be dead about now. His eyes narrow and nostrils flare, and suddenly months of bullshit goes up in flames like dry brush.

"Get your hands off her," he snaps, "or I'll break every finger."

Music to my goddamn ears.

"You"—he addresses Alessia as I unwind—"were supposed to be alone and waiting."

"But instead I'm with my fiancée."

She's good at this.

"Not anymore," he flatly replies.

Alessia doesn't catch on right away, not realizing I'm the "not anymore."

The only thing that'd make what plays out next better is popcorn. And Riley.

Run all you want, baby. But I'll find you, soothe your worries, and then spank your ass pink. And you'll love every second of it.

My father whisks Alessia up and hauls ass out the door. Leaving me to crawl over to where I tossed my cell and call for an update.

CHAPTER 32

MY MEN DESCEND ON MARIETTA, Ohio, as out of place as lotus in a wheat field. And, as I sit over a pot roast dinner in Riley's grandparents' kitchen and field rapid-fire questions about my relationship with their granddaughter, I fully admit I'm a class-act asshole.

Though they act like I'm some heartbroken fuckup.

"Riley must have had a good reason to dump you, son," her PopPop admonishes me.

"George, stop pressing him," Mema interrupts. "Do I need to remind you you were twenty minutes late to our first date?"

"She never lets me forget it."

I take another mouthful of pot roast, and my stomach rumbles with pleasure. New York's finest restaurants have nothing on Riley's grandmother's cooking. If I wasn't so goddamn frustrated at how easily my girl's evaded me, I'd enjoy the home-cooked meal more.

"You cheat on her?" Mema demands.

I cough as a slice of meat clogs my windpipe. And here I believed George was the cutthroat.

"Martha," George scolds.

"He's handsome as sin. I bet women flock to him like bees on honey."

I clear my throat. Then tell them the truth—not about the women, who've suddenly lost their appeal—but why Riley left me. "My father is an important man in the Italian community and has an old-fashioned mindset. To strengthen our family, he arranged a marriage for me."

"You're married?" Mema looks six seconds shy of snatching my dinner plate away.

"No. I was engaged."

Their eyes shoot daggers at me. If Riley is half as loyal as these two, I'm a lucky man.

"I convinced my father the engagement was bullshit, and I broke it off." I roll back in the dining room chair. There it goes again—my fucking heart.

No more red meat.

No more dead ends that lead me no closer to her.

"She left me because she learned the truth."

"What did you expect, Al?" Mema asks softly.

"I told her I loved her." A fucking first. And every day she's gone, the feeling grows *worse*.

They look at each other.

Mema reaches over and pats my fucking hand. Like I'm a dog that needs consoling. Or a brokenhearted asshat who lost the best thing that's ever happened to him. "When she calls us, is there anything you'd like us to say on your behalf?"

I stifle the few choice descriptions that immediately come to mind.

"Tell her ..."

Please come home.

I miss you, baby.

I love you.

"That after she talks with me, if she still wants to leave me, I'll let her go."

"You're a romantic," Mema says, looking at me like she's seconds away from swooning. "If you love someone, set them free. If they love you, they'll come back."

Even PopPop eyes me with a hopeful gleam.

They'll sing my praises when Riley calls—because she will call, right? And if her grandparents are convincing enough, she's bound to talk to me.

But as for setting her free and waiting for love to bring her back? Fuck that.

<hr>

A KNOCK INTERRUPTS MY MISERY.

"What now?" I snarl.

My office door opens, and Tommaso appears. "An envelope for you was just delivered." He closes the distance between us, and then comes around the desk to stand next to me.

"By who?"

"Some kid. The men tried to grab him, but he tossed it into the driveway and took off on his moped."

I pick it up. *Sandro* is scribbled on it in familiar, practically illegible handwriting. When I get my hands on my soon-to-be-dead twin ...

Scowling, I tear it open and read:

Asshole,

Congratulations on your failed engagement. Guess if I'm attending the wedding, I better give you what you want before you kill me. And what you want, brother, is probably indulging in pistachio treats by now.

Renzo

I toss the letter onto my desk. The room seems brighter, and my chest lighter.

"Time to bring my girl back home," I tell Tommaso.

Willingly, I hope.

If not, so be it.

CHAPTER 33

CHASING EXTREMES LEADS NOWHERE.

If I'd listened to logic, I wouldn't be hiding in an apartment dating back to Roman times and cursing a man who redefines extreme.

An engaged man.

Did he think I'd be okay with that? Or was he hoping I'd never find out?

"Stronzo," I mutter, walking over to look out the kitchen window while making a note to look up the definition—though I hope it means asshole.

Luna is on the street below, clinging to a handsome man in a suit like a koala to a tall tree. He struggles to peel her off, glancing around, clearly uncomfortable with her affection. But then she whispers something in his ear, and suddenly he's kissing her, his reservations carried away on the breeze.

I grin. Dante Lucchese doesn't stand a chance.

My heart pinches.

But I've learned a crucial lesson. At my weakest and most vulnerable, I sought refuge in the shadow of Alessandro's power. Now, at my strongest and most grounded—having fully recognized and embracing the darker sides that make me who I am—I stand with my feet firmly planted. Heartbroken or not, I'll never be the shattered woman I was back in New York. It took a kidnapping to set me free, a lying mafioso to show me what unconditional love really is, and the turmoil of the last few months to come to terms with myself.

Do I still love him? Yes. Will I survive without him? Absolutely—surviving is what I do, right? Though I fear this time, my broken heart will never fully heal.

The apartment door bursts open, and I jump and spin.

Luna enters in a flourish.

I look past her.

"Chill. I'm alone. Dante thinks I'm visiting an elderly aunt." She dumps a bag on the round table and begins unpacking trays of food. I move beside her and place enough food to feed an army inside the apartment refrigerator. The bottle of wine I open immediately and pour two glasses.

I've no doubt that, if it hadn't been for Luna, Alessandro would have located me by now. But Renzo was right, hiding in Italy on the next island over, was a clever decision. I keep a low profile and am careful while walking the small cobblestone streets when I do venture outside.

It's been two weeks. Tomorrow, I'll take a huge risk by heading to a nearby resort, where I'll use a phone to call my grandparents. My grandparents shouldn't be worrying about me. I'm also curious if Renzo was right—did his deceitful twin search Marietta, thinking I'd run home? Did Alessandro terrify my grandparents with his menacing glares and demands? Are they now questioning how I ever got involved with a monster like him? No one dares deny him anything.

But I'm denying him me.

Feel that, stranzo?

Luna removes the tray from my hands. "You look ready to murder that meatball platter." She secures it in the refrigerator, and then turns toward me, her eyes filled with animation. "I've got news. But you'll want to finish your wine first."

My eyebrows lift.

She tugs my elbow and forces me to sit. My stomach knots as she takes a seat across from me. "Dante's flying to New England next week for a Beneventi wedding. Did you know?"

I reach for my wineglass. "About his wedding? No."

"Evidently, it was a huge secret."

Understatement meet cruel reality.

"Her father's an influential politician. The Eleven are thrilled with the arrangement."

"I'll blow up the balloons," I mutter.

She rambles on, mindless. "Dante says it's a love match despite—"

I hold up my hand. "No."

"It's not?"

Not unless he lied about loving me. "I said no because I ... *can't* ..."

"Is it because of the age gap? He's what, thirty-eight to her twenty-three?" She makes a face. "Dante refuses my advances because he's much older. He treats me like a baby, even when I do everything imaginable to make him see I'm not."

I don't ask her to define imaginable, and Dante didn't exactly refuse her advances less than ten minutes ago.

"Wouldn't it be romantic if Alessandro swooped in here, apologized for being a dick, then brought you to the wedding?"

"What?" I screech. But my racing mind quickly catches up to everything she's said. Age gap? Who is thirty-eight?

"Wow, Alessandro really pissed you off, huh?"

I place the wineglass on the table. "Luna, this is really important. Which Beneventi is getting married?"

She laughs. "Did you believe it was Renzo?"

"Who, Luna?"

"Our new capo di tutti capi is marrying Alessia Amato."

"Sebastiano Beneventi?"

"The one and only. Poor girl."

The kitchen closes in on me. "Not Alessandro? You certain?"

She gives me a puzzled look. "There was a rumor ... but I'm positive. The announcement was made the day after Don Lucchese's funeral."

I'm overwhelmed by it all. He's the most terrifying man I know, yet a dutiful son caught in an arranged marriage. He's engaged but in love with me. And now, for reasons I can't comprehend, Fate has spared us.

Alessandro isn't getting married—his father is.

What does that mean for us?

Luna glances at the small decorative clock on the wall. "Shit, I'm late. We don't need my father asking questions about where I've been."

"Thank you for risking so much for me," I tell her.

She flashes me a smile, looking like a girl on the verge of womanhood. "Women must always stick together, don't you think?"

I consider everything I've been through, dead canaries and all. How much easier life would have been if this had been the case. "Absolutely."

"See you tomorrow," she says, and races off in a flurry of movement.

The apartment feels empty without her presence.

I move to the window and sip my wine, watching her step onto the street and quickly disappear toward the bus stop. She's carefree in a way I'll never be yet, like me, in love with a mafioso she never should have encouraged.

As I turn, my elbow hits the window frame, spilling wine onto the floor. Sighing, I perch the glass on the sill, grab a dish towel from the sink, and clean up the mess. After rinsing my hands, I return to the window.

I lift my glass, but movement below catches my eye—a man stepping out of an expensive car. He pauses and looks up toward the window.

And in that moment, my entire world turns upside down.

He doesn't have to say the word this time.

I'm already on it.

Run.

<hr>

HE'S COME FOR ME.

Did he see me? Does it even matter? He's here, outside the apartment, miles from where he should be. I don't need to ask why—I've been preparing for this moment.

I grab my prepacked bag, containing clothes, essentials, and the money Renzo gave me, then dash to the bedroom at the back of the apartment. Climbing out onto the slate overhang, I carefully inch sideways along its pitch, wary of the long drop below. Reaching a flattened rooftop, I scramble to my feet and break into a run.

Questions race through my mind. How did he find me? What does he want? Can I ever forgive him? His distrust led to my kidnapping, yet he was the one who deceived me all along. I had confided my darkest secret to him—how my father's secret engagement devastated me almost as much as his murder. Knowing this, why would Alessandro keep me in the dark about his own engagement?

Because he's a possessive control freak who never wanted to let you go.

Because he knew he'd lose you.

I reach the edge of a neighboring balcony. Unlike the villa's balcony, this one is built from stone with a flat granite floor. More importantly, a winding staircase of the same material descends to the backstreet below.

Pausing, I glance over my shoulder, but there's no sign of him. I frown. Chasing me used to be one of his favorite games. Did I misread the situation? Has he not come for me?

Disappointment weighs heavily on me, but I shake it off. No, Riley, that's not the right way to think about this. I push aside the swirling emotions and focus on making my way to the street.

Once there, I head left and follow the side street parallel to the one leading to the bus stop. As I draw closer, I turn the corner and slip into the shadows, waiting for the next bus to arrive.

Five minutes later, with my heart in my throat, I board a nearly empty bus. I did it. I've escaped him—again. So why am I crying?

The driver watches me with a look of helpless concern. I offer him a smile I don't feel, then wipe my eyes with the back of my hand and take a seat at the front.

How much sadness can a person endure? My mother, my father, even my undeserving best friend—all gone. I had no control over losing them. This feels different. Trembling, I reconsider my decision. Maybe I should at least hear him out and offer him a chance to explain, even though he denied me the same consideration?

The bus driver's muttered exclamation cuts through my thoughts. "Cosa sta facendo questo pazzo?"

I glance up to find the bus isn't moving.

The reason why stands in the middle of the street and blocks the road, arms crossed like he's daring the driver to run him over.

Our eyes connect through the windshield.

"Drive," I tell the man, as fight-or-flight instincts kick in, and I've already chosen the latter.

The driver honks the horn and gestures animatedly.

Alessandro's glare could melt steel. I hold my breath as he charges forward and rounds the bus to the side door. Fist tight, he pounds on it, demanding entry.

"Non vengo pagato abbastanza per questo," the man declares before jumping from his seat and disappearing down the aisle. Leaving me to tame the monster.

"Riley," Alessandro bellows, his voice cutting through the dull hum of the bus. "Open the goddamn door."

Slowly, I slide out of my seat and move toward him, facing the storm head-on. "This entire time, you were engaged?"

"Let me explain, baby." His voice softens, pleading.

I stiffen at the word. "Don't baby me."

"I'm not fucking engaged, okay?" Desperation clings to his words, and I fight the pull to give in. "I never wanted to be. I just needed to find a way out."

"You lied."

"I kept you in the dark," he growls. "There's a difference."

"Not in my mind."

We lock eyes through the grimy bus window, tension thick enough to drown us both. Behind us, a horn blares impatiently, but the world outside feels miles away compared to the battle raging between us.

"Open the door, Riley," he urges, quieter now, raw. "Or do you plan on hashing this out here?"

I bite my lip, hard enough to taste blood. A part of me wants him to suffer, to feel the same sharp hurt he's inflicted on me. But another part still hopes, and wonders if this is it—the moment when love conquers everything.

Right. Just overlook the fact he's a mafioso, a cold-blooded killer, and a possessive lover with control issues.

But he's also the man I love.

I sigh, the weight of my decision settling in my chest. If I open this door, I know my future won't be painted in rainbows or butterflies.

He presses his hand against the glass, his voice breaking through the fog of my thoughts. "I didn't want to lose you. I won't lose you. Capisci?"

The ache in his tone twists something inside me. Reaching behind, I tug the switch, the door creaking open—and sealing my fate.

Before I can process it, he's there, scooping me up and pulling me into his arms, holding me so tight it hurts.

"Thank fuck," he breathes, and I let myself get lost in the chaos of him, knowing it's the only place I truly belong.

I HAVE her exactly where I want her.

By my side, in my bed, at my command.

The latest addition to the Beneventi famiglia—though she's insisting on a long engagement.

"Take off your dress," I tell her.

She nervously glances around the hallway leading to my office. "Now?" she murmurs, though I spy the excitement in her eyes. "Your family are visiting."

"They can wait."

"Or discover us making love right here in the hallway."

Making love. The phrase used to set me on edge. I'm a man who thrives on control yet couldn't get a grip on my fucking feelings. Hell, I wasn't certain I had feelings of the tender sort before I fell for Riley.

I don't correct her. Even if this will be a quick, hard fuck, in one shape or form, I'll be loving her.

She flushes a gorgeous shade of pink as her hands find my belt. My girl's suddenly on the same page. I let her take me out and stroke me. Watching her get off on pleasuring me the same way I do when I go down on her sweet pussy.

The thought alone makes me hard.

"Use your belt," she mutters, positioning her arms behind her back.

Fuck, the crazy shit I want to show her. The limits we've yet to test.

This world isn't for the meek. And ask anyone, I'm not the easiest man to please. Why she trusts me is a goddamn mystery. But every day, I try to live up to that trust.

I carefully wrap the belt around her wrists, push her back against the wall with a thump, and rip the neckline of her dress clear to the waist.

Her lips form an "O."

Never will I grow tired of the sight. "Come to daddy, my babies."

She laughs. "You're obsessed."

"You're the most beautiful thing in my life." I lean in and lick her jawline, then leave a trail all the way down to a breast. "And my dirty fuckdoll to do with as I want."

"If you'd stop talking ..." I frown. "... and get busy pumping me full of come." Her eyes flash, and in this exact moment, I realize I'm truly, thoroughly fucked. "I want it dripping down my thigh when we go back to the party."

Jesus. I've died and gone to hell.

"Keep mouthing off," I growl, "and I'll punish you."

"Still talking?"

I hoist her up, anchor her on my hips, and drive home so hard, her back slides up the wall.

"Finally," she gasps.

I crash my lips into hers, shutting her up. I thrust into her and set a frantic pace. We're both sweaty and flushed by the time she crests, chanting my name as I push her over the ledge.

Alessandro. *Alessandro.*

I relax my hold and allow gravity to pull her fully onto me. I hiss and curse, and then do what she demanded I do and fill her womb with my seed.

We take a moment to catch our breath before I gently set her on her feet.

"You hurt me," I tell her, more vulnerable than I've ever felt in my life.

Alarm fills her expression. "I did? Where?" Frantic, she looks me over until I grab her hand, place it over my heart, and end her worries. "Here."

"Alessandro," she whispers. Then she balances on her toes and kisses me.

A man can grow used to this softer bullshit.

Finally, she breaks away, and then blushes as she glances down at her ruined dress.

"Think anyone will notice I've changed?"

I take in her wild hair, pink cheeks, and as I release her wrists from the belt, the chafing found there, then I lie.

"No one will look twice."

* * *

Riley

"CAN'T KEEP his filthy mitts off you, can he?" Renzo comments, sauntering up to stand beside me the minute I return to the party.

My mouth falls open, but I hastily compose myself. "I just spilled a drink on myself."

"And I just shot myself in the arm."

I steal a glance at his cast, the result of a mysterious bullet wound and the surgery that followed, then let my gaze drift down to the all-too-familiar monitor around his ankle. "Can you do me a favor?"

"Only for the woman who tamed that asshole," he says, nodding toward Alessandro, who is speaking to Alessia. Whatever he says makes her look away, while he resumes angrily scrolling through his phone.

My eyes widen as his father swiftly closes the distance between them. I'm terrified for Alessandro, and with good reason. The capo di tutti capi of the Eleven is not only handsome and wickedly charming but also notoriously cunning and, according to rumors, quite skilled with a chain saw.

Don Beneventi says something, then snatches the phone from Alessandro's hand.

I start to step forward, but Renzo grabs my arm. "You think you can protect my brother from our father?"

We watch as Alessandro leans back, smirks, and says something in return. Then both men study whatever's on the screen with rapt attention.

Renzo chuckles. "As you were saying, what favor?"

"When you escape this time, don't jump."

"Maybe I'll stick around awhile?"

I search his expression to see if he's serious. "Alessandro would like that."

Renzo's expression turns serious. "You really love the asshole, don't you?"

I chuckle. "I really do."

Suddenly, I'm pulled into a warm hug.

Just as quickly, Alessandro is at our side, escorting Renzo away from me. "What the hell?"

Renzo straightens up. "She's a keeper, brother."

Alessandro's gaze softens as our eyes meet. "And that's exactly what I plan to do."

THE END

Renzo's story, DIRTY MAFIA TORMENT, is next!
Here's a quick taste of my troubled, oh so naughty hero.

Renzo

The bedroom's a goddamn mess.

Evidence of her struggle is everywhere; tangled sheets, a broken lamp on the floor, the slackened ropes that bind her ankles. A shard of glass rests beside her on the mattress, and I can tell she used it to pick away at the Shinbari binding her wrists.

I've got Elia Seraphina Lombardi trussed up like a flamingo ready for the fire pit.

I close the bedroom door behind me. "Miss me?"

She glares daggers. Because she can't reply, I've gagged her with a silk tie.

It'd be easy to say the devil made me do it because I never claim responsibility for anything, my motto being if the fools in my life believe they can outwit me, fuck 'em while they figure shit out. In this case, I claim full responsibility. There are consequences to actions, so my father likes to remind my twin and I. This girl needed a Beneventi-worthy wakeup call.

I get that I'm memorable, and she clearly hasn't forgotten me. In the four years between luncheons, she's only gotten sharper, hungrier for my presence, and twice as relentless.

Spying on me turned into a game of dodge and evade once she caught me staring earlier. Did I use it to break up the monotony of my day? You bet I did. Teaching her a lesson became my afternoon entertainment.

I escaped to the kitchen and seconds later, she came in for a glass of water. I took a piss and she lurked outside the door, waiting for me to exit. When I ducked into the library though, she was already there, seated on sofa and pretending to read. I gave her points for that. It wasn't until she followed me upstairs like a lovestruck pup and into a guest bedroom at the far end of the hall, where no one could hear her scream, that took sprung my trap.

Did she struggle while I subdued her? Fuck, yeah—I've scratches on my arm and chest to prove it. Cursed me to hell and back, too, not knowing I've been there a time or two. But to her credit, not a scream or even a whimper escaped her lips.

She's on her stomach now, same place I left her when I escaped downstairs to mingle, her pink feathered cocktail dress riding up over her hips.

I pause and admire my work. The rope is an intricate masterpiece, winding between her thighs, cinching her waist, parting her perfect breasts before splitting over her shoulders where it then intertwines with the other end and around the wrists behind her back.

It's my first attempt at Shinbari. The art form's meant to be visually appealing. But the way the rope pulls her shoulders back and showcases her big fucking breasts is so erotic, my dick notices.

Sixteen, and a stunner.

How did I miss it?

She glares at me from over a shoulder, and I remind myself she's in this predicament to learn a lesson. Nothing more, but especially not because I'm designating her as my latest distraction.

I sit on the mattress beside her. "Bet you regret following me around like a desperate virgin."

Her green eyes narrow.

"Watching my every move. Stalking me." I pluck a feather from her dress. "A little bitch in heat, aren't you?" Goosebumps prickle her skin beneath as I trace the feather across her bare arm. She's prettier now that I'm really looking at her. Curvier, with a flat stomach and legs that go on for miles.

They're bent now, wrapped up like a gift.

Good thing I don't do teen virgin.

She squirms, and the colorful ropes draw tighter.

"So tell me," I lean over to whisper in her ear. "Am I your crush or your ruin?"

She jerks her head sideways in an attempt to headbutt me.

I laugh, loving the fight in her. "Looks like you traded in your puppy dog vibe to be my little fucking pony girl. Is that what you were hoping? To be my little plaything, to be bridled and ridden?"

Her emerald eyes flash with...interest...

No way.

A curious fucking hellion.

"You're a virgin, right?" I demand. Not sure why I ask or why it's important. It just is, because rumors are circulating.

The Twelve are in Rhode Island for a pissing contest disguised as a luncheon. Every capo is puckered up with big guns drawn, hoping to gain favor with Don Lucchese. Because with the new succession rules come new opportunities. My godfather will nominate two men for the Twelve's vote to succeed him after his death. My father, a top earner and ruthless enforcer, will be one name, I'm damn sure of it. It's been predictably boring watching the other capos compete.

Rumors are circulating that Don Lombardi will be announcing during the birthday toasts the deal he made with Carlo Accardo. His daughter's hand in marriage for gold. *Actual* fucking gold bars. Everyone knows Don Lombardi is drowning in debt and a gambling addict. Still, Don Lucchese will welcome the marriage, seeing it as an acknowledgment to the fragile peace he struck with the traitor Accardo, a former *famiglie* affiliate and Chicago power player, whose brother's loose lips nearly got his entire family slaughtered years ago.

My father put Pascale down.

Fast forward to the present where Don Lucchese has forgiven them. No doubt the wise man stacked his gold bars neatly on top of that peace.

Though rumors haven't stopped Elia Seraphina Lombardi from being up our asses. Specifically my ass, Sandro's just an innocent bystander.

Sixteen, and still a hellion.

She nods, flushed, as she struggles against the ropes.

My gaze rakes over her body. The mafiosi downstairs would be flattered by the attention. Some might take advantage of her vulnerability. If they opened their eyes and saw her like I do now, melon-size breasts, flat abs, perfectly groomed pussy hidden by the tiniest purple triangle patch...

A picture of her forms, her in a lifeguard's swimsuit and running across a California beach. Gorgeous breasts bouncing and midnight black hair billowing from the ocean breeze.

I shake my head, regretting my horny teen years and the nights spent jacking off to old Baywatch reruns. Still, discovering a bombshell like Elia Seraphina Lombardi hidden beneath that horrid pink dress might be the biggest surprise of the day.

I've two choices; spring her free or peel the offensive material off her for a closer look.

No choice, jackass.

The game we've been playing was entertaining while it lasted, but it's time to cut her free. Lombardi will demand her presence for his big announcement and send men to locate her. Still, I go for cutthroat, because kindness isn't a winning strategy when dealing with a stubborn, lovesick girl.

"I'm not interested. Period. No more butting into private conversations. No trailing after me like a teenager does her first crush. No antagonizing my brother or spying on men who murder for a living.

And, as a general warning, stop involving yourself in everyone else's business. The consequences will be more severe than being bound and gagged for an afternoon." She doesn't even flinch, her expression impassive. "Stick with the children, understand? Leave me the fuck alone. Or you won't find yourself in a comfy bed next time but in the Beneventi dungeon."

We lock eyes, and I curse beneath my breath.

Is that fucking defiance I see?

I ignore the warning bells. Clasping her arms below the elbows, I help her onto her knees. She sways, and my fingers swipe across her skin. Warm breast greets me like an electric bolt to the balls.

Her throat bobs as she swallows hard. From my touch? Or the situation she's found herself in, in general?

"Enough," I grind out. "I'll ungag you but think twice about screaming because as much trouble this will cause me, I'll be double for you. Nod if you understand."

Her head bobs.

I can't untie the silk tie quick enough.

Her tongue darts out and swipes across her lips.

Fuck. That's hot.

I shift on the mattress, distancing myself.

"Why Shinbari?" I hear her croak.

I freeze. "What?"

"Why tie me up in such an erotic way?"

Bound and gagged for hours, and this is her first comment? No demands to be untied or worse, banshee screams. Instead, she questions my bondage technique? Do I pat myself on the back, or run?

Her eyes flash and my lips draw tight. Because I spend the majority of the afternoon thinking about her similar reaction.

I was right about her, and that interests me.

"Listen, Elia," I warn her.

"It's Fina."

Well fuck me blind. "You're lucky, Fina, that I didn't anchor the tail end of the rope to the ceiling."

She looks up at the hook directly over the bed. Yeah, my father likes keeping his guests entertained. What sixteen-year-old virgin's into kink? What kind of fucking poetry is this hellhound reading?

Drawing on my inner Sandro, I face her. "Curiosity gets you killed in the Life."

She answers with poetry. "Entombed by whom, for what offence. If Home or Foreign born. Had I the curiosity. Twere not appeased of men."

"Jesus Christ."

"No, Emily Dickinson."

She's lost her damn mind.

Her head cocks. "You blow with the wind yet remain alive and thriving."

"Barely alive," I mutter, "and hardly thriving."

She shifts on her knees and straightens. Her breasts swaying and my mind playing vicious tricks on me. "Point is, Hot Pants, you do as you will without consequences."

Until I turn twenty-one.

Until my motherfucking destiny becomes inescapable.

On my eighteenth birthday, my father sat me down in his leather-clad library, the air thick with cigars and aged whiskey. His steely gaze pinned me to the chair, unwavering, as he mindfucked me. "You have until your twenty-first birthday to get it out of your system." By "it," he meant all the sex, drugs, and rock 'n' roll I could handle. Understanding that numbness wasn't truly the goal. Escape. Relief. Freedom from the crushing weight of expectations was.

Because when you're Sebastiano Beneventi's son, The Life is your only destiny.

It's like my father sees straight through me, knowing my mind isn't wired like Sandro's. I'm not just some hormone-fueled kid with a rebellious streak a mile long. There's something deeper, something restless, simmering beneath my skin, a hunger for the unpredictable, a thirst for the forbidden. I crave the burn, the sting, the electrifying charge buried in the raw and the real. If curiosity killed the cat, I've died ten times over. But what'll truly kill me is the soul-crushing predictability of the famiglie. Because no matter Don Lucchese's promises of change, mafiosi will always be mafiosi. And I curse the day I'm officially one of them.

"Experiment. Test your limits," my father commanded, his voice a low growl of authority. "But don't be a stupid little shit. Don't get caught, don't get hooked, and don't fucking die. When your time's up, you'll step up as the Beneventi heir. Capisci?"

He meant proving myself, either as an earner, an enforcer—or both, if you're Sebastiano Beneventi.

The clock in my mind is always ticking, even when the weight in my wicked soul wishes for time to stand still.

Less than two years to appease my darkest impulses. Less than two years to indulge every craving.

Then the cage closes around me.

She licks her lips once more, capturing my complete attention. "You want a taste of my dick, baby? That why you tracking my bed partners?"

She rolls her fucking eyes. "Curiosity is why I've befriended you."

"That what you call this?" I gesture between us. "Befriended?"

Her sigh fills the room. "You think I'm in love with you?"

"Well...yeah."

She laughs, and my balls shrivel at the sound.

"Why else be up my ass for years?"

Her laughter dies and her expression sobers. "You need to marry me."

"What?" I'm not often shocked, but what the fuck?

"Not now. When I turn twenty-one. But you'll need to present your father with the idea this afternoon so we can announce it."

I'd like to rip Don Lombardi's throat out. A hug is out of the question. She's still bound and an erotic sight I'll be jerking off to for many nights. With a slight shake of the head, I give her the same hollow lie I tell myself. "A lot can happen in five years."

"So, I should ask Massimo?"

"Massimo?" I stupidly exclaim. "You're in contact with him?"

She shrugs a shoulder.

I frown. What is it about her approaching fucking Massimo Grassi for help that irritates me?

"He's my best option."

That fucking right? "But he already turned you down?"

"No. He offered me a better alternative. His words, not mine."

I laugh. "Me?"

"Sad, but true."

"You were pursuing me."

"Pursuing? Yes. Offering you my tender heart?" Her face contorts. "Absolutely not."

I'm hurt. "Why not?" I demand.

"As entertaining and deliciously wicked as you are," she tosses her long black hair over her shoulder, "I'm out of your league, Hot Pants."

I think I'm in love.

She gives me this look, her emerald eyes slicing through my defenses, her body a weapon she doesn't even know how to use. "We'll marry then divorce when I turn twenty-two."

I choke on my own breath. I've just been outplayed. Instinct takes over, and I quickly untie her and push off the mattress like it's ablaze. "You said you were out of my league."

"Well, I'll take you over Accardo."

Bitch-slapped. That's what this feels like, with me being her bitch.

She slides off the bed, smooths her dress, then runs her fingers through her long black hair, erasing every trace of struggle. Like our wedding's already a go.

"In case you missed it, I'm uninterested in the Life."

She fiddles with the gaudy pink feathers on her dress, trying to arrange the collar so they don't fall over like wilted weeds. The more she smooths them upward, the more they springs into different directions, every which way but up.

"You're a capo's daughter, for Christ's sake. And now, suddenly, I want in?" Two years too early. Two years of freedom gone.

"You can continue with your lifestyle." She sighs with exaggeration. "Like I said, we'll marry in five years."

"My lifestyle?" I demand.

"Come on, Lorenzo—"

"Renzo."

"Fine, Renzo. I'll spell it out for you. You spend Friday night's at Providence's Sin City and every Saturday getting high and laid at one of several night clubs."

Jesus.

"That lifestyle."

I trace fingers across my chin. My marrying anyone is fucking ridiculous. Being shackled to one woman? Give up all the filthy pleasures the world has to offer? Having to answer for my habits, my kinks, just like I've the urge to do now?

Not happening.

"My father won't agree. Not even if it's Sandro."

Her eyes flash with disgust. "Sandro?"

"It won't be me," I say in a firm tone, hoping she'll drop the idea.

She open her mouth, the fight still in her. As much as I admire it, I'm shutting this conversation down for good.

"My father earns money. Yours pisses it away. If there's such a thing as embarrassment by association, that's how we Beneveti feel about the Lombardis. Do you really expect him to give his blessing to our marriage?"

She stares at the floor, like she'd like it to swallow her up, disappointment carved into every inch of her.

No reason for it to sting the way it does. I barely know this girl.

"Like I said, a lot can change in five years." I open the bedroom door, signaling an end to this discussion. "Give me a few minutes before you follow me downstairs."

I walk out before she can respond, putting distance between us and the ridiculous idea that I'm her salvation.

Wrong bastard to approach for help.

When the only comic book character I identify with is the Joker.

I'm famished by the time I reach my seat. "Where's the clinger?" is the first thing Sandro asks me, nodding toward the empty chair beside the one I'm settling in to. A chair awkwardly squeezed between mine and the mafiosi to my right, when it should be at the far end of the table with the other children's.

"Guess she got tied up elsewhere."

He shoots me a look.

I smirk, giving nothing away. "What did I miss?"

"Roberto Ferrara has an FBI agent in his pocket."

"No shit?" I spear an asparagus with a fork and stuff the tip into my mouth. "Don Lucchese loves strong government connections," I say while chewing.

"Yeah," Sandro replies. "Know what else he loves? Good table manners."

"Not what he told me when I approached him earlier to wish him a happy birthday. He asked about you."

"Damn it." He places his wine on the table, buying the bullshit. "You covered for me, right?"

So fucking gullible.

Finally recognizing the lie, he elbows me hard in the side.

Point made, I shove another asparagus into my mouth.

The luncheon is interrupted by spoons tapping against glasses, signaling the birthday toasts will begin.

Fina appears in a blur of pink.

I wait, ready to lock eyes—and yeah, offer her encouragement. Without so much as a glance my way, she takes a seat with the children.

"Can't believe that bloodhound gave up," Sandro declares. Not a huge Fina fan. She gets beneath his skin like nobody else.

I fill our wine glasses with an expensive Chianti Reserve I

pinched earlier for the Beneventi wine cellar and raise mine high. "Let the games begin."

And they do, amateur hour first. Toast after toast. Boast after boast. Male egos locking horns like rams battling for dominance.

Blah. Blah. Blah.

Midway through, Don Lucchese interrupts to acknowledge my father for his financial prowess. Everyone applauds, and then, timing it perfectly, my father does what he does best, and drops another bomb. He's entering the casino business.

The room hums with excitement, the air practically vibrates.

Except for Bible Belt Benny Manocchio. His face hardens, lips pressed into a razor-thin line, his knuckles whitening around his glass. Benny controls the South with claws buried deep in the gaming business.

Two types of men rise in rank in the mafiosi, the earners and the enforcers. My father's both, and can kill men twice; once financially, sabotaging a rival's financial assets with the click of a finger and secondly, the traditional, smoking gun way. Today, the opposite happened. Overnight, he made every criminal in The Twelve wealthy. Not equally, of course, though no one's complaining.

And no one's dead yet.

Benny has yet to turn a huge profit. And, if he doesn't wise up and raise his glass in toast, his chance to do so is over. Hard to turn profit when your turning up tulips.

Don Lombardi stands.

Snickers ripple through the room, that's how much respect the bastard has.

"Don Lucchese." He raises his glass. "To ensure a new era of peace, I'd like to announce the engagement of my daughter, Elia Seraphina Lombardi, to Don Carlo Accardo."

Silence suffocates the room.

"Accardo's what—fifty-two?" Sandro mutters.

"Fifty-three, with the hygiene habits of a pig."

Judging by the reaction of those around us, we're not the only ones disgusted.

Lombardi shifts, sensing the unease. "He's agreed to wait until Elia's twenty-first birthday." With that, he sits, shoulders hunched, eyes down.

My attention falls on Fina.

She pours herself a wine from a bottle that doesn't belong at that end of the table, and casually sips it. Like she's unaware of the pity-filled glances cast her way.

"In this world, that's how the Life goes," Sandro murmurs, watching her, too.

There's no middle ground in the Life. Escape it or let it sweep you under.

If my goddamn future wasn't so precarious, I'd almost feel bad for her.

ALSO BY MICHELE MANNON

Dirty Mafia Kingdom

Dark mafia romance

Dirty Mafia King

Dirty Mafia Sinner

Dirty Mafia Torment

Dirty Mafia Lover

Deadliest Lies Novels

Dark contemporary with *a lot* of suspense

Rogue

Mercenary

Hit Man

Player

Liar

Bastard

Worth the Fight Series

Sexy contemporary sports romance

Knock Out

Tap Out

Out for The Count

ABOUT THE AUTHOR

Michele Mannon has been writing romance since her first publication in 2012. A multiple recipient of Romantic Times Magazine's prestigious TOP PICKS award, Michele's books always pack a punch, leaving readers laughing out loud or swooning and biting their fingernails at all the appropriate times. Her books have been sold in print, digitally, and on Audible.

She loves the darker shades in romance; the anti-heroes and villains, the angst mixed with a heavy dose of unexpected.

Michele lives on a mountain overlooking the Delaware River, where she can be found with a glass of Riesling in her hand and a laptop on her lap. On occasion, she posts on TikTok @authormichelemannon

For updates on her latest release, sign up for her newsletter at
www.michelemannon.com

Or connect @authormichelemannon